"You leap out of yo
the bells chime at t

Sarah shook her head. "I

He kept going, despite her attempt to interrupt. "I know. But how could you never get used to sounds you hear all day...every day? And there's more. You're always watching the front door of the diner... as if maybe you're dreading whomever the next customer will be."

"Now, that's just silly. I'm just doing my job being prepared for customers."

"You didn't want anyone to know about Aiden...or your last name."

Now she only shrugged. If he hadn't bought her excuse the first time, he was unlikely to buy it now.

"Do you have any idea how many times you looked over your shoulder at the zoo today?"

"I did not."

Why couldn't Jamie stop asking questions? Just because he'd told her his deep, dark secrets didn't mean that she had agreed to share hers. Besides, he was getting too close to the truth. What if he found out everything?

* * *

If you're on Twitter, tell us what you
think of Harlequin Romantic Suspense!
#harlequinromsuspense

Dear Reader,

Hello, Harlequin Romantic Suspense readers! I'm excited to be in my new publishing home at Harlequin Romantic Suspense and to share *Shielded by the Lawman* with you. As a huge romantic-suspense fan myself, I'm thrilled to have the opportunity to write the same type of stories that are on my Kindle or on the tattered pages of my own paperback collection. Sarah and Jamie's story has lived in my thoughts for several years now, so it was a joy—and a relief—to finally get the chance to write it. I hope you'll love these characters and their journey to trust, healing and love as much as I do.

True Blue is a brand-new series for Harlequin Romantic Suspense, but it is also a continuation of the contemporary romance series I wrote for Harlequin Superromance. Bonus! True Blue is about the lives and loves of the brave men and women from a Michigan State Police post. Now with Romantic Suspense, these characters get to face an even rockier—and more sinister—road to forever love. If you can't get enough of the True Blue crew for now, then meet a few more of the gang in my Superromance backlist titles, *Strength Under Fire* and *Falling for the Cop.* Meanwhile, I'll be back at my computer, working on the next dark and dangerous adventure.

I love staying in contact with readers, no matter how you choose to connect. Learn more about me and sign up for my newsletter through my website, www.dananussio.com; connect with me on Facebook or Twitter, @DanaNussio1; or drop me a line on real paper at PO Box 5, Novi, MI 48376-0005.

Happy reading!

Dana Nussio

SHIELDED BY THE LAWMAN

Dana Nussio

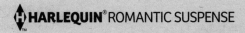
HARLEQUIN® ROMANTIC SUSPENSE

Recycling programs
for this product may
not exist in your area.

ISBN-13: 978-1-335-66188-3

Shielded by the Lawman

Copyright © 2019 by Dana Corbit Nussio

www.Harlequin.com

Printed in U.S.A.

Dana Nussio began telling "people stories" around the same time she started talking. She has been doing both things nonstop ever since. The award-winning newspaper reporter and features editor left her career while raising three daughters, but the stories followed her home as she discovered the joy of writing fiction. Now an award-winning fiction author as well, she loves telling emotional stories filled with honorable but flawed characters. Empty nesters, Dana and her husband of more than twenty-five years live in Michigan with two overfed cats, Leo the Wondercat and Annabelle Lee the Neurotic.

Books by Dana Nussio

Harlequin Romantic Suspense

True Blue
Shielded by the Lawman

Harlequin Superromance

True Blue
Strength Under Fire
Falling for the Cop

Visit the Author Profile page
at Harlequin.com for more titles.

To Randy, for believing in me and supporting my dreams, even when that means you must keep wearing dress clothes and fighting traffic while I'm at home telling stories in my PJs. Thanks for loving me and ensuring that our three daughters didn't starve during deadline mania and, let's admit it, most of the other times, as well. You are my hero.

A special thanks to Officer David Willett, of the Michigan State Police, for patiently answering all my questions, even the strange ones; and to my dear friends Angela Armstrong, for inspiring me through your own true-life romance with a hunky police hero, and Cindy Thomas, for your constant support and superior country-music-festival matchmaking. As always, I would like to thank the real heroes in law enforcement, those who every day don the uniform with dignity and accept the duty and risk of protecting the rest of us. May God go with you all!

Chapter 1

Another day, another death. A continual supply of senseless carnage. Solutions buried deeper than the corpses fallen by their own hands.

Jamie Donovan squeezed his eyes shut and took several gulps of dank air to slow the pulse pounding like hi-hat cymbals in his ears. He would give anything for the pummeling inside his head to let up, even if the deluge pelting his hoodie refused. But he couldn't keep pacing in the frigid early April rain outside Casey's Diner like a despondent person. Did he want someone to call the police on *him*?

So, he yanked open the door and ground his molars as the wind caught it and clanged those obnoxious bells against the glass. He stomped inside and wrestled the door closed. Rain dripped off his coat and puddled on the mat. As if to punctuate his misery, water trickled from his hood to his nose. He brushed it away with a soggy sleeve.

Why had he agreed to come at all? The answer to that was clear, even before nearly a dozen expectant faces turned to him from the line of tables on the far wall. If he hadn't at least made an appearance at the diner tonight, his fellow Michigan State Police troopers would have known he was *not* okay after the events that occurred during his shift. And they'd have had proof that he'd lied when he said he was. How was he was supposed to fake normalcy when the usually delicious scents of frying bacon, cinnamon and fresh-baked somethings were rolling his insides like six-foot swells trapping a boat on Lake Michigan?

"Whoa there, *Hercules!*" Sergeant Vincent Leonetti called out.

The others laughed the way they usually did at Vinnie's jokes, but the sound fell flat. Everyone was trying too hard. They all thought he was just sensitive to the type of case he'd investigated tonight. Weak-stomached even. If they only knew. But because they seemed to need him to pretend, Jamie pushed back his hood and started toward the table.

Suicide attempt. Why did they call them *attempts*? Like a gymnast trying out an amazing, double-twist dismount. That guy's effort wasn't an *attempt*, anyway. It was a frigging success, with blood spatter like a Jackson Pollock painting on the living room wall to prove it.

Jamie had been too late. Again.

Though his face felt hot, a chill edged up his spine and gooseflesh peppered his skin beneath his sleeves. Bile that he'd forced back earlier crawled from his stomach again, lukewarm and bitter. He had to get control.

As he turned his head to the side, he hoped to avoid eye contact with any of the officers who knew him too well and yet not at all.

Her gaze snagged his instead.

Jamie could only stare back at her. Somehow, he managed to prevent his mouth from falling open, but keeping his feet moving toward that table was damn near impossible. Sarah. The petite, ethereal beauty who'd never once looked back at any of the Brighton Post troopers when they'd tested their best lines on her. Whose last name no one knew and whose *first* name they probably still wouldn't know after two years if it wasn't emblazoned on her waitress badge and she didn't have to scribble it on their bills each time she waited on them.

That Sarah was watching *him.*

Stranger still, her haunting, pale blue eyes were piercing him deeper than an RIP bullet at close range. As if she could see everything he was trying to hide from his coworkers. Everything he wished he could forget.

And then it was over. She looked away and tucked those wavy, dark blond tendrils that fell loose from her ponytail behind her ears. That was one of her nervous habits he'd observed. Twisting her gold locket was another. They were things she did when she thought no one was watching. Now she smoothed her apron and grabbed a tub to bus a vacated table.

Jamie blinked several times. Had he imagined their moment of connection? Wow, his mind had really gone off-road this time. His lips lifted as he reached his coworkers, hung his sweatshirt over the back of the lone empty chair and dropped into it.

That he could smile at all after everything that had happened tonight was as surprising as his reaction to poor Sarah's simple glance. Of course, she'd looked at him. This was her table. She'd taken note of him only so that she could drop by an extra water glass and more wrapped silverware.

Anyway, just because he'd secretly watched *her* for months didn't mean she'd paid any attention to him. And he'd watched her, all right. As closely as a witness expected to give expert testimony. What did it say about him that he could describe her impossibly pale skin and dancer-like movements and could almost feel the silk of wavy hair he'd never touched?

He rubbed the damp sleeves of his Henley shirt as much to settle himself as to relieve the chill. He should have known better than to go out in public tonight.

"Did you drive here or swim?" Vinnie asked.

"Both. Did you see how it was coming down out there?"

Kelly Roberts watched him closely. "It wasn't raining yet when we came in."

A few of the others murmured their agreement. He was later than the rest of them, but it wasn't because he'd let tonight's events get to him. That would mean he'd allowed his past to seep into the present again, its persistent spread threatening to smother his plan to help at-risk youth.

"We already ordered, but we can call Sarah over if you're ready." At the other end of the table, pretty boy Nick Sanchez waggled an eyebrow.

"Oh, *he's* ready," Vinnie said, managing to draw a stilted laugh from the others.

"And who knows? Maybe the earth will shift, and Sarah will be primed like an Indy car engine, too," Dion Carson quipped.

Jamie pressed his lips together. He hated the way the guys talked about women when they were off work. About Sarah in particular. No matter how many times he'd called them on it, they never stopped.

"If she *is* primed, you know she'll be coming right over to me," Nick added.

The women and even the men frowned at Nick and then shrugged. Now that the post's resident Adonis, Shane Warner, was married, Nick had the best shot with any woman. Female drivers gawked at him, even when he was issuing traffic citations.

"That's enough, guys. She's a person," Jamie ground out. "Leave her alone."

Chuckles spread around the table. Had they been baiting him to see if he would react as he normally did? Well, he'd passed that test. Yes, he was Jamie, defender of women and hero to lost kittens. A nice guy, and everyone knew where they finished.

"You guys are lucky she's still willing to serve at our table at all," he groused. "And you're lucky I don't recommend all of you for another round of sexual harassment training."

"Please, not that. We can be good." Dion lifted his right hand to back up his promise. "Anyway, we're not that bad."

"And we pay great tips," Kelly supplied.

Jamie nodded. Sarah probably needed that tip money, too. Working the night shift at a diner in Brighton, a southeast Michigan city of less than eight thousand, didn't shout *financially secure*.

The image of her eyes stole into his thoughts again, huge orbs of liquid sky, so striking and yet so…guarded. Were there secrets behind them? Or just regrets, like his?

"Anyway, won't you guys ever give up on her?" Delia Morgan Peterson called from the head of the table. "She doesn't want anything to do with any of you."

"And give up a challenge like that? Never!" Vinnie shoved his fist into the air.

Lieutenant Ben Peterson rested his hand on Delia's slightly rounded tummy. "If the alien here turns out to be a girl, we'll have to protect her from guys like you."

Kelly handed Jamie a menu. "Now would you guys let him order? We'll be paying our bills before his food comes."

Jamie made a show of studying the photos of omelets and pancakes and the extensive burger collection, though he could recite the list from memory. Anything he ate would sit in his stomach like a hunk of granite, but the sooner he shoved it down, the sooner he could go home and wrestle in private with the memories tonight's events had unearthed.

"What will it be?" Dion asked.

Jamie turned to find Sarah standing right behind him, the starched white apron of her pink cliché uniform nearly brushing his chair. She shot a quick glance toward the front door, as she often did, and then set a cup and saucer to his right.

"Decaf?" she asked, already tipping the carafe.

"Never know. He might be in the mood for orange soda tonight," Vinnie quipped.

"Oh." She stopped mid pour and cleared her throat. "Sorry."

"Don't pay attention to him. Decaf's fine." In fact, decaf was the only choice for his insomnia.

"You guys." She tipped the carafe again. "You ready to order?"

"Oh. Right." He chose the same hamburger he ordered at least once a week.

She jotted down the information on the pad inside her black binder, and then she disappeared into the kitchen behind the swinging door.

Suddenly, Jamie wished Sarah, or any of them, had seen through his act as he'd pretended that that nothing was out of the ordinary tonight. It didn't seem right that a human life could have been snuffed out a few hours before and their days would just rumble forward as if nothing had happened. Just another Western burger, medium-well. Another round of coffee refills and jokes they'd all heard before. As if that life had never mattered at all.

"What did you think about that rain?" Trevor Cole asked from the seat to his left.

Jamie rested his forearms on the table edge. "A little early for swimming."

"Right about that," Trevor said. "Lucky it wasn't snowing like it did last week. It's going to be a while before I take my boat out on Kent Lake."

"At least you've got a boat."

"As much work as old *Esmerelda* is, I think she's got me rather than the other way around." But then Trevor leaned close and spoke to Jamie in a low, stiff voice. "You doing okay? Because if you need someone to talk—"

"I'm good," Jamie whispered. A white lie wasn't so bad when they both needed for him to say it.

Vinnie reached over to poke Trevor's shoulder. "You mean *Esmerelda*'s still floating?"

Jamie tried to settle back in his chair. At least they were talking about inane things like Trevor's boat and the big-top theme for Ben and Delia's nursery. The regular stuff of life instead of the tragic consequences of unfortunate decisions and mental distress that played equal roles in their working lives.

"There's some speedy service for you," Vinnie said, as Sarah returned to the table, carrying a tray laden with plates.

"Hope you know we won't be waiting for you to eat." Nick stuffed a French fry in his mouth.

"No. Go ahead. Eat while it's hot."

Vinnie took a big bite of his hamburger and then spoke with a full mouth. "You don't have to tell me twice."

Jamie laced his fingers together and rested his wrists on the table. At least no one was watching him now. He'd only assumed that the others would make a big deal out of his investigation tonight. Most of them didn't even know about Mark's suicide. Didn't know about the guilt Jamie carried over the things a big brother should have noticed but hadn't.

No, he couldn't think about that. Not when his senses were still filled with the pungent scents of a discharged weapon and blood, and the dark images of a crime scene. Not when he needed his coworkers to see that he could shake this off. Needed to believe it himself.

Sarah appeared again, with Ted, one of the owners, trailing behind her. Both carried trays full of food. The other officers ate their meals, their conversations ending or limited to those seated closest to them.

In the cacophony of plates scratching, silverware clinking and ice cubes tinkling, Jamie let his thoughts slip back to that night's grisly discovery. Then further. Even nine years later, he couldn't think of his funny, smiling brother without seeing Mark's lifeless body dangling in the garage.

Regret, the kind that only someone who has known true loss could understand, covered him, filling every crevice with emptiness, hopelessness and damnation. He'd tried to stop reliving the day of Mark's death, but that night's events had cued up the scene again.

"I got this out here as soon as I could."

The soft, feminine voice from behind him startled him from his daze.

Sarah held another tray and indicated the other diners with a shift of her head. "They're nearly finished."

"Thanks. I appreciate it."

He wished he had something clever to say, but as usual, he came up empty. Dion beat him to it.

"I don't know about the rest of you, but I'm ready for dessert," Dion announced. "What kind of pies have you been baking today, Miss Sarah?"

"A bit of chocolate heaven or blueberry rapture?" Vinnie suggested hopefully.

Jamie didn't need to look over his shoulder to know that Sarah's face would be as pink as her uniform. She seemed so uncomfortable whenever anyone mentioned her baking. He wished Ted hadn't let them in on the secret that she was responsible for all the new pies, cakes and breads on the menu.

She cleared her throat. "We have eclair cake with chocolate ganache and just one piece left of the lemon cake with whipped frosting and—"

"Stop right there," Nick interrupted. "Sold. Both."

She bent her head to jot a note. "And for pies, we have apple amaretto, strawberry rhubarb and lemon meringue."

Several of Jamie's colleagues placed orders, and a

few declined in defense of their waistlines. When she reached him, he shook his head. "I shouldn't."

"No, you *should*," Trevor said. "Give him his favorite. The apple. On my ticket."

Jamie didn't bother arguing. It would be too obvious if he turned down free pie. Even if his slice was Trevor's second clumsy attempt to comfort him.

"Sorry. I owed him," Trevor said, as Sarah returned to the kitchen. "And no, I don't owe any of the rest of you anything."

When the waitress rested the dessert plate next to his barely touched burger, Jamie could only stare. Whoever had cut the pies must have flunked division in math because that slice made all the other pieces look like slivers. Had Sarah picked up on Trevor's pity-pie ploy and decided to stuff Jamie in sympathy? He glanced right and left, but the others were too busy inhaling their own desserts to notice his.

From the first bite, Jamie nearly forgot about his awful day and his shaky stomach. He closed his eyes and savored the sweet almond-liquor flavor that counterbalanced the tart apples. The flaky crust melted on his tongue.

"Worth the five extra miles we're going to have to run, isn't it?" Trevor said.

"Oh yeah."

Jamie pushed the burger aside and finished all but the crumbs of the pie. By then, Sarah had returned.

"Great, as always," Trevor told her as she cleared away their plates.

"Yeah, great," Jamie echoed.

"Thanks."

Her voice was soft, but the corners of her mouth lifted.

When she moved to the cash register to print out their bills, Jamie couldn't help watching her again. She was as oblivious to him as she was to her own beauty. To her effortless allure that always had him catching his breath in her presence. If he believed that the earlier moment between them had been anything more than a product of his imagination, he was smoking stuff stronger than the K2, or synthetic marijuana, he arrested suspects for.

His friends were already pulling on their jackets when Sarah returned to drop off their bills. Jamie glanced down at his. He hoped the pie would be on his ticket instead of Trevor's, but only the burger and the coffee were listed.

Farther down the page, her signature was the same— that loopy, feminine cursive that contradicted Sarah's guarded demeanor. But then his fingers brushed a second slip of paper beneath the bill. The azure color of a sticky note was visible through the filmy ticket.

Though she'd probably stuck it there by accident, her grocery list attached where it didn't belong, Jamie straightened in his seat. What if it was something else, like a call for help? Why would she reach out only to him in a room full of cops? He blew out a breath. He really was losing it tonight if he was coming up with damsel-in-distress theories.

Still, he made sure no one else was watching before he flipped over the bill.

Thanks for everything you do. You're one of the good ones.

He read the words twice. People didn't say things like that to cops. Now profanity-laced rants, topped with middle-finger salutes, those messages were more familiar. He studied the note again. No name. And the letters were block-printed. It wasn't even addressed to him. Or any officer.

So how pitiful was it for a twenty-seven-year-old man to tuck that folded square of paper in his jeans pocket, as if it was a secret note from study hall? Jamie decided not to answer that question as he shrugged into his sweatshirt. At the cash register, Sarah accepted Vinnie's money and impaled his receipt on that tiny spike as if nothing had happened. Maybe nothing had, though this time the note in Jamie's pocket made him wonder.

Sarah caught him watching, and she didn't look away immediately. He couldn't have if he'd tried. His pulse pounded so loud in his ears that everyone in the restaurant had to hear it. His palms were as damp as his sweatshirt. With a shy smile, she turned away.

Jamie couldn't stop blinking. He dug in his pockets for his car keys.

The connection had been as short as the one when he'd first arrived. Shorter. Had it not happened twice, it wouldn't have seemed significant. But now he was certain of a few things. For one, it was possible for every nerve ending in a person's body to become instantly alert. The other was that the note folded in his pocket really had been intended for him.

What those things meant was less clear. Could she have overheard the other troopers talking about him before he'd arrived? Could all of this be about pity, after all?

But when he started toward the cash register, Sarah was gone. Ted had replaced her and was checking out the last few troopers. Jamie slowed. Sarah wasn't clearing tables or filling salt shakers, either. Where had she gone? The answer to that and his other questions lay beyond the swinging door that separated the restaurant's dining room from its kitchen.

He couldn't burst into the back, locate her and insist that she explain herself, but he couldn't let her raise these questions and vanish, either.

"Officer, ready to check out?"

Ted waved him over to the counter. Jamie opened his wallet and pulled out his debit card.

Two minutes later, he pulled up his hood and headed outside. The jangling bells jarred him, reviving those same memories that had chased him into the diner earlier. Had he conjured this whole mystery to escape thoughts about the suicide investigation? Had he clung to the distraction because it might at least offer some answers when the other matter remained a black hole of question marks? Either way, he had to know.

He glanced one last time toward the kitchen as the door whooshed closed. Sarah might not be around to answer his questions tonight, but he was about to become Casey's best customer until she did.

Chapter 2

Sarah Cline hated cowering in the kitchen, but it seemed like her only option now. Even if the dishwasher had to be watching her as he sprayed gunk off plates with the pre-rinse hose, she didn't dare look his way. How would she explain herself, anyway? For someone who understood just how critical it was for her to keep a low profile, who knew what she could lose if she didn't, she'd practically leaped on the counter and performed a country line dance in her sensible shoes for all the customers to see.

For all of them? No, her side steps and kick-ball-changes had been for been for just one guy. And she couldn't explain why she'd done it. A *cop*? She'd learned the hard way how much she could trust them. She hugged herself tighter, her thumb tracing the jagged pucker of a scar on the underside of her left arm. It was covered, just inside her short uniform sleeve. Hidden. Like so many others.

She lowered her arms and wiped her sweaty hands inside her apron pockets. From her awkward angle, she could no longer see the officer through the scratched, round window. She couldn't blame him for his curiosity after her odd behavior tonight, so she was relieved when she caught sight of him again as he slipped out into the rain. Relieved and something else. Wistful? It couldn't be that. If anything, regret was the thing pushing down on her shoulders like a lead blanket. Maybe tinged with the same anxiety she awoke to every morning and tried to sleep with every night.

What had possessed her to write that note? She should have minded her own business. She knew better. It couldn't matter that she'd only today realized that "Mr. Jamie," the after-school-program volunteer her sweet Aiden had been gushing over for months, was the same "James A. Donovan" whose debit card she swiped at least twice a week. Or that, from snippets of his coworkers' conversations, she'd learned that something bad had happened to him at work tonight. Or even that the raw expression clouding his hazel eyes was similar to the one living inside her own mirror.

Not one of those things was a good enough excuse for her to meddle in some guy's situation with a note… or even two-fifths of a pie. Getting involved in people's lives encouraged them to ask questions. She couldn't afford that.

Especially not from a cop.

With a shiver, she glanced back at Léon, who was watching her so closely that he'd sprayed water down the front of his apron. He lifted a thick black brow. She frowned at him. This wasn't the first time she'd hidden in the kitchen at Casey's, but usually she was avoiding rowdy customers who refused to accept the word *no*.

But this one…it was all on her.

Shooting one last glance to the front of the diner to be sure he was gone, Sarah stepped into the deserted dining room. She grabbed the tub of refilled salt and pepper shakers, ketchup bottles and containers filled with sweetener packets on her way past the counter.

Ted plucked a peppermint from the bowl by the cash register and popped it in his mouth. "I wondered where you'd wandered off to."

"Just planning the desserts for tomorrow."

She marveled at how effortlessly she lied, but then most things came easier with practice. And at age twenty-eight, she'd had plenty of practice.

"The fuzz boys do something to upset you? Because if they did, I could talk—"

"No, they're good customers."

"Good. But if they get out of line…"

As Sarah leaned into a booth to reset the condiments, she turned away so that he wouldn't see her eye roll. Ted hadn't even hinted that he would ban them for bad behavior. He couldn't turn away paying customers, especially those who appeared harmless.

But she'd made the mistake of trusting the police once and had barely survived to tell the story. She brushed away that thought with a swipe of her forearm over her forehead. Compared to those Chicago officers, this group seemed like choir boys.

When the image of one particular choir member invaded her thoughts, his wide eyes staring back at her, Sarah's hand jerked. A saltshaker slipped from her fingers and skidded across the table, leaving a sticky white mess on the laminate.

"Butterfingers tonight?" Ted asked.

"I'm just tired."

The sound system blared with one of the country ballads she'd once adored, as a singer crooned about a love that didn't exist. Hearts and hope and heaven easily turned to hurt and hits and hell.

She righted the saltshaker and cleared the residue with her cloth. If only it were as easy to erase the other mistakes she'd made tonight. She had one rule—keep her distance from others—and she'd broken it faster than an order up for scrambled eggs and toast.

She moved to the next table, but Jamie's face flashed back at her from the mirrored napkin dispenser. He had kind eyes, she decided, and then shook her head. Why had she chosen *now* to think about that? She must have noticed his eyes before. Maybe because they matched his boyish face. But when she'd really looked at him tonight, what she'd seen had ripped at her heart.

So, blame her odd behavior on the misery in his eyes. That rare vulnerability in a guy whose career suggested a preternatural fearlessness had drawn her in, but that was all there was to it. All there ever could be. Friendships were a luxury she couldn't afford.

Sarah blinked, the absurdity of those thoughts as shocking as her actions tonight. She needed to go home, where she could reclaim her good sense and her survival instinct. She had to remember the truth: She could count on no one but herself.

"Marilyn's late," Ted said.

"Again?"

"She called this time. Car trouble."

She'd moved to the set-up table and was rolling cutlery, but now her gaze shifted to the door. At least there wasn't a crowd of diehards arriving from Salute Lounge. If they had a rush, Ted might ask her to stay until Marilyn arrived. Again.

"You'd better clock out then," he said, as if reading her thoughts.

"I do need to get home."

"Aiden's already in bed by now, right?"

"He'd sure better be, or he'll never get up for school." She wished she didn't still stiffen at his mention of her son's name. It hadn't turned out too bad, anyway, the few times she'd had to bring her son to work with her.

"He doesn't have to. There's no school tomorrow."

"What are you talking about?"

"You know. One of those teacher in-service days. A kid holiday."

Or a single parent's nightmare. What was she supposed to do with her son now? Even her sitter, Nadia, worked days twice a week.

"Bring Aiden with you in the morning," Ted said. "We never get to see him."

"I just don't want him to be bored." Or seen.

"You kidding? He loves it here. Who wouldn't?"

Maybe a six-year-old who'd prefer to play outside? "Why do you know about this schedule change and I don't?"

He held up a sheet of paper. "Local school district calendar. I watch it to know which mornings we'll be overrun with kids and their parents."

But that didn't explain why *she* hadn't known. Had she missed something in Aiden's backpack? She tried to keep on top of that mess, but sometimes she was just too tired. It was easier to curl up with her sleeping boy after she'd carried him down the freezing second-floor walkway from Nadia's apartment to her own.

"Everything's ready for the morning, right?" Ted asked.

"The cinnamon rolls are all ready to go in the oven."

"You made extra, like I asked?"

She nodded, his earlier request now making sense.

"And you'll be able to come in earlier since Aiden doesn't have school? Eight maybe?"

Her second nod hurt a little more. Aiden would be grouchy if she got him up early on his day off.

"Good. Then you'd better get home."

She headed back into the kitchen for her jacket before he changed his mind. She slid it on and pulled up her hood in case it was still raining.

Jamie had been soaked when he'd come in earlier, though the others had been dry. The thought struck her as she stepped out onto the sidewalk, where puddles remained, though the downpour had dwindled.

Why was the police officer on her mind again? Didn't she have enough on her plate without taking on someone else's problems? Bigger problems even than that she'd known nothing about her son's school holiday. Obstacles like caring for a child who deserved a better, safer life than she'd given him, and too many bills with a paycheck that wouldn't stretch. And the ever-present need to look over her shoulder for a boogeyman with a recognizable face, a booming voice and pain-inflicting hands.

As a familiar tickly sensation scampered up the back of her neck, she splayed her apartment keys between her thumb and first two fingers to face off with a possible attacker.

No one was following her. She knew that. Aiden was safe. *They* were safe. So why did every drip of leftover rainwater from the gutter echo in her ears? Why did each crunch of her shoes on the concrete throw off sounds as difficult to place as a ventriloquist's voice? That seemed to come from *behind* her.

She'd made it only to the corner of the storefront when she gave in and peeked over her shoulder. The sidewalk and even the street were deserted. In the lot between Casey's and its nearest neighbor, Langston's Furnishings, only two cars remained. Ted's and the clunker that Léon used to drive himself, the night cook, Marty, and sometimes her to work. At least she wasn't the only one who didn't have a car. She hurried across the parking lot, but as she passed Ted's car, a pair of headlight beams whipped into the lot, the vehicle they were attached to barely slowing to make the turn. The car swerved into a parking space, its driver cutting the engine.

Sarah froze, a squeal escaping her. She needed to run back inside, yet her feet felt glued in place. Instead, she was forced to watch, an unwilling bystander to her own life. The car door flew open, and the driver leaped out and ran right toward her, something light fluttering beneath the figure's hooded raincoat.

As the runner's bare legs came into view, Sarah released the breath she'd been holding. "Marilyn?"

Of course, the waitress would be the one racing in and then sprinting across the parking lot with her apron whipping like a flag behind her. So why couldn't Sarah stop shaking? Why did she have to assume that every fast-moving car would be *him* coming for her to finish the job, like he'd always said he would?

Marilyn didn't even come to a full stop when she reached her. "Sorry I'm late. The babysitter—"

"Ted said it was car trouble."

"That, too."

Marilyn's wry smile suggested there was more to it. Sarah nodded. Single moms had to have each other's backs since no one else did. With a wave, the woman rounded corner to the entrance.

Sarah continued home on foot. It was safer this way. No license plate for police to trace. No checks on the numbers of a driver's license that matched an eighty-year-old woman's profile. A deceased one at that.

It hadn't been Michael running toward her this time, but one day it would be. Safe? They would never be safe. Even if he didn't know where they were—or *who* they were—he would find them. No prison walls would be strong enough to contain that type of hate.

It didn't matter whether he would be able to convince a parole board that he was a safe risk for release or not. Michael's network could fan out like a freeway map. Why had she ever thought they would be able to escape him?

She shivered and pulled her jacket tighter as she neared her apartment building.

She wouldn't allow herself to think any more about a guy who had problems of his own and no time to deal with hers. Her only focus could be on that sweet little boy whose hair smelled of baby shampoo and whose kisses were the most precious gifts she could receive. Without hesitation, she would trade her life for her his.

If she allowed herself to think about any man at all, it would be the one who still stalked her nightmares. The one who'd promised to kill her, and always kept his promises.

* * *

Michael Brooks wedged himself between the car door and the frame and tilted his head back to pitch a mouthful of profanity at the bawling Chicago South Side sky. The least the sun could have done was shine on his first day seeing it from outside the prison gates in six years, but instead, it pissed all over him like the rest of the scum responsible for putting him behind bars.

"Would you get in and shut the door?" his driver grumbled from inside the car.

Michael whipped his body into the front seat so fast the other man flinched, his head cracking against the door. For the first time all day, Michael smiled. Then he brushed rainwater off the paper-thin jacket covering his button-down dress shirt and no-name jeans he'd been presented upon his release.

"Good to see you, too."

He glanced around the interior of the cop's personal vehicle, a foreign-made SUV with many driver distractions across the dash. He brushed his fingers over buttery leather upholstery.

"Nice ride." Nicer than the guy deserved.

When Larry didn't answer, Michael wanted to slug him. He'd been itching for a fight all day, an itch among many that hadn't been scratched for too long. He tossed his measly bag of possessions into the backseat. He had nothing. That was his wife's fault. *Ex*-wife. She was responsible for everything that sucked about his life now. No place to go home to. No feminine heat in his bed. No chance to get to know his son. And most of all, no access to his own sweet nest egg.

She would pay for all of it. When he figured out where

the hell she was. He would find her, too. He had to. She held the key to his future in more ways than she knew.

Larry didn't even look his way as he pulled out into traffic. Maybe he was too scared to risk it. Served him right.

Michael waited through a few stoplights in the tiny community where the prison bus had plunked him, but then he couldn't stay quiet any longer.

"Got anything else you want to say to me?"

Larry's Adam's apple shifted a few times, and then his jaw tightened. "I thought maybe you'd like to thank *me* for coming all the way out here to pick up your sorry ass."

"You joking? I'd still have my own ride if you and your buddy—"

"Hey, if you don't want me to be here, I can…"

"Nah. It's over."

And if the guy believed that, he had a piece of land near Hyde Park with an active oil well in the backyard. Someone as indebted to him as the loser sitting next to him didn't need a reminder of what he owed, anyway.

"Thanks for coming to get me," Michael said finally.

He knew better than to piss off his so-called *allies* when he just might need them later.

"Glad Clint found you a decent place to live," Larry said.

Michael's jaw tightened at just the mention of the second officer's name. This mess was as much his fault as Larry's. "If that's what you call decent…"

Larry made a tight sound in his throat and handed Michael an envelope with cash for the deposit and the first month's rent. "Anything's better than another night inside, right?"

He nodded. Any place would be better than spending another night in that concrete hellhole with fluorescent lights that held the place hostage in constant daylight, with those grating buzzes and steel-door clicks that could wake a corpse, and the rock-hard pad that passed for a mattress. But he suspected he would never be able to sleep again without those lights. Those sounds. That mattress.

"The place will do for now."

Larry pointed to the computer screen on the dash. "Put in your address."

He looked from the contraption to the driver.

"The GPS." Then he slid a glance Michael's way and grinned. "Oh. Right. You probably haven't used one of those in a while. It was an upgrade on this model."

Michael didn't need any reminders of the conveniences he'd missed out on. The things that were this guy's fault. And Maria's.

"Doesn't anyone use maps anymore?" he groused.

He let Larry guide him through the screens to enter the address on that scrap of paper from his pocket. The information on the other side of the crumbled sheet was more important to him, anyway, but Larry didn't need to know about that.

"It's going to take a few weeks to get used to all the changes since you...left."

"Maybe a month."

He wondered if he would ever reacclimate to a world that didn't have prison's clear rules. The order. Inside, each man understood his role, from the murderers holding court at the top of the social hierarchy to the guys playing Susy Homemaker for their meathead boyfriends.

Even he had a place, as a master of demand-chain management for chemical life enhancers.

Outside, he was just an ex-con with nothing at all. At least not yet.

"Have you found any answers for me?"

Larry shook his head, still staring at the road. "You've got to be patient."

"I don't *have* to be anything. I've been waiting for years."

"Give me a little time."

"I got that request to you a month ago."

"Which was a stupid move, if you ask me."

"I didn't."

"Your wife did a fine job of disappearing." He slid a glance Michael's way. "Do you think she might have had a good reason?"

"You believed the bitch's lies, too?"

The side of Larry's mouth lifted, but he didn't say more. Michael's hands fisted at his sides.

"My marriage is none of your business."

"Guess not."

At least Larry didn't point out that he no longer had one of those. Good thing for him because Michael would have punched him in the throat.

"Just let me know as soon as you find out anything, okay?"

"I will." Larry reached for a button on the dashboard, and a storage area popped open. He pulled out a burner cell phone and handed it to him. "So we can keep in contact."

He murmured his thanks, though they would have stayed in contact whether Larry liked it or not. The officer didn't need to know that he wasn't the only one searching for answers. Michael had made some buddies inside who had helpful friends of their own.

Larry pulled the SUV to the curb and cut the engine. "That's the place."

Michael could only stare through the rivulets on his window. The two-story clapboard house with its peeling paint had probably been showing its age in the fifties.

"It ain't much."

That it was a long trip from the apartment Maria used to keep pin neat was one hell of an understatement.

"It's just until you get a job and get back on your feet."

"And until my wife comes home where she belongs."

Larry's shoulders shifted. "Now even if—I mean *after*—we locate Maria, it might be a while before you can convince her to, uh, come home. If—"

Michael threw open the car door and grabbed his bag from the backseat before the jerk could say *ever*. She *would* come back. The police only knew the things his wife had said when she was upset. She always took them back. Always.

"Just let me know what you find out about my wife."

He dodged the land mines of crumbling concrete on his way up the walk. Deciding that the cracked doorbell wasn't worth a try, he knocked hard on the door.

When no one answered, he considered bashing in the window next to it. But since the impact might have been enough to bring down the whole house, he knocked again.

"You sure someone's supposed to be there?" Larry called out the car window.

"The guy said he'd be here...with the key."

Finally, a rheumy-eyed skeleton of a man opened the door a crack and pushed a clipboard out. Michael signed without reading it, plunking down the envelope of cash and reaching for the key in the man's other hand. He could have wrung the weasel's neck for closing his fist and counting the bills before handing the key to him and closing the door.

With each creak as he climbed the apartment steps, Michael reminded himself that this was temporary, like that sentence he shouldn't have had to serve. They would find her, and she would return to him, where she belonged. She would be sorry, too. For saying those things to the judge. For ignoring a court visitation order. But most of all, for keeping him from his money and his son.

The instant he flipped the switch inside the apartment, he wished for his prison cell. Yellow, nicotine-scarred walls encased a sunken, stained couch and matching chair. A lone TV tray served as a side table, but there was no television, only a shadowy mark on the wall where one used to be.

This would be fine, he decided, as he took in the lumpy looking mattress with a coverlet on top. From his bag, he pulled out a three-by-five photo of Maria, smiling on their wedding day, tresses of her hair curling around the lacy, borrowed veil. He always imagined her this way. Smiling. His.

"It won't be long now, sweetheart. We'll be a family again."

Michael's lips formed a grim line. Maybe he wouldn't be able to make Maria understand that he couldn't live without her. But that wasn't the point, was it? He wouldn't *let* her live without him.

Chapter 3

"Welcome back, Officer."

Jamie stopped, the open door still pressed against his shoulder. Sure enough, Ted, the same diner owner who'd cashed him out less than twelve hours before, waved at him through a crush of customers waiting to be seated. Didn't the guy ever go home? And why were there so many kids there on a school day?

Not for the first time, Jamie wondered what he was doing there, even if the mingling scents of cinnamon rolls and bacon already had his mouth watering. He waved back as he realized that his plan might have a hole in it. If Sarah had worked last night, she probably wouldn't be there to answer his questions this morning. And, in the unlikely case that she *was* there, what would he say to her? That they'd exchanged a few strange looks? And a note? And pie?

Despite the line of waiting guests, Ted sidled over and spoke in a quiet voice. "Everything all right last night?"

Jamie lifted a brow. Was it obvious that he was there to scope out a woman? But when Ted squared his shoulders as if bracing himself for a complaint, Jamie suddenly understood.

"Just couldn't stay away." Those words were truer than the guy would ever know.

"We love hearing that." Ted grinned and nodded several times. "We're slammed because the kids are off from school, but we'll get you seated as soon as we can. And don't worry about the cinnamon rolls. Sarah made extra…"

Jamie wasn't sure what Ted said after that. At the mention of Sarah's name, he couldn't help scanning the room, looking for her again.

"Order up, table 21," a feminine voice called out, somehow rising above the din of conversations.

He didn't need the pounding of his pulse in his ears and the weightless feeling inside him to tell him the voice was Sarah's. Sure enough, her head peeked out through the opening where waitresses collected their orders.

Her head was bent at first, but suddenly those pretty blue eyes were staring back at him and widening with something closer to uneasiness than surprise. Then, just like last night, she disappeared into the kitchen.

Well, that was one time too many. He wasn't the one who'd written that note or cut that pie. She'd created all the questions, so it was about time for her to offer some answers.

Jamie squeezed through the line of customers and strode across the dining room, not stopping until he reached the kitchen's swinging door. Before he could talk himself out of it, he rapped on it.

For several seconds, he waited. Through the window, he caught sight of several waitresses zipping past.

When her face appeared in the circle, his breath caught. Only she wasn't smiling the way she usually did when she took his burger order. As the door opened a few inches, he backed out of the way.

"May I help you, sir? I mean... *Officer?*"

"Jamie," he croaked.

She lifted a brow, but her flour-covered hands were gripped together. Though he'd dreamed of someday being this close to Sarah, he'd never imagined the event with anxiety pouring off her in waves.

"I'm, um, off duty," he said.

"I can see that."

"Right."

As he brushed his sweaty palms on his jeans, he mined his memory for that list of questions that had been lining up like a troop formation. The waitress who appeared behind Sarah gave him a reprieve.

"Behind you, sweetie."

"Sorry, Belinda."

Sarah pushed through the doorway and held the door for the other waitress. Once the woman had passed, Sarah slid into the opening again.

"As you can see, Officer, we're a little busy this morning, so..." She stepped back, allowing the space to narrow.

Jamie could feel the answers he craved and his first opportunity to have a real conversation with her slipping away with the incremental closing of the door.

"Wait."

Her gaze lowered to his hand, which seemed to have

shot out on its own to grip the door. Immediately, he released it, but when Sarah's gaze lifted, that look was in her eyes again. Was it fear? Of him?

"Sorry. That's not—" He cut off his words and took an obvious step back. "Look, I'm doing this all wrong. Can we talk? Just for a minute?"

She shot a glance over her shoulder, as if she would welcome any excuse to say no, but turned back to him and nodded. With a wave for him to follow, she stepped out from behind the counter and led him to the hall where the customer restrooms were located. At least there wasn't a line. He was nervous enough without an audience.

Halfway down the hall, she wheeled around so quickly that Jamie had to jerk to a stop to avoid running into her.

"I didn't mean anything by it," she said.

"I don't know what you mean." He did, and that was the hell of it. Those small things he'd built up to Mount Everest proportions meant nothing at all to her.

She shrugged, watching the toe of her shoe as it tapped the industrial tile floor.

"You know. The note."

"So, it really *was* for me." The words were out of his mouth before he could stop them.

"Of course, it—" She stopped herself and gripped her crossed arms over her chest.

"There wasn't a name at the top."

"I just wanted to say thank-you. You know. For your work in the community."

"Oh." Well, she hadn't announced that she found him irresistible, but it wasn't the worst thing she could have said.

"Because I'd kind of overheard about your rough night."

"Thanks," he said, because there wasn't much else he could say to that.

"I just wanted you to know that your work is appreciated. That's all," she rushed to add.

"And I *appreciate* your saying so."

He would also be grateful for a graceful exit. Or an escape route of any kind. Everything made sense now. Her strange look when he'd arrived the night before. Charity, not a come-on. And the pie? She and Trevor had been in cahoots on that one. What kind of police officer added those measly clues up to a sum of romance?

"Well, thanks for clearing that up, but you probably need to get back to your tables." His gaze lowered to the jeans and long-sleeved T-shirt she wore beneath her apron rather than a uniform, and then to the dusting of flour on her sleeve.

"Oh. You're baking."

"I do that in the mornings." She cleared her throat. "And I should get back to it. Everyone seems to want cinnamon rolls instead of pancakes this morning."

That she shuffled her feet then didn't surprise him. He'd mentioned her baking again. But the way she wrung her hands and kept looking over her shoulder toward the restrooms and side kitchen door seemed excessive. How could she expect scrumptious desserts like hers to remain a secret?

"Can you blame them? They smell great."

Her cheeks deepened to a pretty pink. "Do you want me to pack some up for you?"

Again, she glanced over her shoulder. Why she was so anxious for him to leave? Was she hiding something?

Then a door squeaked, and the answer to those questions ran out with a burst of energy and a mop of sandy blond hair he would have recognized anywhere. Aiden?

"Mommy, Mr. Mike said the oven timer—" The boy stopped midsentence. "It's Mr. Jamie!"

He ran right past his mother and launched himself, his face landing soundly in Jamie's stomach.

"Oomph." He ruffled the boy's hair, stalling for both a breath and the chance to absorb these new details. Sarah was not only a mom, but she was *Aiden's* mom, and for some reason, she hadn't wanted him to know either of those things. Why not?

"How're you doing, buddy?"

Aiden beamed up as he eased him back, and Jamie's stomach clenched. How could he have missed the resemblance before? Sure, he'd never seen them together since the babysitter rather than a parent always picked Aiden up from Kids' Space. But even so. The child's huge, almost impossibly light blue eyes were just like his mother's. And his mother's hit him like a gravel truck with a full load every time she looked at him. Which at the moment she was avoiding.

She spoke to her son instead. "Aiden, you know it's not nice to throw yourself at people."

Aiden took another step back, but his mischievous grin remained. "Sorry, Mr. Jamie."

"Thanks. I think I'll live." He held his hands wide. "Hey, I heard you get to skip school today."

"We had a day off, but Mommy made me come to work with her."

"Yeah, moms are mean that way sometimes," she murmured.

"You got to come to work with Mom?" Jamie slid his

gaze to Sarah. "Looks like we have a pretty important someone in common."

She finally nodded.

"And the note was really about this guy?" He gripped the giggling boy and rubbed his knuckles on that blond head.

"Yes, but I'd better—" She jerked to look down at her son. "Wait, did you say, *timer*?"

"Mr. Mike already took out the pies," Aiden announced.

Jamie could have kissed the kid. Sarah wanted to answer his questions about as much as a suspect in an interview room, but her son hadn't learned the art of excuses and wasn't helping her to escape. "That's great that Mr. Mike helped you out."

"Mommy, can we eat breakfast with Mr. Jamie?"

She shook her head so hard her dangling earrings jiggled. "Sorry, sweetie. I still have a few things to finish in the back."

"You said we could leave when the pies were cooked."

"Yes, I did." Then she smiled. "So, we'll finish and then leave right away."

Aiden opened his mouth, but then drew his eyebrows together as he must have realized that he'd won. Or *lost*.

"But I want to stay," he whined.

"Yeah, he wants to stay." Jamie gestured with a tilt of his head toward the dining room. "And if the line out there has moved at all, I'll have a table soon. You don't want me to eat alone, do you?"

Jamie couldn't believe the words coming out of his mouth. They sounded more like something ladies' man Nick or reformed womanizer Shane would say. Not him.

He would have said anything then to convince her not to leave, but she was already shaking her head again.

"Please, Mommy. It's Mr. Jamie."

Her son's words must have made the difference, because she dampened her lips and then nodded.

"Yay!" Aiden called out.

It was all Jamie could do not to shout, or at least grab the kid in a bear hug.

The boy slid past Jamie and scampered down the hall before turning back to them. "I'm going to go tell Mr. Ted."

Sarah watched him go, her eyes awash with the kind of affection that a mother reserves for her child. Funny how Jamie wished she'd look at *him* that way.

She did look back at him then and caught him watching.

"He's so full of energy," she mumbled. "But then you already know that."

"You're right about that."

Again, she glanced at her son, a watchful mother even though he was only twenty feet away.

"Thanks again for being so kind to my son. Making friends is always a struggle for him."

"Really? I don't know why. He's such a great kid."

"I wish the boys in his class could see that."

Jamie brushed off her worries with a wave of his hand. "He'll be fine. You worry too much."

"What mother doesn't?"

He had to give her that. His own parents had hovered over him for months after Mark's death, even to the point of ignoring their own grief.

"Well, I'm glad I've gotten to know Aiden," he said.

"And I know a lot about him…if I can believe half of what a six-year-old tells me."

She blinked several times. "Probably less than that."

Her words were light, but her chuckle sounded strange.

"Okay, then, I'll believe just 25 percent."

She nodded, though from her look, she still wasn't satisfied with that bargain. What didn't she want Aiden to share?

"Then it's good that we'll be having breakfast together."

Her gaze narrowed. "Why's that?"

"So you can tell me which quarter to believe."

This time she smiled, and the slow burn he always felt when she was around edged up a notch.

"I'll be sure to do that," she said.

"And while you're at it, maybe you can do one more thing."

"What's that?"

"You can tell me why you didn't want me to know you were Aiden's mom."

Chapter 4

At the clink of the bells, Sarah startled, her head twisting toward the sound. Another group of customers had squeezed inside the diner's entry area and were waiting for their fill of eggs, pancakes and breakfast meats.

For a moment, she'd almost relaxed. She couldn't afford to do that. Not with Aiden sitting next to her, right out in public where anyone could see them. Not when her back was to the restaurant door as Trooper Donovan had taken her preferred seat facing the exit.

And especially not while in the presence of the officer, who was too curious about her and her son.

She turned back to the table, where Jamie had settled in his chair, his arms crossed. Could he see right through her? Could he sense that she was living a lie?

"I never get used to those bells," she explained, and then licked her lips.

"I hate them, too." He forked another bite of his eggs but didn't lift it off the plate. "They're jarring."

At least he hadn't pointed out that she'd nearly climbed out of her skin over something she heard dozens of times each day. Something that should have been as familiar to her as the shrill of his patrol car's siren probably was to him.

But instead of asking her about it, Jamie took a bite of his pancake. She was grateful for the reprieve but didn't kid herself into believing that the officer's earlier question about her son wouldn't pop up again. If only she knew how to answer when it did.

"Aren't you hungry?"

She glanced down at her plate, where she'd only scooted around her eggs and toast. "Guess not."

His gaze felt warm on her crown as she bent and forced a bite.

"That means your mom won't get to have a cinnamon roll."

"Mom said *I* could," Aiden said, over a mouthful of scrambled eggs.

"Aiden…"

At her warning, her son swallowed and then tried again. "Sorry, Mom. But you said I could if I finished my breakfast." He pointed to the yellow and white mess on his plate, where he still had some work to do.

"Looks like it's going to be just us two then." Jamie reached across the table to give the boy a high five.

Despite the warning bells that should have been clanging in her head, she couldn't resist smiling at the man who'd befriended her son. He was kind, unassuming and— What was she doing? It didn't matter that he was easy to like. Too easy in her case. Jamie was a cop. If she had any sense, she would steer clear of him.

"Can you believe I've never even tasted your mom's famous cinnamon rolls?"

Aiden's eyes were wide. "No way!"

"They're not *famous*," Sarah said before she could stop herself.

She tucked her chin to her chest, hoping her cheeks weren't as flushed as they felt. Over the top for a tiny bit of praise. Her dream of opening her own bakery was a lifetime ago, anyway…when she'd still foolishly believed in happily-ever-afters. She was nobody's fool now.

"Maybe not, but they're always all gone before my friends and I come in at night."

"Well, Trooper Donovan… I mean Mr. Jamie…"

When he grinned at her, a tiny dimple that she hadn't noticed before appeared in his left cheek. The flutter in her tummy took her by surprise. She ruthlessly shoved thoughts about that dimple and the laughter in his eyes aside to consider later. Or never.

"How about just Jamie?"

Because it was easier than meeting his gaze when he was making her so nervous, she turned to her son instead. "He's a grown-up, so he's still *Mr.* Jamie to you."

"Your mom's right about that." Jamie gestured toward Aiden. "Come to think about it, though we've been first-name buddies at the center all year, I still don't even know your last name."

"Aiden Thomas Cline," her son announced importantly.

The pulse thudding in Sarah's ears nearly drowned out his answer. Of course, he'd said "Cline." That and "Aiden" were the only names he'd ever known.

"Cline, huh? I like that."

Though he was speaking to her son, Jamie was looking right at her. The skin on her forearms positively tingled, so she crossed her arms and covered them with her hands. What was the matter with her? She hadn't felt so unsettled around a man since... No, she wouldn't think about that now.

His gaze lowered to her arms, but he didn't comment on them.

Sarah pushed her chair back from the table.

"Looks like you're almost finished, so how about I package some rolls to go? There's still a line over there..."

Jamie waved a hand to brush off her suggestion. "Our waitress can get those. Anyway, weren't you just getting ready to answer my question from earlier?"

"Oh. Right." Ignoring her rushing pulse, she slid closer to the table again. She still didn't know how to answer him, but she refused to do it in front of her child. "Sweetie, why don't you go wash off your face, and then you can have your cinnamon roll."

"Okay, Mom." He hopped up from the table.

Good thing his first-grade logic didn't make him wonder why she would send him to clean his face only to make it dirty again.

When the restroom door closed, she turned back to Jamie, the answer rushing from her all on its own. "I'm not ashamed of being Aiden's mom, if that's what you're asking. He's the best thing I've ever done."

"Sorry." Jamie's hands came up in surrender. "Didn't mean to offend you."

She wanted to ask him just what he *had* intended to

do with a question like that, but she couldn't encourage him to ask more. He knew enough about her already.

"You've met all the guys you work with, right?" She paused, waiting for her words to settle. "If you were a single mom like me, would you want any of them to know details about you? Including your last name?"

His jaw tightened the way it had the night before when his coworkers were joking about her. When he'd defended her.

"Point taken."

"Then we're agreed." She took a bite of her cold toast and managed not to wince.

"If you ever need me to talk to the guys and make sure they remember their manners around a lady, I'd be happy to."

"No! I mean I can handle it. They're not half as bad as some of the guys who come in here."

"Those must be some real bottom feeders if they're worse than Vinnie and Nick."

His jaw flexed again, and she somehow managed to keep from smiling at him. Again. Wait. Wasn't it bad enough that she was enjoying a man's compliments about her baking? And noticing his dimples? Now she was allowing herself to be flattered by his protectiveness. His offer to "talk" to his friends should have been reason enough for her to grab Aiden and sprint through the nearest emergency exit. What did it take for her to learn to steer clear of men who communicated with their fists?

Because she couldn't afford to dredge up memories she'd tried so hard to bury, not when this guy already had her balancing on shifting ground, she waved the waitress over.

"Evelyn, would you mind packing up two cinnamon

rolls for us? Two boxes." She pointed to Jamie and then to Aiden as he reached his seat.

Aiden's smile fell. "But I want Mr. Jamie to come over to play."

From the word, *play*, she started shaking her head.

"Grown-ups don't have play dates." So why did the thought of *playing* with this particular grown-up send shivers up her spine? This had to stop. "Besides, just because you have the day off from school doesn't mean that everyone has a day off."

"Your mom's right again. I have to go to work in a few hours."

"In your police car?" Aiden planted his elbows on the table with his face nestled in his hands, excitement dancing in his eyes.

"Absolutely. I might even get to use the siren today."

The boy's eyes widened. "Will you take Pancake with you?"

"Pancake?" she asked.

Aiden sat taller in his seat. "That's Mr. Jamie's cat. She's orange-brown."

"Nah, she prefers to stay at home and take catnaps," Jamie told him.

"Who names a cat *Pancake*?"

"Somebody who loves…" Jamie began.

"Pancakes!" Aiden filled in for him.

They both pointed to Jamie's clean plate as the busser whisked it away. Sarah could only look back and forth between her son and the cop. How could Aiden know so much about Jamie? And if he did, just how much had Aiden told *him*?

She shoved her chair back so quickly that it toppled over and hit the floor as she stood. She jerked it up and held her breath while it wobbled and then settled. "Too much coffee this morning. Anyway, I should see how Evelyn is doing with those cinnamon rolls."

The waitress emerged from the kitchen, carrying two white paper bags. She handed the first to Jamie as he stood.

"Now, sweetie, you'll want to warm that up when you're ready to eat it." She gestured toward Sarah as she handed her the second bag. "But I'm sure your friend here will give you the specifics."

"Thanks for the suggestion," Jamie said.

He was counting out bills from his wallet, which was a good thing, since Sarah wasn't ready for him to look her way.

"Let me get that." She reached for the check, but he pulled it away.

"Don't think so. Departmental rules. You wouldn't want me to get into trouble for accepting gifts, would you?"

She reached for her purse, heavy with the tip money that would keep her account from flatlining later this morning. "That's not a thing. Wait. Would you really?"

"Want to risk it?"

She frowned but lowered her arm. "Well, thanks. Then I'm sure Evelyn will help you at the cash register, and you—I mean we—can get out of here."

"Sure thing. Want to run up there with me, buddy?"

Her son didn't even look her way before trailing after his hero. The funny thing was she couldn't blame him. There was just something about Jamie Donovan. An unassuming quality that could tempt an unsuspecting person to trust him. That might charm someone who wasn't careful into sharing her secrets.

Neither of those things could ever happen. She had to protect Andrew—no, *Aiden*—as always. And she would.

Still, when Jamie slipped out the front door and her son skittered back her way, Sarah's shoulders slumped forward. Her hands gripped the chair back for support. Relief. That had to be what she was feeling. She'd wanted him to leave, and now he was gone. That was a good thing.

So why did one part of her, no matter how small and ridiculous, wish that he would stay?

"He's back!"

Aiden and his mom were just on the other side of the gaggle near the diner's front door, but Jamie could have heard that excited voice all the way from the kitchen. Sarah had slipped one arm into her rain jacket, but she stopped and stared.

As Jamie opened and closed his hand in a wave, Sarah's gaze darted away from him, while Aiden was waving as if they hadn't crossed paths in months. Well, at least one of them was happy to see him again. The other one wasn't thrilled at all. Jamie had predicted both things as he'd stood outside on the same sidewalk where he'd paced the night before. Only instead of wishing he could run from the building and escape from the thoughts pursuing him, this time all he'd been able to think about was going back inside.

To the woman who'd all but booted him to the literal curb with his bakery bag.

He glanced down at the white sack just as Aiden managed to snake through the crowd to reach him.

"Hi again, Mr. Jamie."

Sarah caught up with them before he could respond.

Her arms were gripped tight over her chest, though one of her jacket sleeves still dangled empty at her side. She spoke only to her son.

"I said to wait for me."

"But Mr. Jamie is back."

"I see that."

She lifted her head and pinned Jamie with her questioning stare.

"I'd just thought of something," he said, and then cleared his throat.

That *something* had seemed like a far better idea while he was still outside, his shoes resting on last night's puddles that had dried to a crusty mud. But he couldn't just watch her pulling away after spending the past year dreaming up ways to get closer to her. When his questions multiplied exponentially with every vague answer she gave. And when each moment with her made him crave another.

"That you can play before work?" Aiden asked hopefully.

"Not today. Sorry. But I was wondering if you," he paused, his gaze darting to Sarah, "and your mom… might like to join me for a day at the Detroit Zoo on Saturday."

"The zoo! Really?"

Aiden's squeals caused several diners to turn toward the commotion. In contrast to the boy's body, which vibrated with excitement, Sarah stilled.

"That's nice of you to ask, but I don't think—"

"Please, Mom!"

She shook her head, her gaze darting to the door before settling again on her son. "Sorry, Aiden."

The boy crossed his arms. "But I want to go."

"Not this time."

"We never get to go to the zoo. Never ever."

Sarah tightened her jaw as if preparing to correct her son, but then her shoulders slumped.

Jamie swallowed. He was a jerk, wasn't he? Worse maybe than even the lechers she dodged at work every day. What kind of guy used a child to get to his mother? What kind of *person* invited them on an adventure a struggling single mom couldn't easily afford?

He still had so many questions. How did the two of them end up here? How could Aiden's father have left him? Left *her*? Most of all, though, Jamie wanted to know what put that stark look in her eyes. But just because he regretted not asking Mark enough questions before it was too late, that didn't make wanting to know things about Sarah excuse enough to manipulate her. She deserved better than that. Better than *him*.

"It was just an idea," he began.

"Please…!"

This time Aiden's plea was so drawn out that it sounded like two syllables.

Again, Sarah shook her head, and when she spoke again, she didn't look at Jamie.

"It was so nice of you to ask, but I always work the day shift on Saturdays." She finally met his gaze.

"Well, not this Saturday."

They all turned at the sound of Ted's voice. When the restaurant owner had slipped past other diners to reach them, Jamie wasn't sure.

Ted patted Sarah's shoulder. "Marilyn can take your shift. She owes you, don't you think? And every kid needs a trip to the zoo, right?"

He gave an exaggerated wink and then patted Aiden's

shoulder. Sarah's side glance suggested she didn't appreciate Ted's matchmaking any more than she relished Jamie's invitation, but she sighed.

Aiden must have noticed the change, as he was bouncing again.

"So, can we go, Mom? I want to see the new penguin exhibit and the tigers and the Kodiak bears."

Whether it was because her son had just listed some of the most popular exhibits at the Detroit Zoo as if he'd been researching them or that their arguments had worn her down, she nodded.

"Yes, we can go."

The words rang in Jamie's ears. He'd won. He would get to spend a full day with a woman he'd dreamed of and a child he adored. She'd required some convincing, but they would have a great time on Saturday. He would make sure of that. So why did he get the feeling he was just one in a long line of people who'd taken something away from Sarah Cline?

Chapter 5

At the grind of metal on metal and the burst of frost-bitten air on the back of his neck, Jamie turned from his desktop computer to the steel door that separated the squad room from the parking lot. He hated that the hair on his nape lifted and that he was tempted to cover the monitor so that his fellow troopers wouldn't see it.

He was being ridiculous. Nobody cared about the mundane information he was typing into the fields of the property-damage accident report. Now the stuff he'd been searching for a few hours earlier, information about a certain young waitress—his fellow troopers would have been very interested in *those* details. That is, if he'd found anything. And he hadn't.

It didn't surprise him that of the forty-two "Sarah Clines" an online directory listed as living in Michigan, Indiana and Ohio, none had a Brighton address. Those

lists were always incomplete, especially for more tran-
sient populations. But that was only the first dead end
he'd hit tonight. She had no social-media profiles. No
embarrassing photos that popped up under a name and
image search. He didn't have her Social Security number to prove it yet, but he would bet she didn't have a
bank account or a credit history, either. It was as if two
years ago she'd dropped out of the sky into Livingston
County, and part of him was afraid to ask why.

"Hey, Donovan." Nick Sanchez shook the rain from
his hair as he barreled through the doorway. He shoved
his radio into a slot in the charging station.

Jamie nodded. "Sanchez."

"You don't usually beat the rest of us back to the
post."

"Still have a few reports to finish." Those would have
been completed, too, if he'd stuck to splitting his time
between clocking speeding motorists and knocking out
reports while parked at the US 23 exit near Hartland.
Instead, he'd sneaked searches on the Law Enforcement
Information Network, LEIN, which could land him in
big trouble if anyone noticed, to hunt down details on a
woman he had the hots for.

"Busy night?" Nick asked, as he continued to watch
him.

"Just a few property-damage accidents and a minor
personal-injury accident."

"Unlucky you. I just had a few stranded motorists
and one DUI, but she's already cooling her heels at Livingston County Jail. Report's submitted with all the i's
dotted and the t's crossed."

Jamie gave him a sardonic smile and then turned

back to his own report, which was no more than half-way complete.

"You doing okay after last night?"

He startled, as Nick had moved closer to him without his notice. For someone in a career where noting details could make the difference between waking up in the morning and being stretched out in a drawer at the medical examiner's office, he needed to pay closer attention.

"I asked if you're doing okay after—"

"Oh. Sure. Sure." He cleared his throat. "Anyway, I can't believe all of that happened only yesterday. Seems like a long time ago."

He could say that again times ten. So much time seemed to have passed, but only he knew how little that had to do with the suicide call. What would Mark have thought when he saw how easily Jamie had compartmentalized thoughts of that unfortunate guy's death?

"Glad you're bouncing back. It was a tough call."

"I'm good. Really." But because the images were rolling back faster now than he wanted them to, he changed the subject. "You said the suspect was female. Did it at least take some of the sting out that *you* were the one Mirandizing her?"

Nick's eyebrow lifted, but his smile still widened, his suspicion over the question losing to his cockiness, just as Jamie had predicted it would.

"She and my mom might have gone to high school together, but to your question, she didn't fight the cuffs too much."

"Did he mention that she puked in his car, and he had to have it hosed down?"

Both men turned to find Shane Warner standing in his street clothes just outside the men's locker room. Shane had come by a few moments before, barely waving as he'd rushed in to change out of his uniform.

Nick shrugged, his grin remaining. "Details, details. Anyway, somebody's gotta pick up the slack now that you're all domesticated."

Shane slid into his jacket with a fluid movement that no longer hinted at the gunshot wound he'd sustained a year earlier. The wound that had briefly put him in a wheelchair *and* had introduced him to the physical therapist who would become his wife.

"Domesticated?" Nick repeated with a laugh. "I'll have to tell Natalie you said that. She thinks I've got a ways to go before I'm presentable in polite society."

"Did you leave the seat up for her to fall in last night?" Jamie asked.

This time the other officers looked his way, their expressions skeptical. Okay, he wasn't usually the one who fired first in their banter wars, but if the past twenty-four hours had taught him anything, it was that things could change. Sometimes more than a guy could predict in his best dreams.

"Well?" he prompted, and then turned back to the screen so that no one would see his stupid grin that had nothing to do with his question.

"I'm not a barbarian. But close."

"So, Donovan, what do you think about that almost barbarian blowing off his friends…again…to go home to his new wife?"

Jamie turned his head to the side to answer. "Oh. You know, I don't think I'm going to be able to make it, either."

"You, neither?" Nick said. "You don't even have a good excuse."

They had no idea. "Sorry, man. Busy tonight."

"Busy, huh?" Shane asked.

Jamie didn't say more, and, despite the looks they had probably trained on his back, he knew they wouldn't ask. It was a guy code kind of thing. A few of them hadn't even mentioned they were dating someone until they mailed their wedding invitations.

The door opening a second time saved him from expanding on that thought. He might have fantasized about Sarah for months in ways that would put some of his fellow troopers to shame, but that didn't mean his wayward thoughts had taken him *there*.

This time several troopers poured through the door, rain dripping off their outer coats and waterproof covers that protected their uniform hats. Third-shift troopers emerging from the locker rooms grimaced as they passed them, their wet and likely busy shift on Michigan's highways only beginning.

Vinnie Leonetti shoved his hand back through his black hair, which was so wet it looked as if it had been slicked with hair oil. "Guess we're the ones swimming in tonight. Good thing the third-shift folks always ride in pairs. They'll be ready to meet up with Noah and his ark."

Lieutenant Ben Peterson only shook his head at him. "Just don't give up your day job, okay, buddy? The comedy circuit isn't ready for your brand of humor."

The truth was that Jamie wasn't ready to be with any of them tonight, which he had to admit was strange. These men and women were his best friends. They were his most fervent supporters. His *people*.

But for two nights in a row, he'd wanted to step back from them. Last night because his own secrets were peeking from behind the dark curtain of his memory, and tonight because of hers. They were also already watching him too closely after his case last night. They were too familiar with his habits, his triggers.

He couldn't spend another evening under the close inspection of a group of professionals trained to sniff out secrets and identify liars. Not when he was searching for the first and, if asked enough questions, might do the second.

So, he waved away the additional invitations and returned to the form on the monitor. He had plenty of screen time ahead of him at home tonight, as well. He didn't care how many roadblocks he faced. Before Saturday, he intended to know everything there was to know about Sarah Cline. And what he couldn't find out online, he was just going to have to ask her in person.

Sarah aimed her digital camera at the five-hundred-pound western lowland gorilla as it lounged on a low branch in the Great Apes of Harambee attraction. The animal paid no attention to the man and boy making silly faces at it from the other side of the glass.

"Do you think he can see us through the window, Mom?" Aiden asked.

"I don't know. Can you see him?"

The boy drew his eyebrows together and rested his hands on the glass as if that would help him answer her question. He must have remembered Jamie's warning not to disturb the animals by pounding on the window, as his touch was gentle.

"Yes. I can see him."

"Well, it's just a thick window. He can see you…if he wants to, anyway."

Sarah turned with her camera and caught Jamie and Aiden in a goofy pose, one of many moments she'd captured on her memory card during their three hours at the Detroit Zoo. From the first frame, she'd convinced herself not to be jealous of the two of them together, even if Aiden's smile was so wide that he'd reopened the tiny split in his chapped lower lip.

She was just content being able to play with her son while disappearing into this crowd of animal lovers. They seemed to be invisible to the world, and today she would pretend that was true.

Now she couldn't resist grinning at the boy, who kept waving at the unimpressed gorilla.

"He just agrees that you two look ridiculous, and he's trying to ignore you."

"Hey, I'm offended."

Jamie pursed his lips in a deep frown that slid into a grin as he nabbed her son under the arms and swung him in a low circle. With the backpack he was being secretive about on his back and a first-grader swinging from his arms, he narrowly missed a mother pushing an empty stroller.

"Oh. Sorry, ma'am." He lowered Aiden to the floor again.

"Why can't you two relax like Mr. Silverback in there?"

Sarah gestured toward the habitat just as one of the three bachelor gorillas winged a banana peel at the glass next to where her son and his friend stood.

"Look, Mom. He threw a banana."

"Sure you want us to relax like *that*?" Jamie asked.

The creature nibbled on its banana as if it wasn't responsible for the smear on the window.

"Maybe not *exactly* like that, but he knows you're out there, and he knows a couple of poser primates when he sees them."

"Us?" Jamie leaned forward and allowed his arms to hang loose like the chimpanzees they'd visited a few minutes before. "Ooh-ooh-ooh."

Aiden imitated him, and soon the two of them were chasing each other out of the exhibit and into the rest of the African Forest habitat. Sarah hushed them, but she was laughing again by the time she caught up with them. In fact, she'd laughed so hard all day that she'd had to remind herself to keep up her guard.

"The animals are wondering why you guys get to run around free while they have to stay in their habitats."

"You kidding? Some of them are probably just wondering if we'd make a tasty lunch." Jamie ruffled Aiden's hair. "I happen to think we'd be delicious."

Oh, he'd be delicious, all right. Sarah blinked, the thought as unexpected as the sensation that skimmed up her arms like a caress. What was that about? She zipped her light canvas jacket higher, though it had no chance of keeping her warm now.

"Right. Delicious," Aiden said.

She would have admired the way her son tried to match Jamie's stride as they continued to the Asian Forest habitat, but she was too busy trying not to notice how Jamie's biceps strained against his jacket. She had no more business paying attention to his muscles than she had noticing how his eyes sparkled when he told a joke. And the way he spoke to and *listened* to her son, well, a woman might find that terribly sexy if she wasn't careful.

But she *was* careful. At least she had been until this

week, when she'd written Jamie that note and sent her own world careening off its globe stand. She needed to return to the controlled, safe spin of that world, and she would…after today. She wanted to give Aiden this one carefree day. The kind of day all children deserved to have and her son had been denied because of her poor choices. She would give this to her son, at least this, even if it meant spending time with a police officer whose company wasn't as unpleasant as it should have been.

To ensure that she kept her thoughts where they belonged, she grabbed the camera hanging from a strap on her wrist and centered her son 's image in the LCD screen.

"I can't believe that you're still taking pictures with a regular camera," Jamie said, as he dropped back to stand next to her.

Her hands jerked just as she clicked the button. "Now look what you made me do."

Jamie stretched his neck to get a look at the image on her screen. Aiden's face was a blurry blob, with an even fuzzier red panda lazing in a tree in the distance. "Sorry. It's just that most people use their phones these days. Anyway, you wouldn't have missed the shot if you weren't always so jumpy."

Always? She kept her expression steady, but her hands betrayed her and shook again. She deleted the second blurry image and took a few clearer ones, but she couldn't as easily wipe away his confession that he'd been watching her. If he had been, what else had he witnessed that she hadn't wanted anyone to know?

"Anyway, I like my camera," she said, to fill the awkward silence. "It takes better photos than a phone. At least my phone. Not everyone can afford a fancy new one every time the cell companies hype the latest model."

"Don't I know it."

At least he didn't ask more about the phone she did have. She could only imagine what he would think if he saw her burner feature phone, which barely had a camera at all.

"If those last few shots are any clue, I can do as good a job as you."

Before she could answer, he stepped closer and extended a hand for her to pass her camera to him.

She held it away from him. "I do perfectly well on my own, thank you very much."

"I'm sure you do, but you haven't been in any of the photos with Aiden today."

Not from any other day, either, but he didn't need to know that. What reasonable excuse could she offer for her fear of including photos of herself with Aiden, even on her own camera? She would tell him whatever she needed to though. How could she live with herself if Michael recognized her in a picture, and it led him to her son?

Jamie lowered his hand, then reached into his jacket pocket and pulled out his cell phone. "Here, I'll try mine."

"No!" Her gaze shot to her son and then back to Jamie, who was watching her too closely. She cleared her throat. "I mean…well, sure."

She pulled the camera strap off her wrist and held it out to him. He returned the phone to his pocket but didn't reach for the camera. She lowered her arm to her side.

"Just wanted to keep all the photos in the same place, so I could upload them to my computer."

"Makes sense."

His expression said otherwise.

"I also don't like my face splattered all over the internet."

"You think I'd do that?"

She'd been avoiding his gaze, but now she couldn't help looking at him. Was that hurt that flashed in his eyes before he hid it behind a neutral mask?

"No," she said, and then pressed her arms to her sides. Worse than that she'd said it, she meant it. She didn't know him at all. How could she know what he would or wouldn't do?

"Oh, I get it. I'm not big on social media myself."

"Thanks for understanding. It's just so… I don't know…invasive."

"I agree, but I also would never share anything without permission. Crappy thing to do."

Again, she believed him too easily. That reason alone should have sent her running for the zoo exit, tugging Aiden along with her. Her track record for believing lies was epic. But because she had learned not to trust her instincts, she held her camera out to him a second time. Maybe he would never plaster her photos all over social media, but this way she could be sure. This way all the photos would be on *her* memory card.

She was relieved when he accepted the camera, but as he closed his hand over it, his fingers accidentally brushed hers. A wave of tingles danced over her fingertips, and her stomach clamped tightly. She jerked back, but even shoving her hand in her pocket wasn't enough to dull the sensation. Her mouth was so dry she had to lick her lips. What was wrong with her? She wasn't that silly teenage girl anymore, so why was she acting like *her*?

"Oh. Sorry."

He fiddled with the camera's picture review button and ignored her. She might have received a jolt from that errant touch, but she was the only one.

"I can't remember how to use one of these things," he said after several seconds. "You're going to have to help me out."

"You've got to be—"

Just as she pointed to the LCD panel to instruct him, he looked up from the device and grinned.

"Now do I have to wear one of those black capes over my head when I take the photo so that the light doesn't get inside?"

It took her a few seconds to realize he was talking about old-fashioned cameras, and then she stuck out her tongue at him.

"Hey, I'm not old enough to remember shooting tin-types, but you do you," he said.

She couldn't help laughing with him, and he snapped a photo of her before she could stop herself. Her face heated. He was supposed to be taking shots of her and her son, and Aiden wasn't close to being in that frame.

"What was that for?"

"Couldn't resist."

"Well, try." And she would *try* to slow her racing pulse and will the heat to drain from her face.

Aiden saved her from having to say more. "Mr. Jamie, can we see the tigers now?" He pointed to the exhibit across from them.

"Absolutely, buddy." Jamie turned to Sarah. "I mean if it's okay with your mom."

"Let's go see some tigers," she said. Jamie insisted on taking a few shots of her and Aiden together as they stood with a snoozing tiger in the background. She was strangely at ease, whether posing on the other side of the camera or falling into step beside Jamie and Aiden on the long walk to the Polk Penguin Conservation Center.

After they entered the center, where the low lighting made photography difficult, Jamie let the camera hang from his wrist.

Sarah weaved through the crowd, ensuring that Aiden was no more than a few feet ahead of her, but as they stepped through the tunnel where water enclosed them and majestic aquatic birds swam over their heads, she stepped back and rested on one of the benches. Aiden zipped back and forth, following one speedy swimmer, but Jamie sat next to her.

"He's a great kid."

She smiled as she continued to watch the child.

"It's a tough job being a single mom, isn't it?"

She turned to look at Jamie, who he was watching a pair of macaroni penguins chasing each other through the water.

"It's not so bad. And Aiden's worth every bit of the effort."

She hoped the conversation would end there but knew it wouldn't.

He cleared his throat. "Is, uh, Aiden's dad in the picture?"

He still wasn't looking at her, so she couldn't just shake her head. "No." She paused, considering whether to say more. "That's a good thing."

"Separated?"

This time she could feel his gaze on her and couldn't help smiling. He'd never considered the other possibility—that she and her child's father could have never married.

"Divorced."

"Where is he now?"

She shrugged. "Never far enough."

"I bet there's a story there."

"Not an interesting one."

She waited, since she didn't expect him to buy that one, but instead of asking more, he jumped up from the bench and jogged over to Aiden. They stared at the tunnel top and pointed to each bird as it swam overhead.

"Which species do you think that one is?" Jamie pointed to a leisurely swimmer. "Macaroni, king, gentoo or rockhopper?"

"It's a king penguin. See those bright orange feathers on his head?"

"Ding! Ding! Ding! You're right."

He turned to Sarah, who'd taken a few steps closer. "You didn't tell me your son was so smart."

"If you get me started bragging about this kid, I won't be able to stop."

"Thanks for the warning."

She must have been grinning as widely at him as he was at her when Aiden tugged his sleeve.

"Mr. Jamie, how come you know so much about penguins?"

"My younger brother, Mark, used to love penguins. Everything about them."

His lips were still lifted, but his smile no longer reached his eyes. A lump settled low in her stomach. She'd seen that stark look before, and now she had to know.

"Used to?"

"He's gone now." He cleared his throat. "It was a long time ago."

"I bet there's a story there," she said, repeating his words.

He only shrugged.

He had a story, all right. Maybe even as painful as her own. And though she had no business sticking her nose in anyone else's personal life when she had so much to hide herself, God help her, she wanted to know about his.

Chapter 6

"You see, I *do* think of everything."

Jamie added the last few packages to the snack cakes, chips and cheese puffs already piled on the bench between him and Sarah late that afternoon. No more than twenty feet away, Aiden dangled from a monkey bar on the zoo playground, oblivious to the bounty of junk food he was missing or the two adults keeping a careful watch over him as he played.

"You weren't kidding," Sarah said. "You had all kinds of surprises in that backpack of yours."

Sarah was grinning as she rifled through the packages, which had no more than trace vitamins in the lot. In fact, she'd been generous with her incredible smiles all day, and he found he would do anything if it would continue to inspire her charitable spirit. Sure, she'd had her uncomfortable moments, like when he'd pulled out his phone, but there were a few times that she'd relaxed around him and had fun.

It had made her nervous that he'd tried to take a photo with his phone. Now he couldn't help wondering which would bother her more—that he'd planned to use her photo for an internet reverse-image search to look for more information on her or that he'd had every intention of keeping the shot so that he could see her face whenever he liked. He shook away the thought that both might worry her equally. He reached for his backpack instead.

"There's more." He pulled out three juice boxes and a handful of wet wipe packets, the kind that came as a necessary bonus with fried-chicken carryout. Next, he unzipped the front pocket. "And now for *la pièce de résistance*."

He pulled out three zipper bags that now held smashed white-bread sandwiches with peanut butter and jelly oozing out from all sides. "Well, that didn't go the way I'd planned it."

"Résistance, huh?" she said with a grin. "I think I might be able to resist."

Despite Sarah's joke, when Jamie dropped the bags on top of the pile, she reached for one. She held it out in front of her and examined the messy plastic.

"Let me guess. *Grape* jelly?"

"Wow. You're good. Psychic or something?" He grabbed a candy bar, ripped it open and bit off the end.

"More like with a six-year-old, I'm an expert on jelly smears. Anyway, thanks for lunch."

"You're welcome. Think Aiden's ever going to eat anything? He said he was starving."

"With a whole playground available to him?" She

sneaked another peek at her son, who'd moved on to the rolling slide. "Doubt it."

"Then more for us."

Sarah unzipped the sandwich bag and carefully peeled the bread off the plastic. She took a single bite, chewed it and swallowed. She was so preoccupied with the boy on the playground that it was a few minutes before she took a second bite.

"Don't worry," Jamie said, before he could stop himself.

She peeked at him with her side vision. "It's just a little flat. It tastes fine."

"Not the sandwich. I mean about Aiden."

She slowly turned his way. "Moms worry. It's what we do."

"I mean right now. I'm watching, too, so you can relax. I won't let anything happen to him. I promise."

"That's nice of you, but Aiden and I are fine. Just the two of us."

Those were also the most revealing words Sarah had ever spoken to him. This mother and son were used to relying only on each other. If he ever hoped to get closer to either of them, he needed to take his time and earn Sarah's trust.

"Oh, I know. You two are great."

He opened a bag of pretzels and started eating, peeking over at her every few seconds. Each time he found her watching her son. He had so many questions for Sarah, but getting information from her was like trying to open a safe with an Allen wrench. They were alike in that way. He understood her temptation to lock secrets deep inside, so maybe if he opened up about his, she would trust him enough to share some of hers.

"Aiden's always such a comedian," he said. "Sometimes when he's telling one of his knock-knock jokes, I can almost see my brother, Mark, telling one of his."

Her eyes fluttered, and then she shifted so that she was facing him with one knee up on the bench.

"How long ago did your brother pass away?"

Pass away. He swallowed. Like *commit suicide,* her words were the kind that people used to whitewash bloodstains, an attempt to make some sense of incomprehensible loss. They offered the grieving no relief. At least Sarah was inviting him to talk about it, which was more than most people did.

"I can't believe it's been nine years now. Mark was a freshman in high school." He waited for the inevitable question: How? When she didn't ask, he answered it anyway. "He hanged himself."

"Oh, God. That's awful. I'm so sorry."

Her voice was so filled with emotion that he couldn't help looking over at her. Her eyes were damp as she stared back at him, like windows into a soul that had known its share of sadness. But when he would have expected her to blink away the compassion he saw there, to return to her familiar, unreadable mask, Sarah met his gaze with a strength and surety that surprised him.

"How old were *you*? That must have been awful for you to lose your little brother."

Jamie swallowed, heat welling behind his eyes. He'd been asked to recall the story dozens of times, but few seemed to remember that he'd just been a kid, too, when it happened. A kid who would never be the same.

"It was just before my eighteenth birthday."

"I'm so sorry, Jamie."

Her repeated words were barely above a roughened whisper.

He could have told her about being the one to find Mark. About struggling to cut down that godawful rope. He could even have talked about how he'd sobbed between breaths while performing CPR, though Mark's skin was already cold. But Jamie didn't want to share any of the macabre details with her. He wanted her to know about Mark. Just Mark. The person no one would get to know now.

"I loved being his big brother," he began. "Though I suppose I should have been jealous of him. He was better at…well, *everything* than I was."

She grinned back at him. "That can't be true."

"Oh, it was. Like we were both on the varsity soccer team, but I came off the bench as an outside defender, and he was starting center-mid."

"If I knew anything about soccer, I would be really impressed, right?"

"Oh, yeah, you would." Strange how he never talked about Mark to anyone, and now he couldn't stop. It was as if his brother would disappear completely if he didn't share these stories with her.

"He drew everyone to him. Guys. Girls. Especially girls. He had this gift with the ladies that the rest of us…" As his words trailed away, Jamie shrugged. "Anyway, he'd just started high school, and he'd already been elected freshman prince on the homecoming court. Me? I was voted 'nicest' in the Senior Superlatives."

Sarah squinted her eyes and watched him for so long that he couldn't help shifting on the bench. Would she conclude that Jamie really had been jealous of his brother, when he would have traded the use of his feet and hands just to have one more conversation with Mark?

But she only smiled again. "Nicest. I can see that. Aiden sure thinks you're a nice guy."

Even if she didn't say whether or not she shared that opinion, *nice guy* didn't sound so bad when she said it. "Maybe. But Mark...now *he* was amazing. Great athlete. Life of the party. Class clown."

"And under all of that, he was sad, wasn't he?"

Jamie blinked, as she'd pointed so easily to the truth that had evaded him until it was too late. He swallowed a few times and then nodded.

"His comedy routines must have been an effort to cover his sadness. He never said a word about it. To anyone. But the more I read about suicide, the more I recognized that he'd demonstrated plenty of warning signs."

"What kind of signs?"

"Oh, he was sleeping more, but not drastically more. And when he decided not to go out for lacrosse that spring, it was supposed to be so that he could focus on soccer for the fall." Jamie paused, self-accusations becoming an acid burning his insides. "There was even a good excuse for him to hang out less with his friends, since his perfect grades were slipping a little. All those signs, and I missed every damn one."

"Anyone could have missed those signs. Anyway, you were a kid, Jamie. Didn't the adults in his life miss them, too? Your parents? Teachers? Coaches?"

"He was my little brother. My...*responsibility*." His voice betrayed him by cracking.

He planted his elbows on his knees and rested his head in his hands. What had he been thinking, reopening old wounds to convince her to share some of hers?

Did he believe that the blame would just bounce off him this time instead of imbedding and infecting?

"This explains a lot."

Jamie sat up straight. He wasn't sure what he'd expected her to say after hearing his sad story, but it wasn't *that*. "What do you mean?"

"About the other night. The rough call the other officers were talking about before you came in. It was a suicide, right?"

"Yeah. I was too late." *Again*, he almost added.

"That must have triggered some memories."

"I guess so."

"The others know about your brother, don't they?"

He closed his eyes and recalled the faces stationed around the table the other night. As he opened them again, he shook his head. "A few of my superior officers know about Mark. I had to share my past during the interview process. I told a couple of my close friends, like Shane Warner, too. But none of the officers at Casey's the other night knew about it. I'm pretty new to the Brighton Post."

"Even if they didn't know, they were still worried about you. I told you I overheard them talking."

He remembered that, all right, though that humiliation paled when compared to his vulnerability now. "They were probably just concerned about the rookie who took a tough call. A case like that is hard on you no matter how many years you've worn a badge."

"Either way, isn't it nice to know that your coworkers have your back?"

"It is."

"But the other night is only part of what I'm talking about," she began again. "Your decision to become a cop. Your volunteering with kids. Didn't your brother's death directly lead you to those choices?"

Jamie blinked several times. No one had ever put it as succinctly as that, but he'd been asked about that possibility during his job interview after graduating from the Michigan State Police Recruit School and again when he'd volunteered at Kids' Space.

"Am I right? Or had you been planning a career in law enforcement since you played cops and robbers as a kid?"

"You're right. I did decide to enter law enforcement… after. But not immediately after. I spent most of that time in an alcohol-induced stupor, though before Mark died I didn't drink."

"You were mourning. And angry. And acting out."

"My parents must have thought so, too. I was getting ready to graduate, and they forced me to delay college for a year, while I worked through intense grief counseling."

"Looks like you made it through okay."

"I guess. It was during that time I decided to study criminal justice instead of engineering. I also had this idea of starting an organization to help troubled kids like Mark. That idea hasn't gotten off the ground yet, but I hope I'll be able to do it someday."

"You will."

Jamie could only stare at her. She barely knew him, and yet she seemed to believe in him without any proof. Did he even believe that much in himself?

Sarah wasn't looking at him when she spoke again, but she was smiling. "Yep, it all makes sense now. I think Mark would be proud of you."

Would he? A knot formed in Jamie's throat, and his

eyes burned. He hadn't let anyone see him cry in years, and yet he was tempted to release his stranglehold on his emotions right in front of her. That was enough to propel him from his seat, though he pretended he was only taking a closer look at Aiden, who waved from the bouncing bridge. Jamie couldn't allow himself to be that vulnerable, and he couldn't let anyone get close to him. He would never risk losing someone he cared about again.

"Ever thought you might have missed your calling as a psychologist?" He looked back at her from over his shoulder. "I feel like I should lie down on your couch or something."

"You've met my son. Do you really think you'd get to lie back on my couch and tell me all your problems?"

Images of other, much more pleasant activities he could share with her on a sofa sneaked into his thoughts then, shaming him. How could he go from sharing his deepest secrets about Mark with her one minute to imagining her smooth skin, soft feminine curves, and hair that would feel like silk beneath his cherishing hands, the next?

Even if this was Sarah, and these images were vanilla ice-cream compared to the crème brûlée of his usual fantasies about her, there still was no excuse. Those private daydreams had been almost acceptable when she was out of his reach, not sitting next to him on a bench, close enough that he could brush her arm if he found the guts to do it. Aneled if he stretched to reach her over the food pile. She hadn't given any signals that she would welcome his touch, either. So why did he get the sense that *her* touch might heal his wounds, and his might salve hers, as well?

"Now you've heard my sad story," he began. "I was hoping that maybe you would tell me yours."

"I suppose I could—"

He could only guess what she'd been about to say, as she cut off her words and jerked her head to watch Aiden racing toward them from the playground. Oddly, she shifted away from Jamie as if caught doing something she shouldn't have been.

He gripped the edge of the bench, trying not to show his frustration. He'd practically gutted himself to get Sarah to trust him enough to speak, and she still hadn't shared a single thing with him. Now the opportunity to learn anything about her had passed. His heart sank with the realization that he might have missed his only opportunity to truly know Sarah Cline.

Chapter 7

"Aiden, stop!"

Sarah leaped up from the bench and reached out to catch her son's arm before he could launch himself at Jamie just like he had the other day at the diner. But the child had too much momentum going to even slow. As her hands came up empty, Sarah regretted feeling relieved that Aiden had chosen this moment to show up and interrupt their conversation. It was too risky for her to even thinking about sharing those things in the first place.

At least this time Jamie caught Aiden in his arms.

"Whoa, buddy. What's the rush?" He lowered the boy to the ground.

"I'm hungry."

Jamie grinned. "You said that earlier. Then you went off to play, and we wondered if you'd ever come back."

Aiden wasn't listening, as he'd already caught sight of junk food on the bench.

"Snacks," he called out with glee, and then turned to Sarah. "Mom, can I have some? Please!"

"Yes, but just for today," she said, as she sat again.

"Can I have *two*?"

"You can even have three, if your mom says it's okay," Jamie said.

Her son looked to her for confirmation. When she nodded, he came to her for a hug. "Thanks, Mom."

As soon as Sarah released him, he plowed through the pile, choosing a package of snack cakes and two bags of chips. He wisely skipped one of the remaining sandwiches.

Once Aiden sat on the end of the bench near Jamie and ripped open the first package, Sarah started scooping up the leftovers.

"Let's get rid of these, so none of us are tempted to have more."

Sarah lifted Jamie's backpack and shoveled the tiny bags inside. When she reached the sandwiches, she paused and looked to Jamie, who shook his head.

"Doubt those will get better with age."

"Probably not."

He dumped them in the trash can near the playground entrance. By the time he returned, she was zipping the final compartment closed. She left the wet wipes out for Aiden to use when he was finished.

She rested the backpack on the ground. "I need to get those things out of sight. If I keep eating them, my waitress uniform's going to stop fitting."

"You don't have to worry about that. If there's someone who can make even a pink dress with an apron look fantastic…"

Jamie stopped himself and looked away. Sarah shot a glance at Aiden, who was blessedly oblivious, before turning back to Jamie, whose neck was ruddier than it had been, even from the chilly breeze. He clearly regretted saying those words, but she wasn't as sorry as she should have been to hear them. In fact, tingles spread over her arms and the tops of her thighs.

What was wrong with her? First, that tiny brush of his hand, which still made her tummy feel weightless when she thought about it, and now *this*? Over the past few years, she'd forgotten she even had hormones, and she couldn't afford for them to peek their ugly faces out today. Not with him.

Because her cheeks burned, and she couldn't look at Jamie, she peeked at Aiden, who was busy shoving the chocolate snack cake in his mouth.

"I don't know why Ted and the other owner swear by those silly uniforms," she said, to fill the awkward silence and let Jamie off the hook at the same time. "They're like wearing a starched pink tent."

"I feel like that about my dress uniform, though it's blue instead of pink and all straight instead of tent-like."

"So, in other words, it's completely different." She hated that she could imagine him in one of those crisp blue state police uniforms and that the word *fantastic* easily came to mind. Since when had she started to find men in uniform attractive?

"Well. Yeah," he said with a low chuckle.

This time when he smiled at her, she felt it all the way to her toes. Where earlier they'd been sitting in companionable silence with their junk food buffet, now there was a sudden intimacy between them and no barrier to ease it. She needed to scoot farther from him, or at least put Aiden between them, but she found those were the last things she wanted to do.

Jamie did it instead, clearing his throat and sliding closer to Aiden. He ruffled the boy's already messy hair. "Guess I should be getting the two of you home."

Aiden's expression turned from contentment to agony in a nanosecond. "No. Not yet. Please! We still need to see the, uh…the sloths." He grinned as he finally came up with an animal they hadn't visited that day.

Jamie shook his head as he stood and zipped his jacket. "We can see the, uh…*sloths* the next time."

"Next time? When?" He was bouncing again as he gripped his hero's hand.

Jamie turned to Sarah for support, and she held her hands wide, but couldn't stop the grin pulling at her lips.

"Haven't you learned yet not to make empty promises to a kid?"

"Oh. It wasn't empty."

"What do you mean?" The guess already playing in her thoughts had shivers shimmying up her spine.

"We can come again. If it's okay with you. I know *I* want to."

He'd been looking down at Aiden, who still clung to his hand, but as Sarah came to stand on his opposite side, he turned her way. His gaze was warm without being intimidating. He continued to watch her, and she was surprised to find that she didn't want to look away, either.

"I know some people go away, but I'm a stick-around kind of guy. I stay. I can be a good friend, too." Then he gave a firm nod. "I'll be here if you…if either of you… need me."

* * *

Michael slammed his fist on the tabletop so hard that the teenager with blue-striped hair and cutoff straws in her ears gaped at him from behind that shrieking espresso machine.

"Damn technology," he said with a shrug.

"Don't I know it. The Wi-Fi's been messing up all day."

No matter what she'd said, the barista didn't know the half of it. Even with the old tablet Larry had lent him, the one with a faulty on/off button and an allergy to the internet half the time, Michael hadn't found a bit of usable information on Maria's whereabouts. Even when he'd managed to get past his own technical ineptitude, he hadn't been able to come up with anything more than a few websites for personal records and criminal background checks. Those charged tidy fees, all requiring credit cards, which he no longer had to because of *them*.

If his so-called friends had been doing their jobs and using their extensive resources to locate Maria, he wouldn't have to be there on a Saturday, wasting money he didn't have on overpriced cups of coffee just to get the free Wi-Fi. His other contacts on the outside, the ones Larry and Clint didn't know about, hadn't done any better.

Between the hours he would squander at the corrugated cardboard plant, where ex-cons worked for slave wages, and the concrete barriers he'd already smacked into on the information superhighway, he was never going to find her.

Or his son.

Or his money.

Not necessarily in that order.

If only he'd listened when Maria had talked about her parents. They'd banished her from their country club lives the minute she'd chosen him over them. Sure, her dad was dead now, but had her mom opened her arms and wallet to Maria once she'd pulled her vanishing act? She had produced a grandchild, after all. He bristled at the thought of that woman cooing to his kid. She had no right. Andy was *his*.

Just like Maria was.

"So, whatcha looking for online?"

Michael startled, shocked that Striped Hair had slipped around the counter to stand behind his shoulder without his notice. If he'd lost his edge like that when he was still on the inside, he would have ended up as an inmate's plaything or with a shiv in his back.

"Because I might be able to help," she continued. "Generation Z and all."

Her smile promised that she would help him out, all right, no matter what generation she was part of. He took a moment to admire all that high, tight ripeness. He was already well aware that tapping some of that jailbait could take the edge off. He'd had his share of offers— and mutually satisfying deals—during his gig visiting high schools. Right now, though, the kid wasn't worth the headache. Or the risk.

"Thanks. But I've got it."

"Whatever. Just like my parents. Too proud to admit they don't know something."

She rolled her eyes and swished away to let him know that what he'd missed had nothing to do with helping an old fart with technology. He shrugged and adjusted himself to relieve the pressure. He'd waited this long, and he could hold out a little longer.

Only one woman could satisfy this jones, anyway. Oh, yeah, Maria would satisfy, too. He would possess her just as he had that first time, when she was about the same age as Striped Hair and the rest of the nubile caffeine dealers he'd crossed the past few days at different coffee shops. When they were back together, he would remind his wife just what she'd missed.

But he had to find her first. Apparently, he would have to do it alone. He propped the tablet on its stand, tapped to wake it again and typed in the names Paul and Amy Norris. He hoped he wouldn't need his former in-laws' middle initials, since he had no clue what those were. But only one search result included both names. He clicked on it and found Maria listed, as well, under the name she'd carried before he made her his. The address was familiar, too, the same house where he'd helped Maria to climb out the window so many times.

Just as those gated walls of their exclusive subdivision had failed to keep the Norrises' daughter inside then, they had no chance of keeping him out now. Either "Mom" would tell him everything she knew about where Maria had disappeared to, or he would beat it out of her.

This was almost too easy. He smiled at the tablet just as a low-battery message appeared, but the screen went black before he could plug it into the outlet. He managed to avoid throwing the piece of crap against the wall, especially with several new customers coming in to fill up the empty tables around him.

Still, Striped Hair's words replayed in his thoughts. *Too proud...* Maria's parents were definitely that. She wouldn't have been invited back into their Christmas card photo, at least without *years* of groveling.

Besides, her mother was the first person who police

would have questioned when Maria had blown off her court date. Even his duo of Barney Fife investigators could have figured that much out. And if Her Majesty had known anything about Maria, she already would have shared it with investigators. No way she would have lied for her daughter and risked any of her beautiful money.

Michael fisted and unfisted his hands on the table. It had already been four days since his release, and he was no closer to finding his wife. With that godawful apartment, all he'd done was trade one cell for another, this one without bars. If he had to stay there much longer, counting flies on the wall, he would go mad.

He had to keep it together. Hadn't he spent six years planning for this moment, this meeting? He couldn't give up yet.

So, if her Mommy Dearest wasn't the one who'd helped Maria to vanish, he had to figure out who could have done it. Maria didn't have the brains to do it all on her own. She wouldn't have left her parents at all if he hadn't shown her that they were just trying to control her. But who else? She was an only child, just like her parents, so she had no aunts and uncles. Well, one great-aunt, but a little old lady couldn't really help. Maria didn't have any friends, either. He stopped as the image of her one childhood friend appeared in his thoughts. The chick with frizzy hair and big glasses he'd once seen leaving their apartment when he'd returned home from work. His blood threatened to boil over again at the memory of Maria's hiding things from him like that, but he had to recall the woman's name. Tammy or Tina or something. The name began with a *T*. She'd shown up again at the hospital after that argument Maria had started had resulted in an accident. Terri? Tori? Had Maria stayed in contact with her, even after he'd explained that she should cut ties to the past if she wanted to prove she loved him?

Just the thought that she might have gone behind his back to stay in touch with some ugly friend had his nostrils flaring. His jaws ached from gritting his teeth. Just another way she'd betrayed him. Another way she'd failed to love, honor and obey. Something else she would answer for when—

Wait. *Tonya.* That sounded right. He didn't know the woman's last name, either, but it couldn't be that hard to find, with an unusual name like that. Easier, anyway, than tracking down a woman who'd vanished like smoke in a fan.

Tapping the screen and spreading his thumb and forefinger to enlarge the text the way Larry had taught him in that ten-minute tutorial, Michael launched another internet search. This time, he would check out some of those yearbook websites that kept popping up. This might not be the answer he needed, but at least it was something. He would locate this Tonya and force her to give up what she knew. For her sake, she'd better know something.

He grinned at the kid behind the counter, the one ignoring him now. Striped Hair would have to find some other dude to satisfy her daddy complex because he wasn't interested in any strange. He needed to save his strength, anyway. It was only a matter of time now until he had a night to remember with his own little wife.

Chapter 8

I'll be here... Jamie's words played in Sarah's thoughts like a music stream on repeat for most of the half hour drive from Royal Oak to Brighton. Aiden barely made it from the zoo to nearby Interstate 696 before passing out in the backseat of Jamie's midsize SUV as they headed west into the remaining pinks and oranges of a spectacular sunset.

"That's amazing." Jamie lowered the visor so that he could see to drive. "The whole day was amazing."

"It was," she managed to reply, because it had been.

Jamie tried a few more times to start a conversation, but he must have given up as he flipped on the radio to an alternative rock station out of nearby Windsor, Ontario. Even the music provided Sarah no escape from her troubled thoughts as Lisa Loeb's voice crowded the car, crooning about a lover asking her to *stay*. Without knowing their story, Jamie had offered to be a constant in their lives, as well. The idea was unsettling and yet somehow comforting. If she had any sense at all, she would focus on the first emotion and banish the second.

She was so busy settling the matter in her mind that she didn't notice they'd pulled into the parking lot outside her eight-unit apartment complex until Jamie threw open his door, filling the car with light. Again, she wished she would have asked him to drop them off at the restaurant, where she and Aiden had walked to meet him that morning, but he'd insisted on an address this time, saying he didn't want them to walk home in the dark. She couldn't argue with that.

Aiden didn't even stir, his head resting against the window, until Jamie opened the back-seat door and unbuckled his seat belt.

"I can get him," she said, as she climbed out and rounded the back of the vehicle. Her stomach always tensed at the idea of letting anyone enter her apartment, especially the sketchy repair workers her landlord always hired, and here she was considering letting a cop inside.

"Let me help, Sarah." He paused for a second and then added, "Please."

"Okay." She grabbed her bag from the hatch.

"I'm sleepy," the boy mumbled, as Jamie lifted him and wrapped his legs around his waist.

"Well, you can go to right to bed…as soon as you brush your teeth."

"I don't want to."

"We'll be superfast. I can't be responsible for you getting cavities."

Even nervous as she was, Sarah couldn't help smiling as her son whined again, but finally rested his chin on his friend's shoulder. Jamie could be persuasive, as she was discovering herself.

After a few steps up the walk, Jamie looked back to her and moved his index finger back and forth, looking for directions. If he was shocked by her dingy two-story building, little more than a sixties-era motel converted into apartments with tiny kitchenettes, he didn't show it. He didn't even wrinkle his nose at the ever-present, garbage smell from the dumpster.

She pointed to the metal staircase on the end closest to the leasing office. At the top of the stairs she pointed again.

"Last apartment on the left." She didn't know why she bothered saying it that way. There was no *right*.

Jamie stopped in front of her apartment, stepping aside so she could unlock and open the door and flip on the overhead light. Once she closed the door behind them, she automatically started through the series of locks, beginning with the one in the doorknob, then sliding the chain and turning the three dead bolts.

He didn't comment on all the locks, and he made no pretense of asking where the bathroom was. He simply continued to the back of the apartment, choosing correctly between the two closed doors on opposite sides of the kitchenette.

He hit the switch for the light and then turned back to her. "If you get his bed ready, I'll help him with his teeth."

She rounded the tiny dinette and braced herself as she turned the knob to Aiden's room, the apartment's only bedroom, since hers was the pullout in the living room. She released a breath as she opened the door. The room was almost clean, compared to its usual chaos. Aiden hadn't even balked that morning when she'd insisted that he clean up his room before they went to meet Mr. Jamie.

She stepped inside and turned down the stars-and-planets comforter on the bottom bunk of the set she'd purchased, hoping that one day her son would get to have a friend sleep over. So far, it hadn't happened. From the cheap dresser that stood next to her own, she pulled out a set of cowboy pajamas.

"Nice digs, buddy," Jamie said from the doorway.

Sarah's hands shook as she closed the drawer, causing her to drop the clothes on the floor. She scrambled to pick them up, stopping just short of bumping into Jamie, this time with Aiden riding piggyback.

"Our boy here was a quick brusher." He squatted to let Aiden climb off his back.

"This is my room." Aiden gestured to the space, which had a complete set of eight planet decals arranged in order, the sun itself nestled in the corner near the closet.

"Hey, this is really cool."

"I have Pluto, too, but Mom put it in the drawer, since it's not a real planet anymore. You should see the ceiling when the lights are off. It's covered with stars. They glow in the dark."

"Now that I have to see. Let's hurry and get you into your pj's so you can show me."

"I'm not sleepy anymore."

But his yawn contradicted his words. Jamie guided him to the bed and crouched next to it.

"I can see that, but I really do want to see your stars."

Not certain what to make of the dampness in her eyes, Sarah stepped out of the room and closed the door to a crack to let them have the full effect of the darkened "sky."

No more than five minutes later, when Jamie emerged from the room, Sarah was already sitting at the kitchen table, the coffeemaker brewing and two mugs resting in front of her. Her mouth went dry when his gaze moved to the mugs, but he didn't comment on them as he closed the door behind him. She should have sent him on his merry way, but she wasn't ready to do it yet.

"He didn't make it past showing me the Big Dipper and the Little Dipper," he said in a low voice. "I can't believe you made star patterns."

"The sign of someone with a lot of time on her hands."

"Or someone who really cares about a little boy, who loves the stars and planets."

"That, too."

"I hope you didn't mind me putting him to bed. I know bedtime rituals are Mom territory."

She only smiled, since everything was "Mom territory" in Aiden's case. "I'm sure he loved it, even without story time."

She gestured toward the mugs. "I figured after our long day, I at least owed you some coffee. Decaf, of course."

"First, you don't *owe* me anything. I had a great time today. It looked like you and Aiden did, too." He indicated the coffeemaker with a wave of his hand. "And I can't let you serve me coffee when you're off duty. That would be like me writing you a ticket when I'm not in uniform."

She shifted. Maybe this was a bad idea, after all. Maybe the warring part of her that said she should send Jamie on his way had been the right one. But how she'd longed for a bit of adult company, just for a little while. "Oh. Sorry. I didn't mean to presume."

"Presume what?" He crossed to the counter, where the coffee had just finished brewing. He grabbed the pot and carried it back to the table. "I just meant you didn't need to *pour*."

He filled her cup and then his own before returning the pot to the warmer. "You drink decaf, too? Am I not the only insomniac in this room?"

She shook her head. "I'm just a busy mom. If I get the opportunity to sleep, I don't want to take any chances that I'll be lying there awake."

He scanned the kitchen and then glanced out into the living room area, now illuminated by the lamp on an end table. She couldn't help wanting to see the place through his eyes. Would he find the used furniture and repurposed decor trashy? Would he notice that once again there were only photos of Aiden in this apartment, never the two of them together?

His examination was slow, the same way he'd looked at her the other night at the diner, when he thought she wasn't paying attention. She had the same disconcerting feeling she'd experienced then, that he would somehow see and know everything.

"This place is great. Did you decorate everything yourself?"

"Of course not. I hired the priciest decorator I could find and allowed her to choose only high-end furnishings."

He pursed his lips. "Learn to take a compliment, would you? Every time someone praises your baking, you nearly run and hide in the kitchen."

"Thanks."

"Speaking of your baking, you don't happen to keep any of those cinnamon rolls around here, do you?"

"There's no way I could eat those things all the time."

"If I had your baking skills I would be eating pies and cakes for breakfast, lunch and dinner," he said with a grin. "Have you ever considered opening your own bakery?"

She shrugged. "A long time ago, I did. But then real life kicks you in the teeth, and you make other plans."

His gaze narrowed, so Sarah smiled to soften her comment. She hadn't meant it literally, but she still had to push aside thoughts that juxtaposed with her sweet memories from the zoo that day. Of singed skin and the jagged edges of broken glass. Of lame excuses offered for all the cuts and bruises.

"But Aiden is my life now," she continued. "Even if I had the money, I don't have the time to think about starting my own business."

"It's okay to have dreams for yourself, you know. Even moms can have them."

"I know." And she did, but Jamie, someone who barely knew her, was the first one who'd ever said it to her. Even her parents had always wanted her to live her life for them and their expectations rather than for herself.

"Anyway, I thought we were talking about food. If you're hungry, I could make you something. That is if your *healthy* meal has worn off." She frowned at her son's bedroom door. "I should have given Aiden dinner before he went to bed."

"He was too sleepy to eat, but I bet he'll be ready for breakfast in the morning. And you don't have to feed me."

Jamie's gaze moved from her kitchen cabinets to her son's door, as if he worried he'd be taking food out of Aidan's mouth if he accepted a meal.

"Just soup and sandwiches. I need to eat, too."

"You mean the peanut butter and jelly didn't hold you over?"

She shrugged. "Pretty sure I won't be craving one of those again for a while."

"I could eat," he said. "But let me help."

She would have turned down his assistance, but he was already up and opening her lower cabinet, locating a soup pan. There were only inches between them. Somehow, they worked in tandem, him pouring the can of vegetable soup into the pan and her slicing cheddar for grilled-cheese sandwiches. It was so different from when she'd been married to Mark, and dinner had to be on the table by the time he walked through the door or there'd be hell to pay.

Soon, they had a quick meal set out, next to their cooling cups of coffee.

"Thanks for dinner."

"It's the least I could do after today."

"I told you that you don't owe me anything. Heck, I practically had to beg you not to cancel."

Because that was true, her lips lifted.

"But if you're determined to thank me somehow, you could tell me the story you started at the zoo earlier."

Her stomach tightened, and she twisted her locket round and round. She'd known he would ask again if she invited him to stay for coffee. Had she kept him there because she wanted him to know her story, at least the small part of it she could share? If that was true, had she lost her mind?

Jamie was a cop. That was both the beginning and the end of the argument. If he was a good one, and she suspected he might be, her skeletal stories would never be enough for him. If he was a bad one, well, she'd already seen what they were capable of doing, or not doing, if it suited their needs.

"I told you my story's not all that interesting. It's not even unique."

"I like ordinary stories."

She couldn't help smiling at that. He was making it awfully hard *not* to share at least something with him, and part of her believed he would understand.

"Short version? Sheltered girl. Cocky and exciting older guy. A family who hated him. Teen pregnancy. Marriage on her eighteenth birthday." She ticked off each fact by tapping her index finger on the edge of the table. "And…go figure…the guy turned out to be a jerk, and it didn't end well."

"That's the short version, all right." He blinked a few times and then glanced over his shoulder to the closed bedroom door, as if calculating Aiden's age and the amount of time he would assume had passed. "*Teen* pregnancy?"

She breathed in and exhaled slowly, hoping her facial expression gave nothing away. "I had a miscarriage."

"Sorry to hear that."

"It happens." Not usually the way it had to her, but she didn't share that part.

"That doesn't make it any easier."

She could only nod at that, a knot clogging her throat. Even years later, she had to recall that loss in medical terms to prevent the memory of it from forcing her to her knees.

"But then that little guy in there came along, and that part was good, right?"

"The best."

"I get the idea that there's more to your story than that digest version."

Sarah had lifted her mug to sip her coffee but lowered it again without drinking. "Why do you say that?"

"I don't know, but all of those locks on your door give me a hint. Five?"

She followed the direction of his pointing finger. "You might not know this neighborhood, but it's not winning any safety awards. As a cop, you should be applauding my taking precautions, anyway. I'm a single mom. I can't be too careful."

"Oh, I applaud them, but don't you ever wonder if you're too cautious?"

Sarah crossed her arms and pinned him with her stare, but her heart pounded as if she'd just sprinted all the way from the zoo. "How can someone be *too* cautious?"

"It's not cautious. It's *nervous*."

She'd kept her voice steady before, but now she didn't dare try to answer. She hugged herself tighter and let him have his say.

"You leap out of your skin every time the bells chime at the diner."

She shook her head. "I already—"

He kept going, despite her attempt to interrupt. "I know. You tried to explain that, but why aren't you used to sounds you hear all day, every day? And there's more. You're always watching the front door of the diner…as if maybe you're dreading whoever the next customer will be."

"Now that's just silly. I'm doing my job, being prepared for customers."

"You didn't want anyone to know about Aiden."

She opened her mouth to interrupt again, but he shook his head.

"Or your last name."

Now she only shrugged. If he hadn't accepted her excuse the first time, he wouldn't buy it now.

"Do you have any idea how many times you looked over your shoulder at the zoo today?"

"Not that many."

She hated that her voice had lifted an octave as she spoke. Why couldn't he stop asking questions? Just because he'd told her his deep, dark secrets didn't mean that she had agreed to share hers, even if for a moment she'd been tempted. Besides, he was getting too close to the truth. What if he found out everything? Could she still protect Aiden if he did?

Why hadn't she listened to her instinct and told him goodbye in the car? Or better yet, at the diner before they'd even begun to trade stories.

"I told you why I'm careful. I'm trying to be a good mom. Trying to protect my son." She stared him down this time. It was the most honest thing she'd said to him all day. She dared him to question her this time.

He only watched her for several seconds, as if waiting for her to squirm.

"Is that all it is? Or are you running from the law?"

Chapter 9

Rapid blinking. Eyes that looked down and to the left. Though his training told him to expect whatever Sarah said next to be a lie, Jamie was ready to buy it. He needed to, and she clearly needed him to. Otherwise, why had she tried to so hard to defend herself?

But then that tight hold she had on her crossed arms loosened, and the sides of her mouth softened.

"Do you think I'd be dumb enough to willingly hang out with a cop when I'm on the lam myself?"

He might have pointed out that she hadn't willingly done anything. That it had taken from persuasion both of the guys in her apartment right now. But he couldn't help smiling at her words.

"On the lam? Watch a lot of old cop shows, do you? Maybe *Dragnet*?" He tilted his head, weighing her words. "Guess you're right. It wouldn't be too smart."

Or it might be brilliant, a disagreeable part of him countered. *A criminal hiding in plain sight.* Was she following the old adage of keeping her enemies closer than her friends? He had to admit it wasn't a bad idea, even if technically she hadn't sought *him* out. Still, he barely knew her, and he'd hidden from his fellow troopers the fact that he'd been searching for answers about her. What would he do if he discovered she really was a fugitive?

Sarah didn't say more but piled their dishes together and set them next to the sink.

"Here, let me help." Jamie pushed back his chair and joined her in front of the sink. There was barely enough space for the two of them to stand shoulder to shoulder there, but he pulled out the dish towel threaded over the oven door handle and dried the dishes after she washed and rinsed them.

The easy silence they'd shared while preparing the meal was noticeably absent, replaced by an awkward tension. When his arm brushed hers, Sarah startled so much that the bowl she'd been washing clanked on the sink bottom.

"Oh. Sorry," he said.

"It's okay."

Clearly, it wasn't. She didn't even look up from the suds-filled sink as she said it. Not once since she'd made the joke about spending time with a cop had she met his gaze. But as if it was the one thing she couldn't resist, she glanced over her shoulder toward the front door. The one that wouldn't have opened without the help of a battering ram and plenty of weight behind it.

When she turned back to the sink, Jamie studied her until she glanced sidelong at him.

"Tell me the truth, Sarah. If it isn't the police you're

afraid of, then what—or who—are you hiding from?"
His jaw tightened and his molars ground. "Is it *him*?"

This time, instead of answering, she made a strange
sound in her throat, and the glass she was rinsing slipped
from her fingers and shattered on the stainless steel on
the empty side of the sink. Shards of glass shot out
against the four sides and slid down the garbage disposal.

Reflexively, Sarah reached for it, but Jamie caught
her hand, then stretched past her to shut off the water.
She gripped the edge of the sink and closed her eyes as
her shoulders slumped.

Suddenly, memory snapshots rushed at Jamie from all
directions. All those examples he'd given her and more.
That raw look in her eyes, the one she thought no one
could see. Well, he'd always seen it, even if he'd been
too dense to understand it. Now the same chimes that always jolted her clanged in his ears, loud and discordant,
and with the bottomless feeling in his stomach, he *knew*.

Lovely Sarah, the ethereal beauty who'd invaded
his thoughts and captured his dreams was also one of
the bruised faces behind the sterile statistics of women
preyed on by an intimate partner. Only she was somehow
still here, when many had fallen to those hateful hands.

Her arms were trembling visibly where she'd braced
her hands, and he longed to reach out to her, but he
sensed that she might not want to be touched. Instead,
he pulled out the chair where he'd been sitting because
it was easier than scooting to the other side of the table.

"Here. Sit."

"But…" She gestured toward the mess in the sink.

"Let me get it. Do you have rubber gloves?"

She pointed to the lower cabinet as she lowered herself in the chair. He slid on the gloves and placed slivers

of glass inside the cracked bottom. Then he pulled the trash can from beneath the sink and dropped it inside.

"I can do that, you know."

"I know." He picked up as many pieces as he could and then dampened a paper towel to collect the rest. "But let me help, okay?"

He was talking about far more than shards of broken glass, and she must have understood that as she watched him for several seconds before looking back to the table. A few heartbeats later, her chin lowered as if she could no longer balance the weight of her secrets.

Her "okay" came so softly that he would have missed it if he weren't straining his ears to catch any sound. Fury spread through him, making his hands, face and neck hot. How could some idiot she'd trusted with her precious heart have betrayed her like that? And why had he been allowed to keep breathing if he had?

"What did he do to you, Sarah?" Jamie whispered, as he moved to the seat across from her and sat. Of its own volition, his hand stretched out to brush hers. She flinched before he even touched her, so he slid it back.

He cleared his throat. "Where is he now?"

"Right now?" She glanced over at the stove clock. "Probably locked in his cell for the night."

"He's incarcerated?"

"Yeah."

The tightness in his chest decreased by tiny increments. The guy couldn't lay his hands on her. At least for now. Jamie didn't kid himself into believing that would be forever. He'd witnessed too many of the failures of the criminal justice system to believe that many felons ever got the sentences they truly deserved.

Unable to stay seated, he stood and paced into the living room, the tiny space squeezing tighter around him. He turned to find her staring at him, not at his face but lower. He followed her gaze to his hands. They were fisted at his sides. He forced them to unfold and wiped his sweaty palms on his jeans, ignoring the sting from where his nails had dug into his palms.

"Aren't you supposed to be a *peace* officer?"

"What do you—" He cut his own words off, took a deep breath and released it. She had to know that the thoughts going through his head weren't close to peaceful. What was wrong with him? Hadn't Sarah already known enough men who controlled their world with their fists?

"Sorry." He cleared his throat. "I'm also sorry for whatever he did to you."

Though he expected to see fear in her eyes when she met his gaze again, there was only caution there.

"So I was right that you hadn't shared your *whole* story with me?"

"I might have omitted a few details."

"Care to fill in some blanks?"

"Like an abusive ex-husband in prison?"

"How about the whole story?"

Her own hands, gripped in front of her, held her attention for a long time, but then she gestured for him to return to the table. He sat and waited for her to tell her story in her own time.

"Like I said, my story is an embarrassing cliché. You said you missed signs about your brother. Well, if you looked up a list of warning signs for teen dating violence, there would have been a photo of us on the page."

Her expression tightened, and then she took hold of her locket and started twisting it.

"Like what?" he said. "Did his last three girlfriends have restraining orders out on him?"

She was finally sharing, and even if every word was stabbing him in the chest like a pen knife puncturing his skin, he had to keep her talking. He had to know.

"No, but Michael blamed every one of them for their breakups. Red flag number one. He was also controlling, almost from the moment we started dating, when I was sixteen. He was twenty-one. He didn't like me hanging out with my friends and said it hurt his feelings that he wasn't enough for me."

"Were those the only things?" They were enough to get *his* heckles up, but then Jamie knew the signs. Had witnessed some of the devastation to which they could lead.

She shook her head. "He texted and called all the time to 'check in' and then looked through my text messages when we were together. He had a short fuse. He pressured me for sex…until I finally gave in."

It was all Jamie could do to keep his hands flat on the table, when he wanted to wrap them around the asshole's neck. At least she couldn't see that every muscle in his body had tensed.

"I don't know how anyone could have picked up on tiny hints like those," he said.

Joking, even if it wasn't funny, was better than punching a hole in the wall, which he also was tempted to do. He'd never punched a wall in his life.

"That's just it. Others did pick up on them. My parents. Friends. Teachers. My parents forced me to break up with him."

"Which made you desperate to be with your poor, misunderstood boyfriend."

She cocked her head to the side. "Have you heard this story before?"

He nodded. Too many times for someone who'd been on the job only two years.

"Well, you're right. I said they just didn't know him. He'd never hurt me at that point, except maybe to grip my arm too tight. And sometimes I did say things that provoked him."

She folded her hands on the table. "When I became pregnant when I was seventeen, my parents refused to sign the permission form so that we could get married. They said they would support me and the baby, but only if I stayed away from him. I didn't believe they would cut me out of their lives if I married him when I turned eighteen a month later, but they did."

"How long after that did he start hurting you?"

"Not long. When he realized that my parents really weren't going to help us out, even for the baby's sake."

"But you said you lost the baby."

She nodded, her eyes damp. "A few weeks after we were married."

He was tempted to ask if the time corresponded to the beginning of the physical abuse, but he worried the question might push her too far.

"Did you go the police when the abuse began?"

The words were out of his mouth before he could stop them, and her narrowed gaze told him they'd struck soft tissue.

"No, I didn't. I was ashamed. And he said he was sorry. He promised he'd never do it again." She lifted her chin. "And before you ask it, I didn't try to leave at first, either. By the end, I was convinced I had nowhere to go, and the police wouldn't help, either."

"A lot of victims believe those things."

"Sometimes they're right."

Her pointed stare sliced right through him then. Had the people she trusted failed her? Had the police? Had she been able to trust anyone at all?

"Even your parents wouldn't help?"

"I couldn't ask them. I was too embarrassed. I'd also alienated all my friends. Except one. Tonya." She smiled as she said the woman's name. "She refused to let me push her away and said she would help when I was ready. But I stayed. And stayed."

"Would he have let you go if you'd tried?"

She shook her head. "At first, he said he would kill himself if I left him. Later he said he wouldn't let *me* live without him. But as the bumps and bruises became cracked ribs, a fractured eye socket and worse, I realized I wasn't going to survive, either way."

As she stared off toward the sink, she rested her right hand over her upper left arm and absently rubbed her thumb on the skin beneath it. It was another of her habits, something she did at work with her hand covering the cuff on her uniform sleeve. Now he couldn't help but wonder what was hidden beneath that sleeve.

"That last time, I almost didn't."

At first her words didn't make sense, but when he connected it back to her comment about survival, his breath was trapped in his chest. The image of Sarah's body stretched out on one of those slabs at the medical examiner's office flashed before his eyes, forcing him to squeeze them shut.

That bastard had tried to do that to Sarah.

When he opened his eyes again, she was watching him.

"Sorry. I didn't mean to share so much."

"I did ask for the whole story."

"You did, but you didn't ask for the gory details."

He should have been able to handle those details. He was a trooper at a full-service post, for heaven's sake. He handled many types of cases and had seen plenty of carnage on highways and in homes, most from a polite, professional distance. But this was Sarah. The thought of what could have happened to her would have dropped him to his knees if he wasn't already sitting.

"Well, it's good that he's serving time. Was his conviction for attempted first-degree murder or aggravated domestic battery?"

"You might not want to hear the answer to that one."

He frowned. "What did he plead down to? Jaywalking?"

"He was never charged for any crime for hurting me."

"How is that even possible?" Jamie swallowed. "Did you get one of those Neanderthal officers who told you not to waste anyone's time by pressing charges, since you'd just drop them when the two of you made up?"

"Close. These officers were his buddies. Or at least he was *their* informant. When they caught him doing his side job of selling opioids to teens while working for a copy-machine-service company with contracts at areas schools, they made him work for them. Then, after I'd spent two weeks in the hospital fighting for my life and I was finally ready to fight back…"

Although he knew what she would say, he had to ask. "They shielded their informant from charges so that they wouldn't jeopardize their investigation, right?"

"How'd you guess?"

Jamie could only shake his head. "I'm so sorry."

"As long as he kept providing good information on

his supplier, and perhaps participated in dirty side deals with a few of them, he was golden. But he must have double-crossed them somehow because he ended up in prison, after all."

"Possession with intent to distribute?"

"Six to twelve years. He got lucky, too. If he'd faced the charge for dealing near a school, the penalty would have doubled. And I was lucky that I got a sympathetic judge, who granted my divorce while he was still in prison, because Michigan law makes that tough to get. But when I showed the judge the police reports I'd filed that went nowhere, and the photos…" She paused, shrugging. "Even then, he made me wait until Aiden was born before it could be finalized."

"At least he's never had the chance to hurt *him*."

"He will never get the chance to hurt my son."

She only whispered her answer, but her lethal promise unsettled Jamie. He didn't have to wonder to what lengths she would go to protect her child, whom she'd referred to as hers alone.

She sounded so determined that he couldn't bring himself to mention that her ex wasn't serving a life sentence and would probably be granted visitation upon his release. If Jamie knew of cases where even convicted child predators were granted visitation with their children, Sarah didn't stand a chance of keeping the guy away from their son.

"I'm just glad he can't get to either of you." *At least for now,* the subconscious part of him that refused to be quiet added. "But with him behind bars, I don't understand why you're always watching for him over your shoulder."

"Old habits die hard, I guess. And maybe because,

even before the divorce, he said he had people watching me, in case I was, you know, whoring around like he was sure I would be while he was gone. As if I even wanted any man to touch me."

Sarah blinked, as if that last confession had surprised even her. She shifted in her seat, looking anywhere but at Jamie.

"So that he could continue to control you, even while he was on the inside," he said, avoiding the other sensitive topic.

Her tongue darted out to lick her lips, and she looked back to him again.

"I just always feel as if one of *his friends* is just around the corner, waiting for me."

"That has to be awful, always waiting to be ambushed."

She only shrugged.

"I just want you to know that if ever you're not feeling safe, you can call me. Any time. If ever you feel like one of his friends…" He let his words fall away as she smiled back at him.

"That's kind of you, but—"

"It just seems like everyone betrayed you." He rushed on, interrupting before she could push him away again. "Your ex. Your parents for cutting you off when you really needed them. Those officers, when you could have been—" He grimaced. "No wonder you hate cops. Please tell me these weren't Michigan police officers."

She shook her head. "Illinois. And I never said I hated cops."

"You didn't have to say it. You're an ice princess around all the Brighton Post guys." But even as he said it, so much more made sense now. Of course, she would have been uncomfortable around some of the more self-assured among his trooper friends. They would have reminded her of her abuser. Or maybe of those officers who'd, at best, traded her safety for information, or at worst, to line their own pockets.

"Anyway, I, uh, don't hate *all* cops."

Jamie stilled. He should have been focusing on the details she'd given him that would confirm her story. There could only be so many Michael Clines serving time on drug charges in Illinois state prison, after all. And only so many divorce records for Michael Cline and Sarah Cline. But all he could see were Sarah's fine-boned hands on the table…clasped between both of his. She was staring at their hands, as well, her eyes wide.

When during her story had he forgotten his control and reached out to her again? Jamie couldn't decide which shocked him more, that he was touching her or that she hadn't pulled away.

He held his breath, waiting for her to do just that, then the temptation became too much, and he traced his thumb over the back of her hand. Her skin was as satiny as he'd imagined, more so, though her palms were probably callused from her long days on the job. Her eyes were darker now under the soft yellow light, the rings of her irises almost violet.

He would have stayed there forever, time dangling in a perpetual and voluntary pause. His heart squeezed when only a few seconds later Sarah slid her hands from his.

But even with her retreat, Jamie sensed that something in the room had changed. The air felt thinner. Warmer. More intimate. They'd spent a whole private hour together, with Aiden clear in the next room, but now was the first time it seemed like just the two of them. Man and woman. Alone.

Jamie would have sworn he was the only one who felt it, but the way she crossed and uncrossed her arms made him wonder.

"I guess it's getting late." She pushed back from the table and started toward the door.

Reluctantly, he stood, slid his chair in and followed her. "You're right. I'd better get going."

He collected his jacket and crossed to where she already stood with her hand on the doorknob. The gesture was mostly for show, anyway, since she couldn't open the door without undoing all the locks first. Although she faced him, she wouldn't look him in the eye.

"Thanks again. For everything. Aiden had a wonderful time."

"I'm glad.

"I did, too."

"Then it was a perfect day."

And it had been. Especially since Sarah had finally opened to him and shared her secrets. *All* of them? His natural inclination toward skepticism that had been honed on the job tried to pop its head out again. He wanted to believe that she had told him everything, and yet he of all people knew how deeply secrets could be locked inside and how difficult it was to trust anyone else with that key.

"Thank you for listening to my story and for sharing yours," he said. "Thanks for trusting me with it. And there's one more thing I'd like to tell you."

He waited, both for her nod of agreement and his courage to say the words in case she never gave him another chance.

"You deserve so much more than life has given you. You should have someone who believes in you, listens to you, cherishes you and trusts you completely." He took a breath as he wondered whether even he could fulfill the trust part of that calling, when he still planned to check out her story.

"I know you're strong. You're courageous. You had to be to walk away. To build a life for yourself and your son. And I know you felt you had no one you to turn to."

He paused and took a deep breath, as his next words could push her away. "But you don't have to be alone."

He braced himself for her automatic step back, for the withdrawal he would read on her face, even if she didn't move at all. Their gazes connected instead. Had she inched closer, as well, or did the sudden tightness in his chest just make it feel that way?

Suddenly, all he could think about was gathering Sarah in his arms. He wanted it so badly that the muscles in his forearms ached with the effort of keeping his hands at his sides. But he couldn't reach out to her. This was Sarah. He wouldn't allow himself to touch her. Not without her permission.

"Sarah, could I…" He cleared his throat. "Would you mind…"

His question fell away as she took another step forward, so close that each inhalation carried with it a whiff of her shampoo. The scent brought to mind a field of wildflowers on a late summer day. Her own uneven breaths feathered over his neck, warming his skin.

It would have been enough, just the privilege of standing a whisper away from someone who'd before been like a mannequin to him, set apart in a display window behind glass. But now that live, complex woman he was getting to know rose on her tiptoes and brushed her lips over his in the lightest flutter of a kiss. Jamie was too shocked to move, but his heart didn't receive the message. It thudded in his chest.

He expected her to pull back then, still wasn't sure whether it had really happened or if he'd just dreamed it. Then her lips skimmed over his a second time, and whatever had held him in place before set him free.

His arms came around her naturally, and she slid into that perfect oval near his heart, as if they'd practiced the choreography together for a lifetime. He touched his lips to hers once, twice, and then settled into the plush heaven of her mouth. He dreaded the moment when the muscles in her shoulders would tighten under the pressure of hands, but just the opposite, they relaxed beneath his fingertips in what felt like a gift. Of permission. Of welcome.

Though he was painfully aware of each of their bodies' finite points of contact, he held himself in check. Just one more kiss and he would leave. But then her lips parted for him, giving him access to her sweet mouth, and her tongue tentatively traced his lower lip, and nothing short of handcuffs or a locked cell could have kept him from drawing her even closer.

He drank her in with deep, heady kisses, reveling in her taste and texture.

He could feel her everywhere, soft feminine curves molding to his planes, silken hair brushing against his jaw. Her tiny moan when he shifted his mouth was nearly his undoing. More amazing even than that, beautiful Sarah's arms had slid up around his neck, and she was kissing him back, offering and accepting, following and leading.

Until she stopped.

She didn't jerk away. She didn't have to. Her retreat was subtler than that. Arms that loosened by tiny increments. Responsive lips that ended their conversation without a whisper.

Immediately, he removed his hands from her waist and stepped back, letting his arms fall to his sides. Regret, hot and damning, welled inside him.

"Sorry," he said.

"I think you should go."

"Really, Sarah. I shouldn't have—"

"Just go."

Her voice was shaky, and her shoulders slumped, just as they had when she'd shared her story earlier. When she'd trusted him with it.

Only this time, he was to blame for the defeat in her voice and in her posture. What was he doing? It didn't matter that she'd kissed him first, or that she'd accepted his touch. She was vulnerable. He should have known better. He'd hoped to be her safe place, and he'd just proved that she wasn't safe anywhere.

He grabbed his jacket from the floor and turned to the door, starting on the series of locks. Once he stood on the walkway outside, he glanced back at her through the open door.

"I still mean what I said. You don't have to be alone."

She didn't meet his gaze as she closed the door behind him.

The clicks of all the locks sounded louder than they had before. More final. But that had to be because this time he was on the outside.

Chapter 10

Sarah rested her head against the cool steel of her apartment door, but even that barrier and five locks couldn't block her need to be on the other side. With Jamie.

"What were you thinking?"

She must have lost her instinct for self-preservation, but she could only wonder whether he was still standing outside, staring at the number on her door and trying to figure out what had just happened. Or maybe he had his jacket collar pulled up near his ears, the way he had at the zoo, and had given up and gone to his car. She needed him to forget whatever he believed was happening between them, too, even if part of her didn't want him to.

She stepped back from the door and brushed at the chill on her upper arms that had come from both the ever-present draft and the loss of the heat that had radiated from Jamie's chest. The apartment always felt cramped, but now its walls seemed to close in around her.

She had no one to blame but herself for this funk. From the moment she'd written the silly note to Jamie at the diner, she'd made nothing but mistakes involving him. She'd understood that it was too risky to let anyone get close to her and Aiden. Let alone a man. And a cop. So why had she all but set out a king-size welcome mat, inviting Jamie into their lives? Was the need to allow someone to truly know her worth the risk?

Wasn't it bad enough that she'd nearly confided everything to him tonight? Then she'd lost her mind and kissed him. Only the second man she'd ever kissed, and she'd made the first move. She would ask herself why, but the answers were obvious. She'd kissed *him* because she could think of nothing else, and she wasn't sure he would go through with it. Even after he'd started to ask for permission. That he'd asked at all had made him irresistible.

As if lifted by some invisible force, her hand covered her mouth and her index finger traced the curves of her lips. Her skin was tingly and sensitive to the touch now. Lips that had never been kissed that way before. Thoroughly. Adoringly. Though Jamie had hinted that he wasn't all that experienced with women, he'd kissed her as if he understood her. Gentle touches that enticed rather than demanded. Kisses that made her crave more, something she couldn't afford to do.

Had the sensual woman inside her that she'd believed dead only been sleeping and waiting to be awakened with a kiss, like some modern-day Snow White? She shook her head. If her life hadn't proved that fairy tales didn't exist, she didn't know what would. Now the evil villains in those stories—she could swear by them. Still, she couldn't deny that her skin had awakened beneath Jamie's touch, then yawned and stretched toward daylight. Though his hands had never strayed from her arms and back, she'd felt his hands everywhere. *Wanted* them everywhere.

The truth that she still wanted it had her stalking across the room to the sofa, but instead of sitting, she frowned at the lamp with its too soft illumination. She marched back to the door and flipped the switch for the overhead fixture. Now stark light filled the apartment, showing all the imperfections that had been hidden before, chasing away the romantic cocoon she'd allowed to enfold her. She flitted about, tucking Aiden's toys and books into their proper places, fluffing already plump pillows and smoothing unwrinkled slipcovers.

But all the activity failed to push forbidden images and sensations from her mind. The glide of Jamie's mouth over hers. The gentle pressure of his hand on the small of her back as he drew her intimately to him. Close enough to make her aware that she wasn't the only one who wanted.

Shouldn't that knowledge have terrified her? More than that, why was she allowing herself to become distracted by a man? Why now? She wanted to believe that loneliness alone had caused her long-neglected skin to crave any tender touch. Yet she was most comfortable in her own company now, and the only man's touch she had experienced had been neither tender nor loving.

The feel of Jamie's hands on her skin had been both those things. She couldn't deny that truth any more than she could dispute that her actions tonight had far more to do with the man himself than with her own needs or wants. What was it about Jamie Donovan that drew her in when she should have been pushing him away with both hands? Was it that he'd allowed her to see his vulnerability when he'd shared his story about his brother? Or could it have been his quiet strength, which was utterly masculine without the need to punctuate that truth with his fists?

The image of his tight jaw and gripped hands slid into her thoughts, contradicting her argument, nullifying her excuses. Was he that different from Michael when Jamie had difficulty controlling his anger, even if it was technically on her behalf?

She refused to listen to the voice deep inside that said the two men couldn't have been more different. She wouldn't allow herself to romanticize thoughts about him, to believe that he would never treat her as a possession like Michael had.

At the thought of her ex, her mouth went dry. Had she lost sight, even for a minute, of why they were there in the first place? Had she forgotten her worries over hands that might drag her and Aiden back into her former reality? Or the truth that she couldn't even call her son by his real name?

She'd thought she was different now. Stronger. Smarter. And yet she's just proved that she was no different from the impetuous teenager who'd gotten herself trapped in a prison as real as the one Michael currently lived in. Just how many details had she shared with Jamie today? Were there enough to lead him back to Michael, even without providing his real name? Enough to trigger a chain of events that would lead the man of her nightmares back to her and Aiden? Had she told Jamie because she wanted to get caught?

At the squeak of the bedroom door, Sarah jumped, caught in thoughts too troubling to share. Aiden stood barefoot in the doorway, his hair sticking out in all directions, his pajama top pushed up so that his belly showed.

"What are you doing up, little man?"

"I'm hungry." He rubbed his eyes and blinked several times as they adjusted to the bright room.

She really was a bad mother. She'd let him fill up on junk food and go to bed without dinner. More than that, when had she allowed this situation to become about her and not the child she loved more than her own life?

"Here, honey." She pulled out a chair for him. "I'll get you something to eat."

When Aiden didn't sit immediately, she took out bread, strawberry jam and peanut butter and made him a sandwich. She couldn't let herself smile over those peanut butter sandwiches earlier or think about how much she'd enjoyed that vending machine lunch. Instead, she sliced an apple into wedges and added a few carrots to complete the meal.

When she set the plate on the table, Aiden finally dropped into the seat and started eating. But then he stopped and looked around the room.

"Where's Mr. Jamie?"

"He had to go home."

He dropped the half-eaten sandwich, his eyes filling with tears. "He didn't have to go. Not yet. It's too soon."

Sarah brushed her fingers through her little boy's hair, but he bristled under her touch. He was overtired after his day of adventures, and he wouldn't know about rules of decorum involving single moms and male guests. But it also was a sign that she shouldn't have allowed her son to deepen his relationship with Jamie. No good could come from Aiden clinging to him as a father figure, or her attaching herself to him for any other reason.

"It was late, sweetie, so he had to go. But we had a fun day with him, didn't we?" Definitely more fun than *she* should have had.

"But Mommy, I want Mr. Jamie."

"I know you do, honey."

She was surprised she could speak at all. For no matter how risky any involvement with the man might be, no matter how many times she reminded herself that she should steer clear of him, she wanted to be with Jamie, too. Wanted to feel safe in his strong arms again, to help another broken human being learn to forgive himself.

But none of that could happen. Jamie might have seemed different from any cop she'd ever met. Or any *man* she'd ever met. That didn't mean she could risk Aiden's safety to be with him. She would get her priorities straight for her son's sake.

Sarah gestured toward Aiden's food that he'd barely touched. "Aren't you hungry?"

He poked his sandwich and then pushed his plate away. "Not anymore," he said in a small voice.

"Well, let's get you back to bed then."

She held out her hand, and he rested his tiny one in hers. The message in that gesture couldn't have been plainer as she guided him into the bedroom, nor could it have struck her on a more elemental level. Just as he had since his birth, Aiden relied on her to protect him. She would do whatever was required to keep him safe, no matter what it cost her.

She hated that the cost felt so high this time. Hated that a selfish part of her still wanted to put her needs first. But even if she could be reckless with her own life, she never could be with Aiden's.

For that reason, and a host of others, her son would not be spending more time with the friend he so desperately wanted. And neither would she.

Chapter 11

Michael pressed the doorbell on the yellow brick bungalow, where clay flowerpots lined either side of the porch. Plastic tulips and daisies poked out of the pots as if fake flowers could convince visitors that winter never came to the Midwest.

He didn't need her to answer the door to know she was at home. He'd nearly frozen his ass off in that econobox he'd boosted, waiting all day for her to return from work. If it hadn't been necessary for him to avoid drawing attention to himself, he would have descended on her like a fog the moment she pulled her vehicle into the detached single-car garage. So, she was lucky he'd at least waited for her to get inside the house before showing up on her porch.

Her familiar, too-wide smile greeted him as she opened the door, but it vanished the moment her gaze settled on him. Oh, his wife's little friend knew something, all right. He would lay money on it.

"Michael? Is that you?"

She adjusted her glasses and tucked her chin-length brown hair behind her ears at the same time. Proving she already had the answer to her question, she started closing the door by tiny increments.

"Hiya, Tonnie. It's been a long time."

"It has."

Her expression was neutral, the kind people gave door-to-door salesmen before they slammed the door in their faces. She wasn't going to get the chance this time.

"I didn't know you were…"

"Out?" He held his hands up and rotated them to show they were free of handcuffs. "Isn't it great?"

She licked her lips. "I don't mean to be rude, Michael, but why are you here?"

"Now is that any way to treat a guest?" He used his best smile, but he couldn't keep his jaw from tightening. "Just invite me in, and we'll catch up."

"That's probably not—"

He loved how she froze when he jammed his foot into the opening so that she couldn't shut the door. She was still staring down at his shoe when he pushed past her into the house. She didn't close the door, so he reached around her and did it himself. Good thing she hadn't thought to scream. That just wouldn't do.

"It's too cold to leave the door open," he said, as he scanned the cramped living room with embroidered pillows lining every seating area and lacy things covering the tables and windows. He would bet there was at least one cat around. Probably more than one. "Nice place."

She cleared her throat. "Thanks."

"Look, I just want to talk with you for a while, and then I'll go. I promise."

He waited for her nod and then stepped to the upright piano, where he could examine the collection of framed photos on top. Most were of Tonya with her parents and brothers. Maria was with her in a few of the old photos. Nothing in the past decade or so. A couple shots featured two dark-haired little girls. A small blond boy in enormous sunglasses. Probably nieces and nephews.

Clearly, there was no guy in her life. He'd expected as much from how easily he'd been able to locate *her*, but it was good to have that confirmed. Wouldn't want any would-be protector complicating things by showing up before she gave him the answers he needed.

She was wringing her hands when he turned back to her.

"Do you have anything to drink?" he asked, when she didn't offer.

"Just sweet tea."

That figured. "That'd be great."

He followed her into the narrow kitchen, so she wouldn't get any ideas about running out the back door. Sure enough, the moment she opened the refrigerator, a pair of gray tabbies appeared out of nowhere. They eyed him warily and then started mewling next to the door.

She let them outside and closed the door, but she didn't lock it. "They never stay out long. Not with dinner coming soon."

The side of his mouth lifted. Was that supposed to be her warning that they weren't alone in the house?

She set out a pitcher of tea and then grabbed two glasses from a cabinet. Her movements were robotic, her hands shaking as she poured, but she finished the job and handed him a glass.

"Let's drink it in here."

She led him into the living room without looking back, as if he wasn't making her nervous as hell. Once they were both seated, she sipped from her glass, but her hand shook again, and brown liquid dribbled on her blouse.

"So, what did you want talk about?"

"I don't know. Maybe you could tell me where I might find my wife."

"Oh, my God. Is Maria missing?"

Her surprise sounded almost authentic.

"You might say that."

"How long has she been gone? Do the police have any leads?"

She deserved a round of applause for her performance. He might even have believed her…if he didn't know better. She'd conspired against him all during his marriage, no matter how many times he'd warned Maria that the witch was filling her head with lies about him. She should pay for all her scheming. Later. For now, if he humored her, she might accidentally cough up some of the information he needed.

"Maria couldn't handle the separation, so she divorced me while I was *away.* I guess I can't blame her. Only now I would make it up to her, if I could find her. It's as if she just disappeared…with our son, Andy." He'd added the long pause and the nickname for effect. Tonya wasn't the only one who could show off acting chops.

"I'm so sorry. I didn't know."

She gripped her hands in her lap, but she met his gaze steadily as if she dared him not to believe her. But if she was telling the truth, then he was back to square one, and he refused to go there.

"You don't know where they are?"

"No, I don't." Her gaze slid to the antique desk on the far wall, a few books resting in a neat pile on its corner, but she quickly looked back to him. "How could I? I haven't heard from her in years."

"Sorry to hear that. Now how many years is that?"

He could almost see the wheels turning in her mind over which details she'd already given away. Although she'd admitted to being surprised that he'd been released, that also meant that she'd known he'd served time. She'd also shown no surprise when he'd mentioned their son.

He gripped the glass tighter as he imagined other things Maria might have shared with her over the years. Private things. He had to relax his fingers to prevent the glass from cracking in his hand.

"Just the occasional Christmas card."

"That does tend to come around every year." He couldn't help smiling at her discomfort. She was like a mouse whipping itself into exhaustion, while he was the cat, toying with her.

Tonya shifted in her chair. "But as I said, it's been years since I heard anything more than that from her. Have you tried to contact her mom?"

"I wasn't sure it was worth it."

"Amy's never been the same since Paul died."

"I also didn't figure Amy would give me a chance. She never did before." Even saying the name tasted bitter on his tongue. He'd once thought Maria's parents would be his ticket to easy street. Screw them. He'd found his own golden ticket. "But I thought *you* might. Give me a chance, that is."

"*Me?*"

She shook her head, so he pressed on before she had a chance to speak.

"It's just that you're the only one who understood how in love Maria and I were." He cleared his throat. "Still *are*. That's why you agreed to say she was sleeping over those times so that we could be alone together."

At that, she shrugged, her pale cheeks filling with color. It had been a risk reminding Tonya that she was a part of their relationship. Complicit, you might say. But as much as it might make her more determined not to share Maria's secrets, there was a chance that it might convince her to help him reunite with his soul mate.

Her decision was obvious as she drained her drink and then stood and reached for his. He stood up so that he towered over her, and though she stepped back, she didn't look away this time.

"Michael, I'm happy for you that you're free now. Really, I am. But I can't tell you what I don't know. I don't even know who else you could ask."

"What about that great-aunt she had? The one who'd sometimes send a few bucks in an envelope. She also paid for the crib before our miscarriage. Was it Aunt *Sarah*?"

He'd turned back to her for confirmation, and the way she startled over the mention of the woman's name was all the proof he needed that he was onto something. She glanced at the desk again, then straightened as she turned back to him. Preparing to lie.

"No, Sarah couldn't help." She paused and cleared her throat. "I guess you didn't know. She passed away several years ago."

"I'm sorry to hear that."

He didn't believe it for a minute, either. Just like he couldn't believe anything else she'd said today. He'd once found a letter from her where she'd said she would do anything for her best friend. She was only coming through on her promise.

Now she continued into the kitchen and spoke to him over her shoulder. "You never know. Maria might have just needed some space. Maybe she'll come back on her own eventually."

He stood in the kitchen doorway as she rinsed the glasses and put them in the dishwasher.

"You could be right." And the Easter Bunny was waiting right outside. "Well, thanks for agreeing to talk to me, even if you couldn't help. You were always decent to me. More decent than any of the others."

Until now, he almost added. She nodded stiffly.

Instead of waiting for her to usher him out, he started that way himself. She followed him.

At the door, he surprised her by giving her a quick hug. He smiled as she stiffened under his touch.

"Thanks again," he said as he released her. "For everything."

Her eyes widened as she stepped back, safely out of his reach. Did she realize that she'd given him so many clues, one he would follow up on right away? Where was Aunt Sarah? Because he doubted she was already in hell where she belonged. And what was she doing to help Maria hide his money and his son from him?

Tonya closed the door behind him and turned the lock, but as he passed the picture window, he caught sight of her rushing to the desk and grabbing her house phone and a small book. Was she really going to warn Maria about his visit? Well, he couldn't let that happen.

He rounded the house to the back door. Those two mangy cats were already meowing outside the door. The *unlocked* door. He shooed them away and turned the knob. It didn't squeak, even when he locked it behind him.

She was standing with her back to him in the living room doorway, the phone pressed to her ear. An address book dangled from her free hand.

"Come on. Come on," she pleaded. "You've got to pick up."

His movements felt smooth, practiced, as his slid up behind her, jerked her head back and covered her mouth with his hand, pressing her chin up so she couldn't bite him. The book and the phone dropped to the floor in two thumps as she raised both hands to scratch ineffectually at his wrists.

"All you had to do was tell me where she was and give me the chance to reunite my family. I would have left you to go on leading your miserable life. But you just had to lie for her."

She made several sounds in her throat as she tried to answer. Or maybe just plead for her release. He didn't care which. She'd already said enough today.

"You didn't stop there, either. Now you just had to warn—"

A female voice interrupted him. A sound so familiar that it gripped his heart. His gaze lowered to the phone on the floor. Tonya strained against his hands to look down, too, as if that could stop the sound floating from the earpiece.

"You've reached Sarah Cline…"

Sarah? Whatever else she said, he didn't hear it. With two words, that voice had just answered more questions than he'd been able to even ask since he'd been released. That wasn't some shaky old woman on the phone. It was Maria. He would bet his life on it.

At the beep, he bent at the waist, forcing the petite woman to bend in half beneath him. While still holding her mouth closed with one hand, he reached for the phone with the other. She grabbed for it, too, but his arms were longer. He was stronger and faster, too. He hit the off button, disconnecting the call just as she squealed as loudly as she could. Somehow, her teeth found purchase on the meaty side of his hand near his pinkie.

He yelped as she bit down hard, and he had to press his hand into her mouth to force her jaw to release.

"You bitch!"

He swung his hand back in a hard slap. She did call out this time, but he cut off the sound as his hands gripped her mouth again. She continued to wiggle against him, her hands scratching and pulling, but she was tiring. And perhaps recognizing the futility of her fight.

"Sounds like you weren't lying about one thing. I guess my wife's spinster aunt really might be pushing up daisies now. But even in death, she gave my wife quite a gift. Her name."

Her muffled cry almost made him feel bad for her. Almost. But he, of all people, knew there were consequences for mistakes made in life. These were hers. With her back still trapped against his chest, his hands slid effortlessly from her mouth to her throat. There was something invigorating about the muscles straining against his hands, her pulse pounding against his fingertips. She was fighting him, but it was different this time. More desperate.

Like she was fighting for her life.

"You don't have to—" she managed to whisper, before it became difficult for her to draw breath.

"That's the thing, Tonnie. I *do* have to. If I let you go, you'll call her and ruin the surprise. That just wouldn't do."

She shook her head, trying to deny the truth, but her scratches were becoming less effectual now.

"But don't worry. I'll be sure to tell her you sent me." He grinned as she shook her head again. "That you gave us your blessing to build a wonderful life together."

Her hands slid bonelessly to her sides, and she collapsed against him. Whether it was his hands on her windpipe or his promise that caused her to give up fighting and accept death, he wasn't certain. Perhaps both.

"I'm sorry, but you didn't give me any choice," he whispered to the corpse in his arms.

As he lowered her limp body to the floor, he had this feeling that he was being watched, though the kitchen curtains were closed. Had the lights become brighter? The floor creaked beneath his feet, and those damn cats meowed outside so loudly that people in the next county must have heard them. A strange energy filled his chest, but it only battled with the acid backing into his throat. When he got a look at her face, flat eyes staring back at him, blaming him, the nausea won. He raced to the bathroom and dumped the contents of his stomach in the toilet.

He wiped the basin for fingerprints with the same towel he'd used to wipe his mouth and brought it back to the kitchen with him. He moved efficiently around the house, wiping any surfaces he'd touched, and then, putting on a pair of gloves from her closet, he dumped dresser drawers on the bed, emptied ketchup bottles on the carpeting, unlocked the front door. No one should have been able to trace the crime to him, but he had to be sure. He'd work too hard to finally have this life he'd planned to let a mishap take it from him.

He avoided looking at her face again, even when he returned to the kitchen one last time and left in the dark through the back door. The cats tried to wiggle around him, but he pushed them aside with his foot. At least outside they would have a chance to feed themselves. He wasn't a monster.

"Bye, Tonnie." He closed the door, her address book and her cell phone in his arms.

He still didn't feel great as he cut through the neighborhood, staying out of sight as he made it a few blocks away to where he'd moved his car. He was exhausted but keyed up as well. His cellmate had described having feelings like that after he'd murdered a gas station attendant during an armed robbery. Taking a life had to have some repercussions, he supposed. But it hadn't been as difficult as he would have expected. A necessary task completed. And he could do it again if he needed to.

Chapter 12

"Hey, Sarah, there's a package out at the register for you," Ted called from the other side of the swinging kitchen door.

A package? Her hand jerked just as she was carefully removing the foil pieces that had protected her piecrust during the first half of baking, and her fingertips brushed the oven rack. She yanked her hand back from the burn.

"Ouch. Darn it." She closed the oven door and rushed over to the handwashing sink to run cool water over her two burned fingers.

Ted pushed open the door and peeked inside. "What's going on in here?"

She tilted her hand so that he could see. "You shouldn't make announcements outside the kitchen without first checking to see who has the oven open."

He crossed to the sink to get a better look. "I'll follow that advice if you keep your hands clear of the heat when you're not wearing an oven mitt."

"I'll do my best. Anyway, looks like I'll live."

Ted took a deep breath, closing his eyes and smiling. "What'd you make this morning? Besides the cinnamon rolls, obviously. It smells great in here, whatever it is."

"Apple amaretto pie."

"Isn't this the second time you've made it this week?"

"Is that a problem? Are we not selling enough slices of that type of pie?"

He rolled his eyes. "You know we are. We sell all of 'em. Always. All I'm saying is you don't usually repeat recipes so quickly. Is it a favorite of someone special?"

She'd been continuing to let the water run over her fingers, but at his words, she jerked back her sore hand and shut off the tap.

"You have a big imagination," she said, as she dried her hands on a paper towel.

Ted might have been right, too, but she wouldn't tell him that. He didn't need to know she'd convinced herself that the recipe selection had more to do with a good deal on McIntosh apples, in April, no less, than one police officer's dessert preferences. She especially wouldn't admit that though Jamie hadn't visited the diner in eleven days, she still had to remind herself every time she received one of his texts that she didn't *want* to see him.

"I guess that might be true."

Sarah stared at Ted until it dawned on her that he was responding to her comment about his imagination and not reading her mind.

"Now what package were you talking about?"

"You'll just have to see for yourself."

She frowned. "If you had to come all the way in here and injure me, the least you could have done was to bring it with you."

"And ruin all the fun? Not a chance."

She didn't have to tell her boss that this was her first package at the diner not delivered through the rear entrance in boxes marked Flour or Sugar. One needed friends, other than her boss, or at least close relatives to have gifts shipped to her at work, and she could claim none of those groups. Well, there was Tonya, but she knew better than to send Sarah a gift at work. Anyway, since Tonya had called without leaving a message almost a week before, Sarah hadn't been able to reach her. Though she was beginning to worry, she hoped her friend had a new man in her life keeping her too busy to return calls.

Speaking of new men…the flutter in Sarah's belly suggested that she did have one other "friend" who might have sent a gift, but she squashed that inkling. With as many times as she'd let Jamie's calls go to voicemail and left his texts unanswered in the past eleven days, he'd probably gotten the message that they couldn't be friends. Or anything else.

What would she have said if she'd answered, anyway? That she'd kissed him as if she wanted him to take her right on her sofa, but she hadn't meant anything by it?

"Are you coming or not?" Ted pushed the door open again, narrowly missing one of the waitresses as she swished by, carrying a tray.

Sarah blew out a breath. "Fine."

She followed him out of the kitchen, trying not to picture Valentine's Day candy or flowers on an anniversary. Those were the silly, wonderful gifts other women received all the time. Things she couldn't have and had never wished for. Until now.

The dining room was empty for a Wednesday morning, something she hoped wouldn't become a trend. She and Aiden would struggle to get by if her hours were trimmed.

As they rounded the cash register desk, Ted pointed to a gift bag that had been set on the floor behind it. "There it is."

Clearly, the bag, covered with rainbows and stuffed with tissue paper, had been hand-delivered. It also could have been sent by one of Michael's cronies who'd finally located her, and it could contain a threat. She pushed that thought away, as well. This one time, she didn't want to think about the boogeyman under the bed. She wanted to be like any other woman, enjoying the excitement of an unexpected gift.

Just as she reached for it, Evelyn and Belinda, the two waitresses hanging around on the slow breakfast shift, joined them beside the desk.

"Did I hear Sarah has a package?" Evelyn said.

"Yep, just delivered," Ted announced, grinning.

"Just now?" Sarah couldn't help asking.

But as she scanned the room, she found only regulars, sipping black coffee and poring over newspapers like they'd probably done most mornings for a decade. The guest she'd most hoped to see wasn't anywhere around.

"Come on. Open it," Belinda said. "We need some

entertainment this morning, since we're not making a lot of tips."

Sarah frowned. "What do you do on other slow mornings? Shoot craps in the parking lot?"

The two women only grinned. With her good hand, Sarah grasped the handles of the gift bag and set it on a table.

"Well, aren't you going to open it?" Ted asked.

She stared at the bag a few seconds longer, but finally pulled a huge wad of paper out and peeked inside. A plush gorilla and a bunch of real bananas rested next to each other on the bottom of the bag.

Sarah couldn't help grinning she reached in with both hands and pulled out the creature and his snack.

"A gorilla?" Evelyn exclaimed.

"Do you *like* bananas?" Belinda wanted to know.

"Doesn't everyone?" she said with a chuckle.

Her fellow waitresses might not have been impressed with her gift, but she wouldn't have loved it more if it had been both roses *and* chocolates. The plush toy was a perfect replica of the lowland gorillas they'd visited at the zoo on an equally flawless day. The bananas only added to the memory.

"Is there a card?" Belinda asked.

Sarah didn't need one. No one else could have chosen this gift that held such special meaning for her. Still, her curiosity won out. She hated that her shoulders drooped after she searched the bottom of the bag and came up empty.

"Wait. What's that?" Ted pointed to the gorilla's back.

She flipped the toy over, and safety-pinned just above its rump was a folded piece of paper.

Her heart thudded as she detached it and unfolded it.

Sarah,

Thanks for the amazing day at the zoo. Sorry I was such a…gorilla. Please accept my apology and bananas from this furry friend. You're one of the good ones.

—J

The first part of the message made her smile, but as she read his last sentence, her eyes filled. She blinked rapidly and turned to brush at them, so the others wouldn't see. *You're one of the good ones.* They were the same words she'd written on the note to *him*, the one that seemed so long ago now.

She'd once regretted writing that note, sorry she'd even opened a door to connecting with someone when distance had been central to her strategy for keeping her family safe. She didn't know what to do now with the truth—that she wasn't sorry anymore.

He'd been too nice, too approachable, too easy to know. And he'd really listened. He probably had no idea how attractive those things could be.

Now in true Jamie fashion, he was being gallant in taking responsibility for what had happened at her front door. Didn't he realize he was no more than fifty percent to blame for those heady moments? Didn't he realize there'd been two of them in that apartment, and she'd been as enthusiastic as he was? Had he forgotten that she'd kissed *him* first?

She was surprised to realize that she no longer regretted that as much as she should have, either. There could be no more between them; that was a given. The risk was too great. But she wasn't sorry that she'd had at least one chance to be cherished in a man's arms.

In *Jamie's* arms.

As her fingers gently brushed the gorilla's faux fur, her tender skin reminding her of the burn, Sarah looked up to find her coworkers watching her. Her cheeks heated as she lowered her hand.

"Wow," Evelyn said. "If she gets this choked up over a gorilla and some bananas, can you imagine how she'd react if someone sent a stuffed rabbit and some carrots?"

"What does the note say?" Belinda asked.

"Nothing important," she said, but her hand went automatically to her apron pocket, where she'd tucked it.

"Come on, ladies. Time to get back to our customers." Ted gently guided them away from the table and the gift. "She's a private soul, our Sarah."

As she tucked her gifts back in the bag, her boss stepped closer again.

"It's a really nice gift," he said.

"And he just dropped it off with you?" Her face warmed at the idea that Ted knew exactly who'd left the surprise for her.

"If you're talking about a polite young police officer who wears the biggest smile whenever you pour his coffee," he paused as if waiting for her reaction, "...then *no*."

"I don't understand."

"But if you mean a mop-headed teenager who said some dude paid him ten bucks to bring that bag inside, then absolutely."

"You're rotten." She swung the bag by its handles and allowed it to thump against his calf.

"And for the first time since you've started working here, you're *smitten*."

"That's ridiculous." And unacceptable. And untrue, though she wasn't as certain as she needed to be. "Where did you pick up that word, anyway? Did you steal it from the 1600s?"

"I'd definitely say *he* is," he said, as if she hadn't spoken. "Smitten, that is."

He pointed to the bag dangling from her fingers.

"He's just one of the mentors who works with Aiden at the after-school program."

"Yeah, Aiden told me all about *Mr. Jamie*," Ted said. "But if that's *all* he is, then why wasn't the gift for your son?"

Sarah couldn't answer that. How could she explain that the gift was an apology for a make-out session, when the many texts he'd already sent would have sufficed? When none of those things had been necessary because he wasn't to blame.

"Hey, I haven't seen Trooper Donovan in here all week. Wonder what that's all about."

Ted glanced at the bag again, as if he knew an apology gift when he saw one. At least he couldn't know about all the calls and texts she'd dodged, or all of Aiden's requests for "play dates" that she'd refused.

"I hadn't noticed," she said, though she wondered why she bothered lying. "Anyway, I'd better get back, or you won't have any desserts for the dinner crowd."

"Okay, go do your magic so you can get some rest before your shift."

She practically ran to the kitchen, so it frustrated her that their conversation chased her. Sure, Ted was an old romantic who believed everyone could have the same love story that he'd shared with his late wife, but could he also have been right? About Jamie at least.

Even she hadn't missed the way that Jamie had watched her at the zoo. It had been disconcerting, but a little exciting, too. Had he looked at her that way when he'd been just one of her customers at the diner? Had she been too busy watching for hands reaching out from her past to notice?

She was relieved when the kitchen door closed behind her. She ducked into the staff locker area, so she could put away the bag before the kitchen crew started asking questions.

But before she returned to the oven, she couldn't resist pulling out her phone and checking for texts. She was almost disappointed when she didn't find any new messages.

"The gorilla probably counts," she whispered in the tight space.

She started to tuck the phone in her purse again, but then stopped and opened her texts again. She clicked on the trail of message bubbles from Jamie, read but never answered, and then clicked on the bubble at the bottom. Taking a deep breath, she started typing a reply.

Apology unnecessary...thanks... A BUNCH. J

Before she could talk herself out of it, she tapped the arrow to send. She tried convincing herself that it was only a thank-you, a small attempt at manners in a world where true thank-you notes and letters of apology had all but disappeared. But she was tired of lying to herself. Tired of denying her connection to the gentle man, who had his own scars but had reached out to her, anyway.

As she glanced down at the conversation stream, she braced herself for a moment of panic. Instead, an almost unsettling calm flowed through her.

With that tiny message, she'd opened the closed door

between them at least a crack. If she had any sense at all, she would have bolted it with more locks than could fit on the entrance to any apartment. But for now, instead of running for her life, she was choosing to really live.

Jamie reread the text message on his phone for what had to have been the twentieth time that day, the butterflies in his stomach slam-dancing like they had the first time he'd seen it, ten hours before. Only this time when his thumbs twitched to type a response, it wasn't some uncool phrase like "You're welcome bunches" or a lighter "No prob" that came to mind.

He had a different message to send her, and he couldn't talk himself out of writing it.

Don't you get tired of lying?

Jamie tapped the screen to send the message but didn't bother watching his phone for a response the way he had for all the others over the past week. He didn't care whether or not she answered. Not this time. He turned his phone facedown on the counter and stuck his plate of leftover chicken Parmesan in the microwave.

He didn't know why he bothered cooking. After everything he'd learned that day, and everything he'd guessed since then, he wasn't even hungry.

"She played you for a fool," he whispered to the dark walls.

While he'd thought they'd made some deep connection as they'd shared their stories and their pain, she'd been feeding him a pack of lies, using his need to serve and protect against him.

Now he knew the truth. Not only was there no Michael Cline currently serving drug charges in the Illinois prison system, there didn't appear to be any "Michael and Sarah Cline" married or divorced in that state in the past twenty years.

Sarah Cline—if that was even her real name—had made up the whole story, and he'd swallowed it faster than a goldfish getting its first meal after a week of neglect. He understood why he'd believed her, but why had she lied? To throw him off her trail because she was on the run from the law, just as he'd guessed earlier? To make him pity her? If either was true, her plan had failed. He hadn't stopped asking questions, and he'd never felt sorry for her, though he'd been furious on her behalf. He was still mad. He'd just found a new target for his anger.

The worst part was that he couldn't recall the pain and fear in her eyes, not to mention the passion, and accept that it all was a lie.

He was well aware that suspects could lie about anything when cornered, but until now, he hadn't thought of Sarah as a suspect. That was his first mistake, though he'd made so many with Sarah that it was difficult to count them. Kissing her and wanting her and letting himself believe that she wanted him back were just a few of them. Each one showed he was a lousy cop.

He'd been so busy pursuing her that he'd forgotten to confirm her story. The irony of it was that he'd longed for the chance to earn her trust when he shouldn't have trusted *her*. He'd known better than to let someone get too close, to risk losing someone he cared about again, and yet he'd raced in, lights flashing and sirens blaring, the moment she'd hinted that she might need him.

He carried his plate to the sofa and then set it aside,

letting his head fall against the cushion and closing his eyes. He couldn't breathe. It felt as if his patrol car was parked on his chest. For nearly three weeks, he'd been hiding his suspicions from his fellow officers because of who she was, but wasn't it about time for him to ask for help to find the answers he was positive would be there?

He had grabbed his cell and was scrolling through his contacts, determining which of his friends he would ask, when the phone buzzed in his hand. The screen flashed the name Sarah, and at first, all he could do was stare at it. Finally, he brushed his finger across the screen to answer.

"*Now* you call me back?"

His heart thudding in his ears was the singular sound as he strained to hear her voice, but just as he pulled the phone away to see if the call had been dropped, her reply came through the line.

"I'm sorry, Jamie," she said in a small voice. "For everything."

"What are you talking about?" Could it have been the lies, or was it something even worse than he'd thought?

"I should never have involved you."

Her voice was louder this time, but there was a shaky edge to it. Whatever acidic thing he'd been about to say vanished in the cellular waves.

"What's going on, Sarah?"

"Aiden's missing. He's just…gone."

His gaze slid toward the window, where the blackest part of the night stared back at him. He came off the couch in a move fueled by fear. Her betrayal. His righteous indignation. None of it mattered now. Her little boy was missing, and no matter what Sarah's track record for honesty, he was sure that this time she was telling the truth.

"Now slow down, Sarah. Tell me what happened."

"I just got home from work, and when I went to Nadia's apartment, where she puts him in her bedroom to sleep, he wasn't there. Nadia was in the shower. Door was closed. She doesn't know how long—"

"The door was locked. It had to be locked," an equally panicked female said in the background. "Baby Boy was sleeping."

"They took him, Jamie," Sarah continued, as if she hadn't heard the other woman. "He has my baby. Again."

"Now hold up." Jamie knew his voice was sharp, but he had to get past her panic. "Have you called the police? Because if you haven't, you need to do that right now."

Either that, or he would call it in himself. But instead of flicking through the phone's screens, he pressed the device to his ear, as he waited for the words he was certain would come next.

"I…can't."

The heartbreak in her voice sliced through him. He barely took a breath before stuffing his feet in his shoes next to the sofa and grabbing his jacket off the back of the recliner.

It didn't matter that she'd just confirmed every assumption that remained after all the truths he'd already learned that day. She couldn't call the police because she was on the run from law enforcement. But she had called *him*. No matter what she'd done before, she was reaching out to him now.

"Sit tight," he said, already jogging to the door. "I'm on my way."

Chapter 13

The moment the car pulled into her apartment's lot and took the only remaining parking spot, Sarah released the breath she'd been holding. She hadn't even confirmed yet that the driver was Jamie, but she was sure it would be. He'd promised he would come, and she believed him. She tried not to think about how, with each minute, whoever had taken Aiden had added another mile of distance. And with each mile, the likelihood that they would find her son slipped away.

"Is that your police officer friend?"

Nadia stood next to her in a floor-length flannel nightgown and a bathrobe, staring out the window and watching the same scene. Her neighbor's face was swollen from crying, and she didn't even know the whole story.

"Yes," Sarah said, before the car door even opened.

"Sometime, you'll explain why we couldn't call 9-1-1, and you phoned him instead?"

She nodded as the door opened, and light stretched from the car's interior to the asphalt. A man of Jamie's size and shape slid from the vehicle and started toward the apartments. He disappeared from her sight near the building's center.

"It's going to be okay," Nadia said in a shaky voice. "You'll see."

Nadia patted Sarah's arm to comfort her, though she couldn't know that nothing would ever be okay after today. That the only thing worse than a monster with no face was one she knew intimately but had been unable to stop anyway.

After she'd given Jamie enough time to make it up the stairs, Sarah stepped around the afghan-covered chair and opened Nadia's door. Unlike her own, this door had only two locks, and if what she guessed was true, Nadia might have neglected to secure even those.

"Jamie, we're over here."

He glanced left and right, then hurried toward them, stopping before he crossed the threshold. "Are you sure you want me to do this?"

"What are you talking about? Of course, I want—"

"I mean, whatever you're hiding from, it can't be as bad as—"

He stopped himself, but not before she understood what he was saying. As bad as losing her son. She couldn't think about that now. They had to find him. They *would* find him.

"I mean there's just one of me when you could have a whole team of officers, even multiple agencies, activating all at the same time. Every minute we waste—"

"Lets them get farther away. I know," she said in a tight voice.

"How bad is it?" he whispered.

"It's bad." She copied his tone as she answered his question about why she couldn't go to the authorities. "Are you going to help us or not?"

Jamie reached in his jacket pocket, and pulled out a small notebook, pen and a pair of nitrile gloves. He set the notebook on the back of the chair and then worked his fingers into the gloves. He probably thought she was an awful, selfish person, but she couldn't bring the police into this if they could locate her son without involving them. What good would it do to have them help her find Aidan, only to have them take him from her?

He didn't even look her way as he produced a stack of tiny paper bags from his other pocket.

"For evidence," he explained, though no one had asked. "If the lab would even agree to accept anything like this from me."

He took a few steps forward and stopped in front of Nadia, whose shoulders were still shaking.

"You must be the babysitter?"

She sniffed loudly. "Yes, I'm Nadia Antonov."

She automatically extended her hand, which Jamie denied with a shake of his head. He held up both hands to remind her he was wearing gloves.

"Okay, let's do this as quickly as possible. Maybe there'll be something…"

But his tone didn't offer much hope. Was he already sorry he'd agreed to come without insisting on calling in other authorities, so they could at least file an Amber Alert? Worse, had she decreased her son's chance of escape or survival by limiting the response to his disappearance? She thought she'd been protecting him by keeping him away from his father, but maybe someone should have protected him from *her*.

"Now if I have the story right, Aiden was already asleep when you showered. Was he in the bedroom?"

He pointed to the closed door at the rear of the apartment, built exactly like Sarah's. At Nadia's nod, he stalked back toward the entry. "And you believe the door was locked when you entered your bathroom?"

"I thought it was."

After flipping on the light near the door, he opened it and examined the locks and doorplate. "I don't see any signs of forced entry."

Sarah's chest tightened. Could that mean that her babysitter had been lying about locking the door, or had she only forgotten? Besides Ted, Nadia was the person she knew best in Brighton. How well did she really know her? Everyone had a price. Had one of Michael's friends figured out Nadia's?

But instead of staring down her neighbor, Jamie appeared to be examining the distance from the front door to the bedroom.

"Is there any chance that Aiden might have heard someone knock while the shower was running, and answered himself?"

"I guess he could have." Nadia met Sarah's gaze and then lowered her head.

Sarah swallowed. She knocked on that same door every night she worked, and sometimes Aiden beat Nadia to the door, no matter how many times both women warned him that only adults should answer. Could he have answered the knock, expecting his mother, and opened the door to his abductor instead?

"Is it okay if I check the bedroom?" Jamie didn't wait for Nadia's answer before entering the room, its overhead light still on from when Sarah had found it empty.

Jamie's gaze moved from the rumpled quilt that had been folded like a sleeping bag on top of the bed, to the window with drawn drapes. Then he stepped closer to the bureau, where Nadia's hefty purse rested near a tidy perfume bottle collection. Like the closet door, all the drawers were closed. He jotted something in the notebook.

Sarah had to force herself to stay in the doorway with her babysitter instead of rushing in and upending every bottle and sock drawer, searching for answers. She'd asked for his help. Since Jamie was Aiden's only real chance now, she had to at least let him try.

When Jamie returned to the bed, he paused next to the smallish pillow, still dented from Aiden's usually sweaty little head. Sarah couldn't stop the whimper that slipped from her lips.

"Does anything look out of place, Ms. Antonov?"

"*Mrs*. Antonov. I'm a widow," Nadia corrected as she shuffled into the room and looked around. "I don't think so."

"There are no signs of a struggle here, either," Jamie noted.

Sarah closed her eyes, but she couldn't shake the image of some awful person, someone who Michael knew well, carrying her son out of the building, careful not to wake him so he wouldn't scream. Or drugging him so he didn't have the chance.

When she opened her eyes, Jamie was writing something else down.

"About how long do you usually run the water in the shower?"

"Maybe ten minutes?" Nadia told him. "Why do you ask?"

"That's how long an abductor would have had to get Aiden out of the apartment before you might have heard something."

Instead of writing this time, he glanced back at the bed. "Does Aiden always sleep on a quilt like this when he's here?"

Nadia nodded. "He calls it his sleeping bag and pretends he's camping. I even give him a flashlight that he plays with until he goes to sleep."

"Did you give him one tonight?" He walked around three sides of the bed then pulled off the quilt and shook it out.

"I'm sorry. I can't remember."

Sarah's hands clenched at her sides. First the door, and now her babysitter couldn't remember about the flashlight. How could she have trusted her with her son?

"And Sarah, doesn't Aiden also sleep with a dolphin named Willy?"

"How do you know…" She blinked several times. "Oh, right. He always keeps it in his backpack, so he has it when Nadia picks him up."

"It isn't here, either."

Immediately, Sarah rounded the bed, bent and searched under it herself. Nothing.

"Couldn't whoever have abducted him also have taken Willy?" Nadia suggested in a shaky voice.

"I suppose that's possible," Jamie said, "but would that person also have stopped to take the flashlight and Aiden's backpack, his jacket and his shoes?"

"What do you mean?" But even as she asked it, Sarah hurried out of the room toward the front door. Once she rounded the side chair, she stopped and stared at the spot where Nadia usually stacked Aiden's things for when Sarah picked him up each night.

Everything was gone.

"I don't understand," Sarah said.

"It's pretty clear that, for whatever reason, Aiden left this apartment all on his own," he said.

"Oh my God." She stared out into the night, which seemed to have become darker. "He's out there somewhere. Maybe he's lost. He's probably cold and scared."

"This is all my fault," Nadia announced. "I should never have showered while he was here."

Jamie spread his hands wide as if to calm them. "It's no one's fault. The only thing we need to worry about now is bringing Aiden home."

As a fresh wave of anguish nearly closed off her throat, Sarah rushed for the door, but instead of following her, Jamie hurried in the opposite direction. Back to the bedroom.

"What are you doing?" The last word was almost a shriek, so she took a deep breath, grasping for a calm that wouldn't come. "We already know he isn't in there. He's out there somewhere."

Though she pointed to the door, Jamie continued into the bedroom as if she hadn't spoken. Sarah stomped after him, but he didn't look back. He only stared at the bed as if he expected it to cough up information.

"Jamie, this isn't getting us anywhere."

He raised a hand, signaling that he wanted her to stop. "Let's think about this."

"Don't you get it? There's no time to think. My baby…is missing."

This time he looked over his shoulder at her. "I know. So, let me do this for you."

He shifted the books on the bedside table, smoothed the comforter and even lifted the blanket again.

"I'm guessing this is the first time Aiden's ever run away. He's six. Not an expert yet. He's probably left a few clues."

Jamie crouched down next to the bed, peeked under it and smoothed his hand over the carpet.

"What do you think he left?" Nadia murmured.

"If I knew that, wouldn't I already have found it?" He shook his head as he lifted Aiden's pillow off the bed, fluffing it and removing the child-size imprint in the process. "Sorry. I'm just as frustrated as…"

His words fell away as a piece of notebook paper drifted from inside the pillowcase and landed on the mattress. Jamie snapped it up. On one side was the message Sarah could remember writing herself, reminding him to be good for Nadia, but Jamie barely paused on that before turning it over to the side written in a child's hand with a purple marker.

"He left a note?" Sarah said. "What does it say?"

But before she could get close enough to read it herself, Jamie stuffed it in his pocket.

"Hey, let me see that."

"He's on his way to my house."

She could only stare at him. "Your house? Does he even know where you live?"

"Generally. But he wouldn't know how to get there." His words came out in a hurried clip that mimicked his walk to the front door.

"Why would he know…generally?"

Jamie glanced back over his shoulder, his jaw tight. "Because he *asked* me, and I told him."

"You told a six-year-old boy, who clearly hero-worships you, where you *live*?"

This time he turned to face her. "Okay, it was a bone-headed move, but can you bust my chops for it later? After we find him?"

"I'm sorry. I'm just so—"

"Scared?" He didn't wait for her to respond before adding, "Then your son is probably feeling the same way right now. Are you coming or not?"

She grabbed her coat and followed him out the door, mouthing *"sorry"* to Nadia for all the assumptions she'd made about her.

Maybe Aiden wasn't in the hands of one of Michael's friends the way she'd always dreaded, but he was out there all alone, probably sorry for venturing out on his own. They had to find him. They just had to. Good thing she wouldn't have to do it alone.

Jamie loved Aiden. He'd proved that long before to-night, when he was probably breaking dozens of departmental rules, and maybe a few laws, to conduct this off-the-books investigation. Now, even if he didn't agree with her decision not to involve other agencies, he seemed determined to find Aiden and wouldn't stop until they did.

Whether it was this one huge realization or so many small ones that had convinced her he was someone she could trust, she wasn't sure. But once this was all over, once Aiden was safe and warm and grounded for life for scaring them, she would finally trust Jamie with the whole truth.

Chapter 14

They were never going to find him.

Jamie bit his lip as the realization descended on him in a fog that only made his surroundings appear more opaque as he drove along four-lane Grand River Avenue for the umpteenth time. As he had every time he'd driven this stretch of road that lead past Brighton's quaint downtown, he hoped the six-year-old adventurer would leap out and say "boo" while remaining safely on the sidewalk. But just like each time before, Sarah sat silently in the passenger seat, scanning the sidewalks for her son. And Jamie couldn't find him for her.

"Do you think we passed him and we just didn't see him?" she asked.

Her words startled him. They were the first she'd spoken in more than an hour. He couldn't even give her an encouraging answer.

"Probably not."

"But dark clothes and a navy backpack and jacket weren't the best choices for running around in the dark, were they?"

He didn't answer, but his hands tightened on the steering wheel, though his muscles already ached from being in a constant state of flex for two hours. His head throbbed from straining his eyes to see a tiny figure who wasn't there. Anywhere.

"Now tell me what you said to Aiden about where you live," Sarah said in a tight voice. "And why?"

"I already told you that I said I had a house on First Street near Mill Pond Park, and he said he loves it when you take him to Mill Pond Playground."

"Which means he would remember what you told him." She repeated her earlier words.

She sat straighter in the seat and started tapping her fingers on the door handle in a relentless drumbeat.

"But as I said before, that doesn't mean he had any idea how to get there."

"We always walked when we went there." She shrugged. "We walk everywhere."

"He's six."

"Have you *met* my son?"

"Fair enough."

But because they'd already had this conversation out loud once, and half a dozen times in his head, he focused on the road again. Though at first the situation hadn't seemed quite as sinister as Sarah had imagined it, the likelihood that it could become so increased with each minute that passed and with each mile they covered in this tiny city without locating Aiden.

They were wasting too much time. At this point, he

didn't even care if the Brighton Police Department had already picked Aiden up, and all hell was about to break loose when the officers in his own department figured out how he'd been spending his after-work hours. At least the child would be safe.

"We're not going to find him, are we?"

"Sure we are."

She'd just put words to his thoughts, and yet Jamie couldn't let *her* believe it. She couldn't give up, couldn't lose hope. If she did, he would, too. As if he hadn't already lost his edge here, wasn't far too involved in the case to be of any help in solving it. All his training told him he also shouldn't make

promises he couldn't keep. Still, when she said nothing, he doubled down.

"We have to find him." He cleared his throat. "We... *will.*"

As if mouthing the words could make it true. If it would, he would repeat it all night.

When he patted her shoulder, she flinched and shifted closer to the door. She stared out into a darkness more relentless than the night.

When he'd first arrived at her apartment, she'd still been crying, her body visibly shaking with the panic of the unknown. Then for a while, she'd been too furious with him to remember how scared she was. But she seemed different now. She had this unsettling dry-eyed resignation, as if she already knew the outcome and only awaited the inevitable.

"Why did I even try? I built this whole world to protect him, and I couldn't even do that."

"This isn't your fault, Sarah."

It was his. They both knew that. And if Aiden was

hit by a car or became the victim of a child predator in a crime of opportunity, he would have no one to blame but himself. Just as he had with Mark, he'd failed Aiden and Sarah. He was poison to everyone and everything he touched.

"You've done everything you could to make him feel safe and loved," he told her.

She kept shaking her head. "But it wasn't enough. And then tonight, because I was so worried about getting caught, I've helped to ensure that we won't bring him home safely."

Now that he couldn't argue with. "But we could still call it in now."

Even if it might be too late to help. And even if he'd be in trouble taking policing into his own hands. Would he be fired for this? It didn't matter. If it gave Aiden a better chance, he didn't care.

"Do you want to do that now?" He perched his hand above the button on his steering wheel to activate his phone's Bluetooth connection.

She stared down at her folded hands for a few seconds. "Yes. Do it now."

The light had changed, so after he turned back onto Main Street, he pressed the button. A mechanical voice asked him what he wanted to do.

"Call—"

But a flash of light off one of the store windows caught his eye and cut off his words. Was that just a car light from a strange angle? His heart raced, and his mouth was suddenly dry. He hit the button again to turn off the car's electronic connection and rounded the corner onto First to pull into a parking space.

"What is it? Did you see something?" She twisted her neck to look in the same direction he had.

"I'm not sure."

It wasn't right to get her hopes up. This wasn't the first time he'd thought he'd spotted something tonight. Still, he threw open the door, climbed out and strode back to the intersection. The other door slammed, and her footsteps approached behind him.

He scanned the area where he'd noticed the light before. Nothing. Had desperation willed another image into existence? He turned his head, taking in the whole scene again, his hope sinking.

"It was probably nothing."

"Nothing," she repeated in a shaky voice.

Then he saw it again, not a pair of headlights, but a single light, swaying back and forth as if a walker carried it.

"It's a flashlight."

That didn't necessarily mean anything, either. This was a dog-loving community. Pet owners often walked their dogs at night, carrying flashlights to make them visible to motorists. But Jamie couldn't stop himself from rushing toward what he hoped was the source of the light.

Just past a group of storefronts, he caught up to both the light and the small hooded figure attached to it.

"Aiden, is that you?"

He barreled into the child and gathered him in a bear hug.

"Boy, have we been looking for you."

"I got lost. I couldn't find your house."

Again, guilt stabbed Jamie. What had he been thinking, sharing details about his home with a child who was smart enough to attempt to find him, even if he was too young to try?

"Well, buddy, I wish you hadn't looked for it. You worried everybody."

Worried didn't begin to cover it, but how could a first-grader, who didn't know that evil was often the next-door neighbor to good, even imagine that kind of darkness?

"I want my mom."

Jamie whisked him up and turned just as Sarah reached them.

"Aiden?"

Jamie lowered the boy to the ground in front of her.

"It's me!"

Aiden aimed the flashlight on his mother's face, illuminating what had been hidden in the shadows from the streetlamps. Tears streamed freely down her cheeks, and her shoulders trembled with the intensity of her sobs.

"Don't cry, Mommy. It'll be okay."

As the child reached up to brush her cheek, likely repeating words she'd used to comfort him many times before, she only shook harder, her fear for the worst not yet reconciled with the answer to prayers.

It was all Jamie could do not to gather Sarah in his arms and let her cry out her fears and her regrets until she'd emptied herself of all of them. But she needed more from him now. She needed him to be close and yet keep his distance, to be the friend and let her be the parent.

Seeming uncertain how to deal with his mother being any less than the rock he'd come to expect her to be, Aiden wrapped his arms around Sarah's waist. For several seconds, none of them moved, but finally, Sarah bent and lifted her son into her arms.

"Don't ever, *ever* do that again," she said in a stern voice, and then kissed his cheeks until he squirmed. "You scared me. Scared *us*."

Sarah didn't look at Jamie as she rephrased her words, but she had to feel his gaze on her. There had been an "us" in those hours of uncertainty. In the hopelessness. And now in the rebirth of hope. He didn't know what it meant or even how he felt about it, especially given the questions that lingered between them, but he was ridiculously grateful that she'd acknowledged it.

"I'm sorry, Mom," Aiden said, and then wiggled until she lowered him to his feet. "But I left a note. Just like you do when I go to Nadia's."

"I saw that," she said, though technically she hadn't seen it. "That doesn't make it okay. You should have asked Nadia or me first."

"You would have said no."

None of them could argue with that, and Jamie appreciated that she didn't try. Until today, she wouldn't answer his texts, let alone have agreed to allow her son to go over for a visit.

"We can talk about this tomorrow," she said. "It's late."

"But I'm so cold." He crossed his arms over his chest and shivered visibly. "And I'm hungry. Can we get food?"

Sarah shook her head. "We should just get home."

"Well, you know," Jamie began. "I do live right by here. If it's okay with your mom, we can get some hot cocoa and a snack at my place."

Then before either of them had the chance to answer, he pointed to Aiden. "But you may come to my house only if you promise never to visit without your mom again."

"I promise. Now can we, Mom? I'm *freezing*." He chattered his teeth for effect.

Jamie braced himself for Sarah's coming denial. Not only had she rejected every offer he'd made to her, but this particular one would reward Aiden's bad behavior. Still, he'd had to ask. His insides were scrambled from the past few hours, and he could use some hot cocoa as much as they could. And no matter what he'd found out about Sarah, and what secrets she hadn't shared and maybe never would, he still wanted to be with her.

As she hesitated in responding, he frowned into the darkness. Again, he'd pushed her into a corner. And again, he'd made her be the bad guy with her son.

"Okay."

He turned to face her, wishing Aiden would have picked that moment to aim his flashlight on his mother's face. "Okay?"

"Really, Mom?"

She nodded, her expression and her secrets still hidden beneath the cover of night. "But just for a little while."

Chapter 15

Sarah shifted her sleeping son's head and her tingling arm to make them both more comfortable as they cuddled together on a reclining end of Jamie's overstuffed sofa. With Jamie's brown tabby, Pancake, sleeping on the cushion behind their heads and a fleece blanket covering them both, Aiden burrowed deeper into her as if he needed to be as close as possible to her. She felt the same way about him tonight.

She could have lost him. Just the thought of it robbed her of her breath. She brushed her hand over the blanket and tucked the toy dolphin under his arm, Aiden's warmth radiating through the cloth, assuring her that he was safe.

"He doesn't look like a boy who's just survived a harrowing night," Jamie said from the second recliner on the sofa's other end.

He grinned as he leaned to set his mug on one of the cork coasters spaced along the coffee table.

"He'll get over it a long time before I do." She shook her head and smiled back at him. "Before *we* do."

His head sank back against the cushiony backrest. "You got that right. But I bet he won't sneak out again anytime soon."

"He'd better not."

"Good thing his biggest disappointment about tonight will be that he fell asleep before he had the chance to drink his cocoa with marshmallows."

Jamie brushed Aiden's hair from his eyes in a caress so sweet and gentle that Sarah could almost feel it against her own head. Almost wished she had.

"Why is it that kids' hair is always sweaty when they sleep?" He gestured toward the boy's mess of blond hair. "Strange how that's one of my earliest memories of Mark, brushing back his damp hair as he slept in his toddler bed."

"I don't know, but this one sweats like crazy." She pushed her son's hair off his forehead again and then cleared her throat. "Mark was lucky to have you for a big brother."

They shared meaningful look, and then he took a sip of his cocoa.

"Sure you don't want me to move him to my guest room?" He turned so he faced her, one knee resting on the sofa cushion. "You look so uncomfortable."

"I don't mind. Besides, I can't let him go just yet." She closed her eyes, but when horrific images appeared to her, she had to open them again. "I can't stop thinking about what could have happened."

"But nothing did. He's safe. You both are."

She shook her head, tears welling again, though she'd already shed many since they'd located Aiden. Once she knew he was okay. Only then, once the crisis was over, had she allowed the horrible possibilities that had been dogging her all night to swallow her.

"It could have been—"

"But it wasn't. You got lucky. We both did."

"Because of you." She shifted taller in the seat, and Aiden's head rolled forward, coming to rest on her lap. "I might never have found my son tonight without you. Thank you…for bringing him back to me."

Her voice faltered on the last, but she couldn't help it. He'd returned the most important person in her world to her.

"You're forgetting that it was also *because* of me that Aiden was out at night in the first place." His head lowered. "I should have known better than to give him even a hint about where I lived."

"Learn to accept a thank-you, will you?"

He looked up again. "I'll try."

"You never told me what the note said."

She pointed with her free arm toward his pants pocket, where he'd tucked it hours before.

"Oh. That." He dug it out and unfolded it. "I didn't figure it would be helpful for you to see it at the time."

He handed it to her, and she read it aloud. "'Dear Mom.' He spelled it *D-E-E-R*. Anyway, he wrote, 'I went to Mr. Jamie's house. You always say no. Love Aiden.'"

She swallowed as she read it again.

"I guess it wasn't only your fault. Apparently, I'm a horrible parent who says no." She folded it again and tossed it on the table. "It was good that I didn't see it then."

"He obviously went to great lengths to spend time with me." Jamie paused as if carefully considering his next words. "I wouldn't have come if *he* hadn't needed me."

"Yeah, I got your text." She stared at her hand that rested on Aiden's shoulder, while trying to come up with the right words. What could she say that would make things right? She went with the simplest version. "I'm so sorry. For everything."

"Why did you lie to me?"

"I didn't lie. At least not really."

"I know you did. I looked all of it up, and none of it checks out. Prison records. Divorce records. Birth records. I couldn't find anything about Michael and Sarah Cline. Or even Aiden. Why would you make up some elaborate lie? What did I do to deserve that?"

Each of his accusations burned her far deeper than if he'd raised a hand to her. It would have been easier if he had. At least she would have known how to react to that, would have allowed the muscle memory to take over, the survival instinct to choose flight over fight. Always flight. But this was new to her. This time she'd caused the hurt that was so evident in his words. The betrayal had been hers.

"You didn't," she answered, in a roughened voice that even she didn't recognize.

"I didn't do what?"

"Deserve it." She pressed her lips together, gathering the courage to tell the truth. The whole truth this time. "And you can confirm that everything I said was true. You were just looking under the wrong names."

"*Names?* What are you talking about, Sarah? Wait. Is that even your name?" He didn't give her time to answer before continuing. "I knew it! From the beginning, I knew it wasn't normal to have no credit history. No vehicle. No social-media presence. But I told myself there was a simple explanation. And there was. You're not who said you are."

"Let me explain. Please."

"Why would I believe you?"

Aiden startled in his sleep at Jamie's raised voice, so he tried again in a lower voice. "How would I know that whatever you were telling me wasn't just another lie?"

She opened her mouth to answer, but then lifted and lowered her shoulders. He was right. He couldn't believe anything she said.

He blew out a breath. "Who is Sarah Cline, anyway?"

"Sarah was my great-aunt, my dad's favorite aunt. We were very close. She died right after Aiden was born."

"And you assumed her identity."

"With her blessing, though I know it doesn't make it right."

"Or less of a crime."

She nodded and then waited for him to ask. Even with the inevitability of his question, she couldn't bring herself to volunteer the name she'd kept hidden all this time.

"If you're not Sarah Cline, then who are you?"

"Maria," she choked out. "Maria Brooks."

She waited for him to call her a liar again. But she wouldn't allow herself to look away. She'd kept her secrets for so long, and now she couldn't bear it if he didn't believe her.

"Brooks is your married name?"

He sounded so detached that she almost expected him to pull out his notebook and to interview her the way he would a suspect. Was she one? Would he feel honor-bound to arrest her now that she'd confessed to a crime?

"Yes. My maiden name was Norris. Maria Sarah Norris Brooks."

"Maria," he whispered, and then frowned.

Was he frustrated with himself for trying the name out, or did he think it didn't fit her? It didn't sound right in her ears anymore, either. No longer matched with the person she'd become.

"Please just call me Sarah. It will confuse Aiden. And Maria doesn't seem like who I am anymore."

He nodded. "It really is your middle name?"

"Dad adored his aunt and had insisted on naming me after her. Aunt Sarah never had children of her own but always thought of me as the daughter of her heart."

"Your ex?"

"Michael Brooks. You'll find him at Danville Correctional Facility."

"What about him?" He nodded to the sleeping boy in her lap.

She shook her head, though he hadn't specifically asked if Aiden was his name.

"It's close," she whispered. "His real name is Andrew."

She brushed her fingertips over his soft little cheek. "He doesn't remember being called anything else."

"He looks more like an Aiden," Jamie said.

He asked a few more questions, and she gave as many details as she could, aware that he would check out each of them as soon as he dropped her off at her apartment. This time he would confirm that she was telling the truth.

For several minutes, Jamie said nothing, as if taking time to absorb all the things she'd told him. If she'd be-

lieved that admitting the truth would be like an appointment in the confessional, where she could find absolution
for her sins, she'd been kidding herself. She felt no relief
from the shame. She hated that she'd lied to Jamie, had
given him reasons to assume that she was incapable of
telling the truth.

When the silence stretched too long, she found herself trying to fill the void with words. Any words. "I
thought everything would be okay after the divorce, but
the judge granted court-ordered visitation. For a baby
and his monster father. I just couldn't let that happen."

"So, you skipped out on a court order and have been
living under an alias." He pinned her with his stare. "Do
you have any idea how much trouble you could be in?
And what you've confessed…*to me*?"

"I'm so sorry. Like I said, I never should have involved you." She leaned down and pressed her cheek
against her son's head. But when she sat up again, she
met his gaze, unrepentant. "I had no choice but to disappear and start a new life."

"You always have a choice. And because of *your*
choices, there could be a warrant out for your arrest
right now for failure to comply to a visitation order. Not
to mention the consequences you could face for identity
theft. Even if you didn't hurt anyone."

She shook her head, refusing to give in. "I'd do it
again, too. I couldn't let him near my son. And my
body's going to have to be stretched out at the morgue
before he'll ever get another chance—"

"Another?" Jamie tilted his head to the side. "Earlier, you said he had your baby *again* when you thought
Aiden had been taken."

She could only give a stiff nod and brace herself for

Jamie to put words to the truth that she'd buried in the deepest part of her heart. A truth she never admitted to anyone, even Tonya, though her friend probably had suspected.

"The baby you lost—that wasn't a miscarriage, was it?"

Baby. The word no one had wanted to use at the time. As if they could explain it away by using clinical terms. Those only stole the humanity of her child. Now Jamie's use of that elusive word made her eyes burn and caused her throat to thicken with memories of the life that never was.

"I don't know." She shivered, chilled despite the blanket and the child draped across her lap. "I might have miscarried, even if it hadn't happened."

"What did happen?"

"We'd been arguing for days. He'd already shaken me a few times, but that night he pushed me, and I landed on my side on the bed. I thought it was no big deal."

"How soon after that did you miscarry?"

"I started cramping the next morning. A few hours later it was…over." Her voice wobbled on the last word as that horrible day replayed in her thoughts.

"Did you tell the doctor what really happened?"

"What do *you* think?"

He shook his head. He'd probably taken many statements from domestic-assault victims who'd covered for their abusers. She'd once been one of them.

"It could have been the stress of all the fighting or the fall. Or neither of those things. We'll never know for sure."

"How do you move on from something like that?"

"I did what I had to do," she said with a shrug. "I just

went through the motions, knowing I would never be the same. I was a mother without a child. And unlike some parents, who don't know who to blame for their loss, I *knew*, whether I could prove it or not.

"I didn't leave then. I was still too scared to try. But a secret part of me never forgave him, either. My child deserved at least that much."

Jamie reached out and brushed his hand over her shoulder a few times and then squeezed once before withdrawing. Though Pancake used that opportunity to lean her head in for a pet from her owner, it was all Sarah could do to keep herself from begging him to touch her again.

"I'm trying to understand. Really, I am. But you stayed with him for years after that. Years. You even had another...you had Aiden with him after that."

Though his body was still turned toward her, Jamie looked away then and reached for his mug.

"You don't know what you'll be willing to endure when you don't believe you're worth more than that. Or how you can cling to even the most destructive relationship if you think it's all you'll ever have."

He turned back to her without ever retrieving the mug.

"How could you ever have thought that?"

"You can believe anything if you hear it enough times."

"Then I'm going to tell you again, you deserve more. Better. You and Aiden both do."

"You did say that."

She chuckled as she spoke, but the sound caught in her throat as his hand returned to her shoulder, his fingers splayed over the whole of it. He stared at her with the kind of surety that she'd never had about anything in her life.

"And I meant it. Now *you* have to believe it."

"I want to." It was the best she could do; he had to understand that. But she had one more question to ask, and his answer to it would affect everything else from this point on.

"You said I deserve more. Do you also believe that I should go to prison for what I've done? That I should lose my son, when all of it was to protect him?"

She expected him to pull away now, to remove both his hand and his support this time, as he remembered who he was and what he was obligated to do. The thought of it nearly closed off her throat. What would happen to Aiden if she couldn't be there to put her own body between him and his father…if Michael was ever released? Would her child become a ward of the state or end up in a situation worse than the one she'd tried to escape?

It felt like an eternity waiting for Jamie's answer. The guillotine lifted high above her head, awaiting the signal to drop. She shouldn't have told him the truth, just like she shouldn't have let herself feel anything for him. Now it was too late to take back either of those things. Too late to stuff the words back in her mouth and tuck those feelings deep inside her heart where they couldn't harm her and her son couldn't be hurt as collateral damage.

"No. I don't."

She blinked and stared at his hand, still firmly resting on her shoulder.

"How do you know I'm not lying now? That I didn't make up everything I've said to you?"

"I don't," he repeated. "And yet I do."

"Then what will you do now? Besides check out my story."

Jamie shrugged, but the side of his lips lifted. At least he didn't bother denying that part.

"That's the problem," he said after a long pause. "This is all falling in a big swath of gray, when it's supposed to be black-and-white to me. That's my job."

"It might not be *my* job, but I used to think the same thing. That the good cowboys wore the white hats and the bandits wore masks." She took a deep breath and then released it slowly through her teeth. "But then I had to live in the real world, and nothing was the way I thought it would be."

He nodded. "It's just frustrating that I have to choose between what I know to be right and what my heart tells me is right. Between my job and...well, *you*."

Neither of them had to speak the words that he'd chosen her. That truth was evident in the heightened tension in the room. A bridge crossed and set aflame. There was no turning back.

"I hope you won't be sorry."

Again, she waited for him to pull his hand away, to at least show his disappointment with the internal battle he'd waged and lost. But instead he slid his palm gently down the length of her arm to rest on top of her hand, his longer fingers covering hers. It felt so natural for her to rotate her hand so that their fingers could link.

The connection felt far more intimate than even their heated kisses and her blossoming desire from the other night. She ached over the sacrifice she'd forced him to make, but she couldn't dwell on that. Especially when she'd just placed her hand in Jamie's and put her trust in him. Though if she were honest with herself, she'd known he was worthy of her trust from the start.

There was just something about Jamie Donovan. She'd sensed it from the beginning. Before she'd known anything about him besides his work with her son and his deep reaction to the loss of a man he'd never met. Was it his heroism, a quiet strength that had no need to flex its muscles? Or was it his loyalty to his brother's memory and his determination to repay a debt he didn't owe? Or, perhaps, the kindness he'd shown, first to her son and then to her.

Jamie broke the spell of the moment by unlacing their fingers and standing up from the sofa. He looked at his watch instead of at her.

"It's really late now. I'd better be getting the both of you home."

"You're right." Even if she would have willingly frozen that moment in time.

"Here, let me take him." He shifted Aiden off her lap. The boy grunted his displeasure at being disturbed, but immediately wrapped his arms around Jamie's neck. "He's going to be tired in the morning. Are you going to give him a day off from school?"

She shook her head as she disturbed her sleeping child a few more times by peeling back his arms to slide on the sleeves of his jacket.

"I don't want to change his routine more than necessary. I'll let him sleep an extra hour and have Nadia take him to school a little late."

She paused long enough to pull on her own jacket. She offered Jamie his coat, as well, but he glanced down at Aiden, who looked comfortable again, and shook his head.

"Just bring it. I'll put it on in the car."

As he started toward to the door, Sarah fell into step behind him.

"I also don't want to reinforce that sneaking out could get him a day off from school."

Jamie glanced over his shoulder, his expression a sheepish one. "You mean in addition to getting the chance to visit my house just like he planned?"

"I wasn't going to say that."

"You also could have said no when I suggested it."

"I could have. But, hey, I like cocoa, too."

She'd also been far too keyed up to go home right away. Or to be away from Jamie when in those moments after they'd located Aiden, she couldn't get close enough to her son…or to him. She still felt that way, and the last thing she wanted to do was to return to her apartment, her bed, when all she could think about was staying here. With Jamie.

Chapter 16

Jamie tucked the comforter tightly around Aiden's tiny form, the feeling of déjà vu swirling around him as heavy as his thoughts. But when he pulled back, ducking his head to avoid the edge of the top bunk, two small arms snaked out to wrap around him.

"Good night, Mr. Jamie."

"Good night, little man." He gave the boy an extra squeeze and then released him.

"Thanks for coming to find me."

"You're…welcome."

His breath hitched, but Aiden was already drifting back to sleep. Jamie flipped off the light, but instead of immediately continuing into the main living area, he braced his hand on the door frame and breathed deeply. He didn't expect Sarah to be back yet, anyway, since she'd stopped to check in with Nadia at her apartment down the hall.

With the darkness as cover, he could brush the sweat from the back of his neck, but there was nothing he could do about his pounding pulse. He needed to get out of this apartment. He had to escape from this space and the intensity of the feelings he had for the two people who lived in it.

He'd promised himself he wouldn't get too close, but the panic he'd felt when Aiden was missing told him how completely he'd failed. He still couldn't shake that feeling of helplessness, even with Aiden safe in his bed and Sarah just down the walkway from him. He could have lost one of them tonight. He'd tried to make light of it for Sarah's sake, but they'd been so lucky.

He wouldn't be that lucky the next time, when she decided to run again. And she would run, after all she'd told him tonight. She couldn't risk the chance that he would have a moment of conviction and would turn her in, after all. The worst part was that she'd probably be right.

As if she needed another man to worry about, when she still was convinced that her ex would find her, even if he was still behind bars and even after she'd gone to great lengths to make sure he couldn't. That Jamie was relieved to know there would be no paper trail to lead her abuser to her showed just how far he'd strayed from his honor code.

Finally, he stepped out into the kitchen area.

"Is he already back to sleep?"

He started at the sound of her voice and turned his head to find her leaning against the counter, a glass of water in her hand. Had she been watching him as he'd used the doorjamb to keep himself upright?

"I didn't expect you back so soon."

Nor was he certain how long he'd lingered in Aiden's room, as much delaying facing Sarah again as assuring himself that Aiden was okay.

As he took in her image now, her haunted eyes masking a strength that had been there all along, he couldn't imagine ever wanting to delay going to her. Not seeing her again—now that would be his version of hell.

"Nadia was tired. I can't say as I blame her." Sarah stared down at her hands for a few seconds and then looked up at him again. "You know, I even blamed her when we couldn't find him. She forgave me for jumping to conclusions, but she has every right to be upset."

"We all say things we don't mean when we're under stress."

Her gaze flitted his way, her crossed arms tightening over her chest in a self-protective pose. She'd clearly misunderstood his words, believing that he would report her, after all.

"I guess we do," she said.

His fingers ached with the need to touch her, if only to reassure her that everything would be okay, but he couldn't let that happen, especially now. The situation was different from the one back at his house when he hadn't possessed the strength *not* to touch her, after she'd finally trusted him with her whole story. This was different. There was no child draped over her to remind him to stop, and from the first brush of her silky skin, he would easily forget.

"It's been a long night. I'll check in with you tomorrow."

He started for the door, forcing himself not to rush. From her. From feelings too overwhelming to dissect without space and time.

He felt as much as heard her approach behind him. "Jamie, wait."

He knew he should keep walking until he was outside the door, when she could secure all five locks between them. But this was Sarah, and she needed him. He stopped and waited.

She took hold of his hand, and he turned back to her, his pulse pounding in his ears. At first, he could only stare at their fingers as she laced them together, but then his gaze lifted to a face he'd always thought of as lovely but found more so now that he'd cataloged all her smiles and frowns.

Sarah licked her lips, her eyes too shiny in the low light coming from the lamp across the room.

"I know I've already said it, but thank you. You've been so good to me." She released his hand and slid both arms around his neck. "You...brought my son back to me."

Before Jamie could process her words, she rose on her tiptoes and, for the second time, kissed him first. Only unlike before, when her advance had been tentative, questioning, now she kissed him with a desperation that shocked his senses. Blood pounded through his body with the same reckless need.

He should stop. Think. But how could a single coherent thought clear that fog when her full lips tasted of both pursuit and surrender? When her breasts were pressed against his chest and her hips rolled over his in a dance so exquisite, so tantalizing, that he ached with need for her?

With her kisses, she gave, and he took in greedy gulps of the tastes, the textures, the essence of the woman who'd glided effortlessly from his dreams to his real-

ity. No lips had ever tasted this sweet. No female body
had ever been this amazing or could have fit more pre-
cisely to his.

Seemingly of its own accord, his hand slid upward
from her hip until it covered her small, perfect breast.
Instead of pulling away, Sarah pressed herself into his
palm, seeking relief in his curious touch, clinging to him
as if he offered answers to all her questions.

A voice of reason clamored inside him for caution,
but he was beyond the sway of those flashing yellow
lights. His only thoughts were of Sarah—who wasn't
really Sarah—and his need to make her his, the way
she'd already claimed his heart.

The moment was everything he'd dreamed of. Sarah
wanted *him*, needed *him*, with the same kind of urgency
he felt for her. She was offering herself as a gift, and he
couldn't have been readier or more honored to accept.

But was this really the way he'd imagined it? At the
wrong time, for all the wrong reasons? Even if it felt
perfectly right.

With more strength than he thought he possessed,
Jamie gently unlaced her arms from his neck and took
a step back from her. He tried not to hear her moan of
frustration or see her dilated pupils or hooded eyelids.

"Sarah, sweetheart, we can't do this." He shook his
head. "Not now. Not like this."

She stared at the floor. "Why—"

"Not when a little boy we both love could come out
that door at any minute."

Her shoulders slumped, and she took another step
back. It was all he could do not to reach out to her again.
He hated that he had to make her feel guilty for, just this

once, placing her needs above her child's, but he did what he had to do.

"I'm sorry. I don't know what got into me."

He stepped forward again and lifted her chin so that she would look at him. Then he lowered his hand, to remove the temptation to touch her again. And again.

"Oh, I want you. Don't think for a minute that I don't." He smiled, trying not to notice her lips, swollen from kisses that he ached to continue. "I haven't been able to think about anything but you for months. And more recently, about you and me together. Every day. Every night."

He paused and stared into her eyes long enough to let her imagine just what those nights might entail. "But I can't have you coming to me this way. Because you're *grateful* that I helped to find Aiden."

"But it's not—"

He shook his head to settle the matter. "No, it has to be more than that."

"Jamie, you're not understanding—"

"Look," he said, to interrupt her again. "I need you to think this through. Our senses are on overload tonight. It would be so easy—believe me, *so* easy—to fall into bed now to escape these overwhelming feelings. But then we'll have to wake up tomorrow, and I couldn't live with myself if you were sorry."

He didn't bother telling her that *he'd* be sorry. She had to know that wasn't true.

She shoved both hands back through her hair, and all he could think about was how soft those strands felt when gliding through his fingertips. He crossed his arms to prevent himself from reaching for that silk again.

"Now, I'm going to walk out that door." He pointed

to it over his shoulder. "You need to lock it behind me and go get some rest."

"Okay, I will."

"And do me a favor. Don't look out the window."

"Why is that?"

"I'll be parked outside a little while," he paused, grinning, "and I wouldn't want you to see me pounding my head on the steering wheel."

"Thanks, Jamie." She smiled, and then her expression became serious. "For this, too."

She let him out the door and then stood at the front window as he passed by, hugging herself. No matter what he'd said, he resented those arms that could hold her when he couldn't.

It only frustrated him more that after she had the chance to think rationally, she would never let him touch her again.

Sometimes being the good guy offered no rewards at all.

Chapter 17

Sounds of pounding dragged Jamie from the only con-
secutive minutes of sleep he'd been able to string together
all morning. He blinked several times in the dimness of
his bedroom, which was darkened by blackout shades,
not entirely sure whether the relentless beat had come
from inside his head or outside. Why had he even expected to get any sleep when everything he wanted con-
flicted with the core of who he was? Or at least who he
thought he was.

At least the racket had stopped. Maybe the overag-
gressive door-to-door salesperson had hit some quota
and decided to leave him alone. But as soon as he buried
his face in his mattress, laying a pillow over his head for
good measure, his phone buzzed on the bedside table.

"You've got to be kidding."

He hadn't even pulled a shift since he'd learned those

things about Sarah. Had he already drawn attention to himself by accessing the LEIN database one time too often in his search for details about her? How was he supposed to explain how easily he'd been convinced to detour off the straight and narrow?

He fumbled for the phone and then read the text on its display. As the shimmying words came into focus, he sat straight up in the bed, suddenly wide awake.

Answer your door.

As if to assure him that he hadn't misread Sarah's message, the thuds coming from his front door down the hall resumed. They were louder this time. He tossed the phone on the bed and yanked on his khaki pants and olive T-shirt that had been pooled on top of the shoes and socks he'd worn the night before. After making a quick stop at the bathroom to brush his teeth, he continued into the living room, tripping over Pancake in the hall. Finally, he opened the door.

Though Jamie had known Sarah would be the one on the other side, his breath still caught when he found her standing at the storm door, her cheeks ruddy from the walk to his house.

"Hi."

He licked his lips and rubbed his eyes. "Hello."

"I didn't know you were busy."

At his confused look, she pointed to the corner of her own mouth.

"Oh." He wiped the toothpaste from his lip and then pushed open the door for her. "Sorry. I just woke up."

"Glad one of us got some sleep," she said, as she stepped inside.

"Not much."

He waited for an explanation, but she only stood in his doorway, shifting her jacket back and forth between her hands.

"Sarah, why are you here?" But then a flash from the night before flickered in his thoughts. "Did something happen to Aiden?"

She licked her lips. "He's fine. Nadia took him to school an hour ago, while I was baking at work. She said he arrived safe and sound."

"Then are *you* okay?"

She nodded. "I haven't forgotten all about it, like my son has, but yes, I think so."

"Nadia?"

"We're all fine."

"Then, as I asked before, why are you here?" But as soon as he asked it, several puzzle pieces fitted into place. He'd encouraged her to think about the situation between them when he'd left her several hours before. She'd also known he would be home that morning. And she'd come here alone.

"I thought about it," she said simply.

Those four words should have made him feel as if he'd won the lottery, but instead of tossing confetti into the air, he was suddenly questioning the authenticity of the ticket. Why couldn't he be like other guys and just take the gift that was offered without any regrets?

"But are you sure you've thought long enough? It's not even been twenty-four hours since your son was missing."

"It's long enough."

That she blinked as if his words had stung only made him question more.

"This thing between us, it can't be only about grati-tude," he said, repeating his argument from the night before.

"It's always been about more than that." Then in a low voice, she added, "You *know* that."

"I don't know that." He stalked away from her toward the kitchen doorway and then whipped around to face her, but from a safe distance. Far enough away that he couldn't reach out and touch her. "Even that first note you gave me was you thanking me for the work I did with Aiden."

She blew out a breath. "Fine. Maybe it started out that way, but I didn't know you then. It changed later."

"What changed?"

"I tried to tell you last night." She cleared her throat. "I mean earlier this morning."

She paused, as if asking whether or not he needed her to spell it out, and then nodded. "I got to know you bet-ter, and you're kind. Really kind. You probably have no idea how appealing that quality is, especially to some-one like me."

He did know. That was the worst part. He also rec-ognized how indebted she might feel to him because he had been nice to her and her son. That wasn't a good reason to jump in bed with a guy, no matter how won-derful the idea sounded to him.

"And you're strong," she continued, as if not recog-nizing his internal battle. "Without the need to prove it to anyone."

Jamie could explain that one away, too, but he was losing his determination to do that. Sure, he hoped he was different from her monster ex in nearly every way, but so what? Didn't Sarah deserve to be with someone better than that? And why shouldn't it be him? Because of who he was and what he knew. The thought stole into his thoughts, uninvited, but he tucked it away to think about…later.

Now his only thoughts could be of Sarah, who somehow seemed closer to him, though he was sure he hadn't moved from his spot near the kitchen, nor she from her place near the front door. Close enough that he could almost hear her ragged breathing and the rhythm of her heartbeat. Or maybe those sounds were his.

"You don't have to say more." In fact, he wished she wouldn't. The man she'd described was heroic, and this one was talking himself out of any honorable tendencies as fast as his mind could spin.

"But I need to say it," she said. "When you told me about your brother, well, I thought that there was finally someone who might understand me. Whose scars were as deep as mine."

He nodded. As survivors, they'd connected over both their pain and their resilience.

Though he thought he already knew the answer, Jamie still had one more question to ask her.

"Have you, you know, ever been with…anyone since…"

She saved him from having to finish his awkward question by shaking her head. "I never let anyone get that close."

She didn't speak the rest of her words aloud, but he could still hear them in the weighted silence. Until now. Until *him*. The honor and the responsibility of being the *second* man she would allow in her bed filled his throat with emotion, but it also gripped his chest like a vise.

"When I met you, I was afraid of everything. Even

my shadow," she continued, when he didn't answer. "You helped me to see that I don't have to be afraid."

She stepped in front of the window and gestured widely. "I didn't look over my shoulder once to see if anyone was following me on the walk here."

He had to chuckle at her attempt to lighten the conversation. "Not even once?"

"Well, maybe once," she said with a smile.

When she straightened and turned to fully face him, the light from the window behind her outlining her hair, but casting shadows on her face, Jamie squared his shoulders, as well.

"There's one more thing. You may not believe me after I kept so much from you, but I...*trust* you."

He swallowed. Her trust. It was the thing he'd been trying to earn all along. Sarah, whose hope had been battered and bruised, who'd believed in no one but herself, who'd been running and hiding for years, was putting her trust...in him.

She lowered her gaze to the floor and fiddled with her locket, as if she expected him to turn her away. Didn't she realize that he could never have walked away from her? That even with everything he knew now, he still couldn't?

Because she clearly *didn't* know that, he crossed the room to her in three long strides and covered the hand on her necklace with his.

She tilted her head to look up at him, her tentative expression so different from the determined woman who'd walked clear across town to tell him she was ready to be with him.

"I trust you, too."

No matter how much he meant those words, they

were a test, as well. If Sarah had looked away then, he would have known that she wasn't ready and would have insisted that she return home and focus on keeping her house of cards standing. But she didn't look away. She met his gaze steadily, and then she smiled. Had he ever been happier to lose an argument?

Jamie barely took time to breathe before lowering his head and claiming her mouth in a kiss that was more about unleashed longing than finesse. He needed to proceed with cautious steps that honored her gift and her belief in him. Sarah was blown glass, after all, precious and perfect. She deserved to be handled with care. But how could he hold back when everything about her intoxicated him and made him want to forgo sobriety for good?

For several seconds, he held himself as still as he could, his lips sinking in the exquisite softness of hers, his hand curling around her fingers. Sarah didn't move, either, as if she, too, wished to honor the time-stamped moment when everything between them had changed.

From somewhere outside the secluded world that cradled them, he recognized that he'd kissed *her* first this time. But that only seemed right, since this would be a morning of firsts. Releasing her hand, he gathered her close and glided his lips back and forth over hers. Her fingers slid up his arms to clasp behind his neck, and he smiled against her mouth.

He'd been privileged to have Sarah in his arms twice before, but this time meant so much more. A molehill compared to Mount Rainier. Each touch reflected a decision. A choice to no longer hide from the magnetic pull that had drawn them together from that first day. And she'd chosen him.

He couldn't get enough of her taste, her scent. *Her.* She was kissing him back, too, with a desperation that stole his breath and nearly made him forget his plan to take his time in seducing her. Had this confident, sensual woman been there all along, hidden behind five locks and as many layers of secrets? Had she been waiting for someone to free her?

When his oxygen-starved lungs forced him to pull back and draw in a breath, he touched his forehead to hers.

"I was dreaming about something like this…until you started pounding on my door." He rolled his forehead back and forth against hers. "My dream didn't come close."

Her chuckle was so low and deep that Jamie felt it everywhere.

"If I'd known that dreams could be like this, I would have tried harder to get some sleep this morning," she said.

"Neither of us will be getting any sleep now."

With that, he pulled her to him again and feasted on her sweet mouth. When he brushed his tongue along the seam of her lips, she opened for him with an enthusiasm that was nearly his undoing, though they were both were still fully clothed.

"Slow down, sweetheart," he said with a chuckle. "Have a little mercy. It's been forever."

"Yes, forever…getting here," she murmured, between kisses that she traced over his jawline.

Jamie dipped his head and covered her mouth once again, sliding his hands over the smooth lines of her back. When they came to rest on her lower back, he pressed her to him to show her how much he wanted her. How long he'd waited. Instead of inching away, she lifted herself to fit more intimately against him.

"You're so beautiful," he whispered against her skin, his finger lifting to twirl in a curl that had worked loose from her ponytail. When that wasn't enough, he slid his hand to the back of her head and unlatched the clip, letting that mass of silk cascade down.

She shook her head, allowing all those waves to fall free.

"Aren't you going to show me the rest of the house?"

He couldn't miss the message in her words. The three of them had been there together only hours before. She'd already seen the living room, kitchen and bathroom. The rest of the house meant the bedrooms—the two guest rooms…and his.

"Absolutely. You deserve the grand tour."

But instead of extending his hand to serve as her tour guide, he scooped her up in his arms and started down the hall. Her laughter rumbled against his chest.

"Ooh, smooth move. Did you practice that?"

"Nope. First time. So, prepare to be dropped."

She tightened her grip around his neck and tucked her head closer against him. He didn't know why he was trying to be smooth with her. She knew him. She was aware of his vulnerabilities and his fears. And she was here with him, anyway.

Careful to turn sideways, dip and turn at the correct times, he slid past his bedroom door into the shadowy space with only bureaus and his unmade bed visible due to the heavy blinds. He lowered her to stand next to the bed, where he'd lain so recently, wanting her and beating himself up for sending her away.

Sarah sat on the edge of the bed and then rested her

hands on his forearms. As she leaned back, she pulled him with her until she lay crossways over the rumpled sheets and he was bracing himself above her.

Then she reached up and traced her fingers over the scruff on his jawline until her thumb brushed the sensitized skin of his lips.

"I trust you," she said, repeating those words from earlier.

He swallowed. She had to have been talking about the gift of her body, which alone meant so much. She couldn't know that her words held far more significance for him.

He didn't repeat them as he lowered himself to her, his body fitting perfectly to her feminine curves. Convex to concave. Rolling hills to lush valleys. Then, slanting his mouth over hers, he brought their lips together again. She lifted her head off the mattress to meet him.

Trust. Neither of them had said *love*. It was too soon for that, and he wasn't sure if her feelings could even make that momentous turn. But she had to know that for him, at least, those two words meant the same thing.

Chapter 18

Sarah blinked in the darkness of Jamie's bedroom, her surroundings threatening to become claustrophobic rather than intimate. She couldn't let her misgivings take hold. She wanted to believe she was ready to take this significant step with Jamie, just like she'd told him. But was she really?

They were both right, he about many of the steps that had brought them to this moment, and she that things between them had changed. But had *she* changed? Had she returned to that naive girl who could allow herself to be vulnerable, when she'd spent much of her adult life erecting steel walls around her heart and then, finally, her body?

"Are you okay?"

Jamie's whisper came from near her ear, where he'd brushed his lips again and again. Had he noticed that her mind had drifted from this place, when she'd been convinced it was where she'd wanted to be? She'd had a child, had been pregnant twice, so why did she feel as if she was being invited behind that curtain of experience for the first time?

"Sure. I'm fine," she lied.

She reached for his neck and guided him back to her, kissing him with the type of intensity she hoped might convince them both. He only rolled onto his side, his fingertips brushing through her hair.

"Are you sure?"

He studied her face, his eyebrow lifting as if he didn't believe her. Instead of answering this time, she sat up and lifted the hem of her T-shirt, drawing it up and over her bra. He sat up next to her and stilled her hands.

"Would it be okay if I did that?"

She could hear the smile in his voice as he asked it. Swallowing, she lowered her hands to her sides, gripping the sheet.

He pulled the shirt the rest of the way over her head and dropped it to the floor. Then he reached toward the lamp on the bedside table.

"Would you mind?"

She shook her head and unclenched her hands as he turned the switch, throwing a soft light into the room and making everything happening inside it real.

But instead of immediately looking down at her bra, he stared into her eyes as if searching her soul. When he finally did lower his gaze, his slow, appreciative perusal felt like a caress. She reached behind her and unclasped the hooks, but it was Jamie who gently slid the straps down her arms and lowered the lacy garment to the floor.

"You take my breath away," he said, as his gaze traveled over her again.

The warmth building in private places surprised her, though he had yet to even touch.

He didn't make her wait much longer, lifting his hand and brushing it over her exposed skin and then tracing a funnel pattern toward the peak that most craved his touch. She held herself back from pressing into his palm, but when he followed that same path with his lips and tongue, she arched into the sheer pleasure of it.

With his face close to her heart, he looked up to her and smiled.

"I still can't believe you're here," he crooned, as his fingertips drew lines along her ribs and, lower, to the button of her jeans. "And that you're real."

As she lay back on the bed to make his work easier, it was all she could do not to push aside his hands and dispose of her clothes herself. She couldn't get close enough, couldn't move quickly enough toward a culmination that would ease the painful ache building inside her.

Jamie seemed to have other ideas. He took his time becoming acquainted with each bit of skin as he exposed it. Touching. Tasting. Cherishing. But still dangling the promise of release.

Soon all her clothing was piled on the floor, and he was stretched out next to her, fully clothed and still working magic with his hands. His touch was reverent as he traced the scar on her upper arm. When her frustration humiliated her by becoming an audible sound, he chuckled low in his throat.

"Patience, sweetheart."

But he stood up from the bed then and quickly added

his T-shirt and pants to the pile on the floor. His gaze flicked to hers in a moment of vulnerability before he bent and shucked his boxer briefs.

Then he stood to his full height, lowered his hands to his sides and waited. She couldn't have predicted the perfection standing before her. Broad shoulders and chest. Narrow waist and hips. Perfect. Utterly male. And so ready to give her exactly what her body craved.

Sarah held out her hand to him and smiled when he took it, first resting his knee on the edge of the bed, then climbing on it and settling on his side next to her. She turned and followed with her curious hands the same lines that her gaze had traveled. His eyes closed, his teeth sank into the flesh of his lower lip. Finally, he gripped both her hands in one of his.

"You're too sweet. I…just…can't…"

Instead of finishing his labored comment, he rolled away, opened his bedside table and rustled around in the drawer. He pulled out a small box of condoms. He broke the seal on it and rolled back to her, an embarrassed look on his face.

"A recent purchase. I didn't think I stood a chance. But I hoped."

Her misgivings didn't begin again until Jamie pulled a packet from the box and ripped it open with his teeth. She swallowed, the moment of truth upon her, the opportunity to retreat seeming to be hours past.

He either recognized it or may have been having second thoughts himself as he paused, watching her.

"We can stop. It can be now or later. Or never."

He reached for her hand again, dropping kisses on each of her knuckles and then opening it against his cheek, his own hand covering it.

"The decision is yours. Always."

An immediate lump formed in her throat. This was just Jamie being Jamie. He always thought of everyone else first, especially her. Even now, when to stop what they'd started would cause him a world of discomfort. When other men might have claimed they'd passed the point of no return.

Why Jamie? It was a question she'd asked herself not so long ago. Now she recognized that no one else could have disarmed her with his kindness, could have neutralized her defenses with his vulnerability, could have gently scaled the walls around her heart instead of beating them down. And now he was waiting for her permission to love her, when with no more than a shift of their bodies, they would already be there.

If she hadn't fallen in love with him already, this moment would have sent her into a freefall. But it was too late for that, she realized with a shock. For how long she'd already loved him, she couldn't begin to know.

"Please," she began, but he interrupted her by shaking his head.

"It's okay. Really. Just give me a second."

Tossing the open packet on the bedside table, he sat up on the edge of the bed and dug through the pile of clothes on the floor next to him. He handed her shirt to her over her shoulder, as though he hadn't already seen and touched every bit of her.

"Here." He shook it behind him when she didn't take it.

"I'm not going to need that."

"Well, give me a minute." He dug through the pile again and pulled out his pants. "I'll get out of here, so you can dress in private."

"You're not going to need those, either."

He turned his head to the side. "Look, Sarah, I'm trying to be a decent guy here. What do you want—"

"You," she answered, before his question was fully formed. She sat up on the bed behind him.

He turned around completely this time, his gaze lowering to her chest, which she hadn't bothered to cover.

"I don't understand."

"You didn't give me the chance to finish."

"So…" His voice cracked then, so he cleared his throat and started again. "So, finish."

"Before I was interrupted…" she paused, smiling, "I started to say please…don't stop."

He whirled on her so quickly that her breath came out in a whoosh as her shoulders hit the pillow again, his weight landing heavily—and intimately—on her.

"Now that's a promise I can keep."

He kissed her with a desperation that surprised her, thrilled her. As if he'd lost all ability to restrain himself. To be the hero he must have thought she needed him to be. Now he was just a man who couldn't get enough of her. And that was exactly who she wanted him to be.

His tight jaw reflecting his strain, Jamie plucked the packet off the nightstand. Then he sat back on his feet and made quick work of covering himself and protecting them both.

Sarah held her breath as he settled over her once more.

"Uh, Sarah… I know you said it earlier, but I need you to say it again." He cleared her throat. "I mean…before."

She squinted at him, but then realization dawned. This was Jamie. He would want to be certain she'd given consent. She wouldn't want him any other way.

"Yes, please." She'd intended it to sound funny, but

her words came out more like a plea, which was closer to the truth, anyway.

Though his face reflected his strain, Jamie brought them together slowly, and with a gentleness that nearly took her breath away. And when they began moving together, he made good on that attempt, breathing her in with each of her exhalations and connecting with her in every way humanly possible.

The moment couldn't have been more perfect. It was as if every point in her life—even the darkness she'd fumbled through in a desperate search for light—had led her to this moment. To this man. These touches. These sighs.

Then, as the waves of her need crested and rolled, Jamie tumbled closely after her and their worlds settled again in a froth of contentment, Sarah realized that she'd been wrong. Something could be more perfect. And she knew without a doubt that after being loved by Jamie Donovan, she would never be the same.

"Whore!"

Michael pounded his fists on the steering wheel, then jerked his head to see if anyone had been close enough to the car to hear. But the street looked deserted, another suburb with two-income homeowners, who worked day and night so that they could sleep in those bedrooms and park their cars in those garages. People like those whose kids had once been some of his best customers.

He rubbed his hand, which hurt like a mother, and breathed in and out several times, searching for a calm that refused to come. He'd gotten lucky this time. He couldn't afford to draw attention to himself. Not now.

Not when he was this close to getting everything he'd worked for, planned for…and getting Maria back.

"Oh. Right. *Sarah Cline.*"

But what was he supposed to do? *His wife*, whatever she called herself now, was in that house, spreading wide for some asshole. He'd seen her right there in the window, smashing faces with the dude, as if she didn't give a damn who saw them together.

And now she'd been out of sight for two hours, giving him plenty of time to imagine the worst and plan ways he would make her pay for it later.

How dare she go screwing around! He didn't care if she had some piece of paper from the judge. She was *his*! She'd promised 'til death do us part, and she'd sullied that commitment.

"You don't deserve to—"

No. He couldn't think about that now. It didn't matter that he should rip off both their heads. Even if he'd proved that he could do it. He closed his eyes and laced his hands around an imaginary neck, the strain and the fading pulse still feeling so real beneath his fingertips.

A secret smile played on his lips, and the heaviness in his lap that he'd come to expect whenever he recalled that day forced him to adjust again. And to think that he'd tossed his cookies when it had first happened. He patted the address book that rode shotgun in the car. If Tonya were alive, he would thank her again for making it so easy to find Maria.

But he needed to focus. He'd made mistakes that other day, when he'd lost his temper. He couldn't afford to do that again. No matter what Maria had done. No matter what she was currently doing while *his son* was at school. What kind of mother whored around like that?

Then he answered his own question. One who worked as some crappy diner. One lived in an apartment barely better than the dump he was forced to live in. And one who wasn't even doing well enough to have a junker like the one he was driving.

He still couldn't get over how she'd pranced across town without even checking her surroundings to make sure that no one followed her. Good thing she hadn't, since someone had been following. Well, she had looked back once, almost straight at him, but he'd been careful not to make eye contact. She also must have had her mind on other things. Like the loser in the window.

He would have to address her lack of attention to detail once they were together again, just like he had since their wedding day. But it probably wouldn't take her long to remember that dinner belonged on the table at five sharp and that she should take pride in ensuring that hand towels were straight.

They would have to work on other things, as well. Like her infidelity. But didn't all marriages have their bumps in the road? His hands gripped the steering wheel again as he stared at the window through which she'd been parading her sin, but he forced his fingers to relax.

He needed to be patient, and he'd mastered patience in prison. This wasn't the time to approach her, anyway. No need to have her boyfriend in there try to play the hero and get in the way. Besides, she didn't appear to have the book with her.

No, she had to be alone when he approached her. Back at her apartment, as long as that old woman wasn't around. The one who'd walked his son to school this morning. Instead of her. Little Andy. The same blond boy from the photo on Tonya's piano.

He couldn't wait too long. His asinine boss and his parole officer might not take too kindly to him skipping town, and then the Keystone Cops would be looking for him, as well, still believing that they would get their share of the money.

No, tonight would have to be soon enough, though he wasn't certain he could wait that long. That is, unless Maria deserted his son to go play house with Romeo again.

At the sound of an approaching siren, Michael jerked, whacking his head against the driver's side window. How had they found him? What detail had he overlooked? But a quick peek in the rearview mirror showed an ambulance barreling toward him. He sank down in the seat, anyway. No need to have Maria see him sitting outside if she came up for air long enough to look out the window.

The emergency vehicle drew so close that the sound was piercing, and then the warbling faded away.

But for several seconds longer, Michael stayed low in the seat, staring up at the car's stained roof interior. His visit tonight would still be a surprise. He could almost picture her startled face when she opened the door. Things were coming together now. Just the way he'd planned.

Chapter 19

For the second time that day, Jamie awoke with a start, as a sound from outside dragged him, kicking and scratching, out of a most perfect dream. But as the blaring sound transformed into a high-pitched, pulsing siren and his hand became ensnarled in a tangle of silk on the next pillow, he came fully awake and sat up in bed.

This was not a dream, and it was far from perfect.

"Are the police right outside?"

Sarah sat straight up, as well, the sheet clasped to her chest, as if Jamie hadn't already seen and sampled all the secrets masked behind that scrap of striped cotton. He hated that he'd noticed first the riotous mass of her hair, when he should have been paying closer attention to the panic in her eyes.

He resented his body's automatic response to that first image even more. Why did her lips have to look so swollen and well kissed? Why did that jagged scar on her upper arm seem to call out for his tender ministrations, when he already knew it felt puffy and delicate beneath his lips? Why did he have to crave so desperately someone he shouldn't have had once, let alone again?

That siren was like a megaphone announcing that he'd just made a huge mistake, and all he could think about was pulling those sheets over them and doing it all over again.

"Probably an ambulance," he said. This time, anyway.

But because it was difficult to differentiate among siren pitches when so many agencies and contracted services responded to calls in Livingston County, Jamie had to know for sure. Anyway, Sarah was right; the racket sounded like it was coming from the front yard. He threw back the covers, pulled on his pants and T-shirt and rushed to the living room.

He couldn't see anything through the front window, so he stepped out on the porch barefoot, catching sight of the fire and rescue vehicle before it disappeared around the corner. Crossing his arms against the chill, he started to turn back to the door, but a rusty white sedan, parked just up the street, caught his attention.

Jamie shook his head as he continued through the open door. Another one of the teens in the sub had probably turned sixteen and had received that rust bucket as a gift. He needed to remember that when he drove through the neighborhood.

"Is everything okay?" Sarah asked as he padded back into the bedroom.

She stood next to the bedside table wearing her jeans and bra and was pulling her T-shirt back over her head.

"Yeah, it's fine."

This time. The words repeated in his thoughts, his chest tightening. Next time, she might not be so lucky. She was a fugitive, after all. A fugitive he'd just taken to bed.

Sarah shot a look toward the front of the house, though walls separated her from seeing outside. "I thought for a minute that you, uh…"

"Turned you in?"

She shrugged, her shoulders curving forward.

"No, I didn't. Don't you think that all of this—" he gestured to the unmade bed "—would be tough for me to explain?"

"You're probably right."

He couldn't watch her as she finger-combed her hair and wrangled it back into a ponytail without being tempted to pull out the band and free it all again, so he turned toward the wall. But that only put the bed squarely in front of him, a piece of furniture he would never be able to look at again without picturing so many tender memories with her. As he shifted to escape that sight, as well, he found her watching him.

She gestured toward the digital clock, where "12:15" was flashing on the screen. "It's late. I can't believe I slept so long."

He didn't miss that she'd spoken only of herself, when there'd been two of them in that bed. "You were probably exhausted. I mean, after everything last night," he was quick to add. "You said you didn't get any sleep."

Their gazes connected, and then they both looked away. Morning-after moments were awkward enough without awakening to sirens and fears of arrest.

"Well, I don't know about you, but I'm starving," she

said with a smile. "I have a shift at three, but if you have time, we could get lunch somewhere."

"Sorry. My shift starts at two."

"Oh. Okay."

He hated the disappointment in her voice, but what could he do? He'd worried so much that she would be sorry after they'd slept together that he'd never considered he might be the one with regrets. Even knowing what he knew about her, he'd believed he could still make love with her and live with himself. He'd been wrong.

He couldn't stay in that bedroom any longer. He grabbed their shoes and socks, handed Sarah hers and started into the hall.

"Thanks," she said from behind him, her voice rising and making her response sound more like a question.

In the living room, he sat on the couch where they'd cradled Aiden between them only hours before. It felt like a lifetime. Instead of sitting next to him, Sarah lowered into the side chair and put on her shoes, as he was doing.

"Will you tell me what's going on?" she asked.

"What are you talking about?" He didn't look up from tying his shoelaces.

"What has changed from two hours ago? Or did it mean…nothing…to you?"

The pain in her voice created a physical ache in his chest. No matter what he felt, how could he hurt *her*? How could he allow her to believe that it was only a hookup rather than the single most significant physical experience of his life? Even if it never should have happened.

"I'm sorry." He stood and crossed to the window. "It

was a mistake, but it wasn't you. It was *my* mistake. This can't happen…again. At least not right now."

"Sorry, buddy," she said, suddenly behind him. "You don't get to take full responsibility like some modern-day knight in shining armor. There were two of us in that bed. And I'm a full-grown woman. I walked all the way here on my own."

"But you're not a cop. I am."

"I know you're a cop. And I'm here, anyway. Doesn't that mean anything to you?"

Since answering that might incriminate him, he only paced to other side of the room.

"You'd already told me everything. The identity theft. The violation of the court order. You're a fugitive. I didn't even think about that before I willingly jumped into bed with you."

"Well, willingly is a stretch. You had to be convinced."

He frowned at her attempt to make a joke. "Oh, I was willing, all right. Believe it or not, it's frowned upon for law-enforcement officers to sleep with suspects."

"You think of me as a suspect?"

"I should have."

She watched him for so long that he couldn't help squirming.

"Would you rather I hadn't told you?"

"No. I'm glad you told me." The answer to that one was clear, even when the rest of the truth had settled in murky water. "But the siren reminded me that although no one was coming for you today, the next time they could be. And I didn't do my job after coming into contact with a fugitive, so I'm involved."

She planted her hands on her hips. "I never asked you

to get involved. But no matter how hard I tried to dodge your questions, you kept asking. It was as if every answer made you hunger for more."

He'd felt the same way every time he'd kissed her, but now wasn't the time to tell her that.

"Either way, here we are," he said instead. "And all I'm saying is that you were worried about your ex coming after you, when he couldn't reach you from behind bars, but maybe you should have been equally worried that the police would show up one day at your door."

"Child-custody cases probably aren't top priority."

He shrugged. "Even so, you made me suspicious. There were just too many things that didn't add up about you. What if I'm not the only one asking questions about you?"

"You were just trying to get in my pants."

It was a shot, taken out of pain, and he deserved it, so he quietly absorbed the sting. Maybe on some subconscious level, that was what he'd been doing. So how was he supposed to make it right now, when he'd had her, and it had only made him crave her more? When she deserved a much better friend than he'd been to her?

"So, what happens now that you've received your wake-up *siren*?" she asked. "I said I wondered if you'd I turned me in. Is that what you're going to do now?"

"No." He shook his head to emphasize his point. "As I said, my involvement in this situation is…complicated. But you should turn yourself in."

"Turn myself in? After all I've done to make sure he can't find Aiden and me? Not a chance. I told you before, I'll never let him get to my son."

"But I can help you." Jamie held his hands wide. "We

can figure this out together. I'll make sure that you and Aiden are safe."

"You can't." She spat the words. "Don't you get that? No one can."

That was the worst part. She was right. It didn't do either of them any good for him to make promises he couldn't keep.

"Can you at least let me *try*? I'll do some research. We'll talk to an attorney. Maybe we can mitigate your legal situation."

But she was shaking her head, closing the door of possibility that he was still straining to hold open. "You promise you won't report me?"

He closed his eyes, his black-and-white world tarring and whitewashing at the same time, until he could see nothing but an unwelcome gray in front of him. But he could do nothing about the color. Sarah needed him, whether she realized it or not. He hadn't been there for Mark, when his brother had needed him most, and there was no way he would fail the woman he loved. No matter what it cost him.

Opening his eyes again, he nodded. "And if you need my help, just ask. I'll do whatever I can."

A flash of vulnerability appeared in her eyes, but then she blinked it away.

"You already did the kindest thing anyone has ever done for me. You brought my son back to me last night. I'll never forget that."

Jamie's throat constricted over words that sounded suspiciously like a goodbye. What had he expected? That she would stick around after he'd pried all her secrets from her? Why hadn't he realized that those revelations would make it impossible for her to stay?

"I just need you to keep quiet for a few days, until I figure out my next step," she continued. "Aiden and I will have to keep moving to stay ahead of suspicions. We've started over before. We can do it again."

When he couldn't hold back any longer, Jamie crossed to her and took her by the upper arms, forcing his touch to be gentle when he longed to cling.

"It doesn't have to be this way." *Stay. Please.* He wanted to say those things so badly that he was surprised he was able to hold it in. But how could he beg her to stay when he could offer her nothing right now? Not even a way out of the mess she was in. "We can figure something out."

"*We* can do nothing. And *I* have to fight for my son. Alone."

Jamie flinched, the word striking him faster than a sneak attack from his six. He'd told her she didn't have to be alone. When he'd still hadn't known everything. When he'd still believed he could help repair what was broken inside her. That was before the truth and consequences got in the way.

Alone. The word must have uncovered memories for Sarah, as well, as she stared at the ground for several seconds. When she met his gaze again, a sad resignation filled her eyes. There would be no hope to cling to this time. No salve on old wounds. No smooth possibilities trapped beneath the jagged rocks of past mistakes.

"If that's the way you want it to be," he somehow managed to say despite his clogged throat. Since there was nothing he could do about the dampness in his eyes, he turned his head, so she wouldn't see. "Can I at least drive you back to your apartment?"

"No, that's okay. I've gotten used to walking. And I really could use a walk right now."

Sarah hurried to the door and yanked it open.

Again, he was tempted to beg her to stay, but he couldn't. He had to figure out a solution first. Something that would make it possible for her to be with him.

Unable to watch her go, he stared at his shoes and waited for the door's inevitable click. But it didn't come.

"Jamie," she whispered.

He looked up to find her standing just inside the door, looking back at him.

"I need to know one thing."

He cleared his throat. "What's that?"

"Are you sorry? About…this morning, I mean?"

His breath caught. It was as if she'd keyed in on the conflict that was peeling him apart, layer by layer.

"It doesn't matter," he managed to reply, the truth as tragic as the lies had been before.

"It matters to me."

He licked his lips, stalling. Could he admit the truth aloud, even it if brought into question everything he'd thought he believed?

"Because I want you to know that no matter what happens after today," she continued, when he didn't answer, "I'm not. Sorry, that is. I'll never be sorry."

Aching from having the best moment in his life, and the worst, on a collision course with his fragile heart sandwiched between, he shook his head.

"No. I'm not sorry."

Nothing could have stopped him from going to her and taking her into his arms again. Nothing except the door that she closed behind her.

She didn't look back as she hurried down his driveway and then started up the sidewalk, probably retracing her steps from earlier. He half expected some of his nosier neighbors to be watching out their windows, curious about the woman leaving his house on foot, but the street appeared deserted. Even the junk heap that had been parked across the street was gone now, the new driver probably skipping class to tool around town.

He watched from the window until she was out of his field of vision and then stepped out on the porch, just as he had earlier. From there, he followed her path with his gaze until she slipped out of sight. As soon as he returned to the house, he dove for his laptop.

If there was a way out for Sarah, he was going to find it. And if there was a way he could make things okay for her so that she could stay in Brighton with him, he was determined to find that, as well.

His first step would be to learn more about the tormenter who'd convinced her she had no choice but to run in the first place.

He opened the inmate locator on the Illinois Department of Corrections site and typed "Brooks" in the field for last name. As he started to click the search icon, he hesitated. Was the name real this time? Were Sarah's stories true?

He shook his head, dismissing his insecurities. She might have lied to him, but that was before she'd really known him. Before she'd given him the most precious gift she could have: her trust.

Still, he let out the breath he was holding when a list of names appeared, including "Brooks, Michael E." It was comforting to have his belief in her confirmed.

Now that he was this close, he had to know more about Inmate #LK2341, the creep who'd hurt the woman he loved. As he clicked the name, a page appeared, with front and side prison photos of a dark-haired man at the top. Jamie was strangely relieved to note that Aiden bore little resemblance to his father.

He scanned down the page, using the touch screen, past general information and incarceration location. But when he reached the "Status" section, his gaze froze on the word crime victims most feared: *paroled*. His pulse thudded, and a chill threaded up his spine as he read the date. For a few weeks, while Sarah had assumed her ex was at least safely behind bars, Brooks had been traipsing around, but for a few early-release restrictions, a free man.

Jamie needed to tell Sarah, even if he could already picture the panic in her eyes when he did. She needed to know that the figment of her imagination she pictured over her shoulder could be real now. Could be coming for her.

This didn't have to mean anything, he reminded himself, even as a sense of dread settled in his chest. Sarah and Aiden were living under assumed names. She might have broken some laws, but she'd also covered her tracks. Brooks couldn't know their identities or their location.

But what if Sarah had made a mistake, had accidentally left bread crumbs that could lead the guy to her? If she was right that Brooks would never stop until he found her and made her choose between life with him or living at all, Sarah wasn't safe anywhere.

Chapter 20

Sarah couldn't breathe as she stared down at the Illinois phone number flashing on the buzzing phone in her hand. The same number that had popped up on a call ten minutes before. And another ten minutes before that.

Could it be *him*? She shook head. Why did her thoughts automatically go there? If Michael's friends had tracked her down, there was no way he would call to warn her that they were coming for her. Who was it then? Could Tonya finally have been getting back to her, using a different number than her landline or cell? Or had the police caught up with her, just as Jamie had predicted?

Only when the call went to voicemail could she look away from the display. She tucked the phone back into her apron pocket and gripped the counter next to the cash register.

She needed to put the calls out of her mind. The Illinois area code was probably just a coincidence, anyway, and she could have been freaking out over a robocall offering an opportunity to refinance a student loan she didn't have. She was overreacting, but how could she not after the roller coaster she'd been riding for the past twenty-four hours? After some of her highest highs had connected to her lowest lows, with plenty of jerking turns and corkscrew spins along the way.

She still couldn't believe that just five hours before, she'd been in Jamie's arms, in Jamie's *bed*, speaking with her body things she hadn't yet been able to say aloud. She'd never experienced a more unsettling rush of emotions other than at Aiden's birth. And she'd never known the kind of bliss that Jamie's tender lovemaking had produced in her. A gift she would always cherish.

She loved him. She was certain of it now. Yet before she could even process it, that siren had sounded and reminded Jamie of his duty. The cocoon they'd wound around them to block out the realities of their lives had unraveled so quickly. His sense of honor and her need for survival had put them at an impasse, and neither could give without losing who they were in the process. So, though it would strip away part of her heart when she did it, she had to leave him behind.

As she started back toward the kitchen, her phone buzzed again and lit up inside her pocket. She refused to even look this time. She would just let it go to voicemail again and hope that the caller would get the message.

Only Ted passed by her then and pointed to the light in her pocket. "You going to get that, or are you going to make them keep calling you all night?"

She rested her hand on her pocket, the phone vibrating beneath her touch.

"Well?" He pointed again. "You can take it in the office if you want to."

She nodded and pulled out the phone, touching the button to answer. "Hello."

In case she needed to end the call as soon as the other voice came on the line, she hurried down the hall, out of her boss's earshot.

"Hello, ma'am. I'm calling for Sarah. My name is Detective Evelyn Ryan, and I'm with the Lisbon Police Department."

Just short of the office door, Sarah bobbled the phone and nearly dropped it.

"Sorry," she said, when she righted it again. With her heart racing, she hurried into the room and closed the door behind her.

"Could I have your full name please?" the detective asked.

"You must have the wrong num—"

"Do you know a Tonya Franklin?"

Sarah had been pulling the phone away, preparing to disconnect, but now her hand froze above the button. She guided the phone back to her ear.

"Yes." She braced her hands on the edge of the desk. "Is she okay? Is something wrong?"

"I am reaching out to you because you made several calls to Miss Franklin's home and cell numbers in the past week. Can you tell me the last time you spoke with her?"

"Where is she? Did something happen to her? Was she in an accident?" She couldn't stop the rapid-fire questions. She'd been worried after she hadn't heard back from Tonya, but was it worse than she'd thought? "I haven't been able…to reach her."

"Again, I need your full name before I can provide that information."

Sarah blinked as it occurred to her that the police might have the number of her throwaway phone, but they didn't know anything about her, besides a name that wasn't really hers from her voicemail. It meant she would have to change it again, but she needed answers now.

"Sarah Cline."

The detective asked her to provide address information, as well, and she made that information dup as quickly as she could.

"Thank you, Miss Cline. How do you know Miss Franklin?"

"We've been friends…since we were kids." *She's my best friend.* It was all she could do not to beg her to say that Tonya was okay.

"Then I'm sorry to have to inform you that Miss Franklin was found deceased in her apartment two days ago. Foul play was involved. Apparent asphyxia from manual strangulation. The county coroner confirmed it after the autopsy yesterday."

She shook her head, the words not making sense. "What are you saying?"

"Miss Franklin was strangled."

"She was murdered?" A sob escaped her before she could stop it. Sarah couldn't keep her body from shaking. Her throat constricted and fought for air just as it had once before when Michael had wrapped his hands around her neck and squeezed until she lost consciousness. Now a chair was there to catch her as her legs gave way.

Tonya's death could have been a random act of violence, she told herself. Just an unlucky coincidence in a world where anyone could be a crime victim. But the bottomless feeling inside her announced that nothing about this situation involved chance. And she was to blame for all of it.

"Oh…my God. How could this…happen?" She licked her lips, the tears she wasn't bothering to swipe away making rivulets along her cheeks and dripping off her chin.

"I'm sorry for your loss." The woman paused and cleared her throat. "But I'm sure that as her friend you'll want to help us find her killer."

"I don't know what help I'll be. We'd barely spent any time together…in years."

She held her breath as she realized that photos and documents in Tonya's house might have easily led back to her. She was an awful person. Tonya was dead, and all she could think about was herself. She'd never deserved a friend like Tonya in the first place.

Still holding the phone, she rested her other elbow on the desk and lowered her chin into her hand. Her palm was immediately wet from her tears.

"Why don't you let me be the judge of whether your information can help?" the woman said. "Even a tiny piece of information might give us a lead."

Or send the police to her doorstep. "Okay," she said anyway.

"First, do you know anyone who had a problem with Tonya or who might have wanted to harm her?"

"No. No one. Everyone loved her. I know… I did."

"That's what all her coworkers said."

The detective paused for a few seconds, as if taking the time to scroll through a list of questions.

"Now, Miss Franklin's records show that she dialed this number on April 13, the time suggesting the call might have gone to voicemail. Do you have any idea why she might have wanted to reach you?"

"I'm not sure." To plead for help Sarah couldn't give? To warn her that someone was getting closer to her? "Maybe she was just checking in."

She swallowed as panic clogged her throat. If Tonya had lost her life trying to alert her, then she already knew the why and the *who* regarding the police detective's questions. Only one person would care enough about getting to her to risk killing anyone standing in his way. Unfortunately, she used to be married to him.

"So, you didn't speak to her that day?"

"No, but I kept trying to call her back."

"Then when did you talk to her last?"

"About four weeks ago." Maybe longer, but she wasn't sure.

"Did you often have long stretches between conversations?"

"Yes. Ever since I moved out of state." Too long. Now she would never again hear the laughter in Tonya's voice.

"Then why did you call her ten times and leave five messages over the past seven days?"

The messages. Had she slipped up on one of them and gone beyond the script they'd agreed to when she'd purchased the burner phone? *Hi. It's Sarah. I look forward to hearing from you.* No, she was sure she'd said it just the way they'd agreed, but she'd left a lot of messages in a short time, and her voice must have sounded more worried with each day that passed.

"She didn't leave a message like she usually did when she called." Sarah shifted in her chair. "Then when I called her back, I couldn't reach her, so I kept trying. I started to worry."

"If you were worried, then why didn't you call police and have them check on her?"

"I know I should have, but I was trying not to over-react. I thought she might have had a new boyfriend." There were many things she should have done differently, too many to name.

"Sometimes it's a good idea to follow our instincts," the officer said.

"Excuse me?"

The officer cleared her throat. "I'm sorry, ma'am. But according to Miss Franklin's phone records, her call to you on April 13 appears to be the last call she made."

"You mean she could have died while…" The words were out of her mouth before she could stop them.

"We don't know that. All we know for certain is that there was a struggle, and she made no other calls from her home or cell numbers after calling you."

The woman kept talking, but the words *last call* kept repeating in Sarah's thoughts. She'd been a lousy friend. Tonya had always been there for her, and she couldn't even manage to answer the last call she would make.

"Apparently, Miss Franklin had already been dead for over two days before the accounting firm where she was employed called police on Monday when she didn't show up for work. Tuesday was Tax Day, after all."

"I'm so sorry I didn't call right away."

Sarah didn't need the long silence on the line to know that the detective blamed her and the delay for their lack of leads in the investigation.

"Was there any other reason that you might have been reluctant to reach out to authorities?"

"I don't know what you mean," she said, in the blandest voice she could muster.

"We believe that Tonya knew her assailant because there's no sign of forced entry. And although the house was ransacked, little appears to have been taken. Not the cash in her purse or the gold necklaces in her jewelry box." The woman paused and then added, "The only things missing were her phone and a leather-bound planner that her coworkers said she carried everywhere."

Sarah knew that planner. The one with her address and phone number listed her as "Sarah Cline." The police might have needed more evidence to build a case, but the chill scaling her spine told her everything she needed to know. Michael had murdered her best friend to get to her, and now he would be coming for her.

"Beyond that, we don't have any major leads right now," the detective continued. "Unless you have something else you can tell us that will help us get justice for your friend."

"I'm sorry," Sarah told her. Sorrier than she could have known. For everything.

The detective gave Sarah her contact information in case she remembered anything that might help with the investigation. Though Sarah dutifully wrote it down, she prayed the two of them would never speak again.

"I just have one more question," the detective said, as they were about to end the call.

Sarah had just stood, so she braced her free hand on the desk.

"What's that?"

"You don't happen to know anyone named Andrew T. Brooks, do you?"

Sarah blinked several times, but when she spoke, her voice sounded almost natural. "No, I don't. Why?"

"Well, my office has already notified her next of kin, a brother, but her attorney said he's been trying to find one of the beneficiaries of her will. So far, the attorney has been unable to locate him."

What had she done to deserve a friend like Tonya? Not only had she died trying to protect her, she'd also reached out from the grave to help ensure that she and Aiden would be able to escape from Michael, this time for good.

"Sorry I can't help you. I hope they find him and whoever did this."

Only when she ended the call did she allow herself to drop back into the chair, bury her face in her hands and sob.

Chapter 21

Jamie slammed the door on his SUV and sprinted across the parking lot to the diner. He had so much to tell her and little time to do it before the others arrived. If he hadn't been ready go public with their relationship before, he couldn't do it now, at least until he convinced Sarah to go to the police.

He rushed through the door just as Sarah slipped out of the kitchen, carrying a tray of food. Something looked different about her as she hesitated when she caught sight of him, but she only gave a tiny nod and continued to a table where four guests were waiting to be served.

"Is everything okay, Officer?" Ted asked as he stepped in front of him, blocking his view of Sarah. "Yeah. Sure." He forced himself to lower his hands to his sides, as if a casual stance alone would help him look calmer. "I just need to talk to her."

He didn't need to identify who he meant, as Ted's gaze automatically went to Sarah. At the restaurant owner's cautious look, Jamie frowned.

"It's important. Really."

"I'm sure it is." The older man cleared his throat as he guided Jamie to the side of the dining room closest to the cash register. "Look, we don't want any trouble."

"Trouble?" He followed Ted's gaze to the smattering of customers around the room. A few were sneaking glances their way, while a few more weren't even trying to hide their curiosity. He lowered his voice so that only Ted could hear. "There won't be any. Has there ever been?"

Ted gestured with his thumb toward Sarah, who peeked their way and then continued distributing the plates on her tray.

"I don't know what it is about that young lady that makes you guys so crazy."

Ted didn't know the half of it. He also was right about how Sarah affected Jamie, at least, but he would worry about that later, when he was sure she was safe.

"Look, I need to talk to her before the others get here, and they'll be here any minute."

"Sure. Nobody's business, right?" He pointed down the hall. "Head to the office, and I'll send her back there."

"Great. Thanks."

He was few steps away when Ted called his name.

"That wasn't you on the phone earlier, was it? Because if it was, I don't want you to upset her again."

Upset her? "It wasn't me."

But since the news he was about to share with her was

sure to distress her, he didn't respond to Ted's second comment. No reason to make promises he couldn't keep.

Inside the office, he considered the leather executive chair behind the desk and the two upholstered visitor chairs, but he didn't bother trying to sit in any of them. How could he relax when he had to tell Sarah that her biggest nightmare was now her reality?

He was still pacing around the cramped office, nervous energy making it impossible to stop his forward motion, when Sarah pushed open the door, slipped inside and closed it behind her.

"What's going on, Jamie? You rushed in here like you were being chased."

"I'm not. But you might be soon."

She pinched the bridge of her nose and shook her head. "What are you talking about?"

"He's out, Sarah." He crossed to her and rested his hands on her forearms. "I looked him up on the inmate locator. He was paroled on April 3."

"I know." She slowly stepped back until his hands fell away.

"You know?" He looked closer at her. His earlier impression had been right. She did look different. Red rims ringed her eyes, and pink blotches dotted her cheeks, both indications that she'd been crying.

"Are you okay? Have you heard from him?" He longed to pull her into his arms, but she looked as if she would come out of her skin if he tried.

"I didn't need to hear it from him. The Lisbon police told me." She shoved her hands back through her hair. "They effectively did."

"Why would you hear that from them? That's who

called earlier?" His head shifted. "Wait. The police called *you*, and they told you about Brooks?"

She shook her head. "They told me about Tonya."

"What does Tonya have to do with—"

"Jamie, she's...dead."

"Oh, honey, I'm so sorry."

His heartbeat pounded in his ears as he struggled to order the disjointed and unspoken pieces of her message. A body. A suspect. A motive. But some of her words crowded out the rest and replayed in an ominous loop. *She's dead...she's dead...she's dead.*

He pushed away the words and the rising panic that linked to them. But this time he couldn't stop himself from pulling her to him. She didn't resist, but her arms remained at her sides, her spine straight, unrelenting.

Jamie needed to release her, should give her the distance she seemed to crave. And he would, as soon as he could peel his arms away. As soon as the message could filter from his brain to his limbs that Sarah was right there with him. Solid. Safe. He was an awful person. A woman was dead, someone who loved Sarah, possibly as much as he did, and all he could do was feel grateful that it hadn't been *her.*

"I'm sorry," he repeated, this time for many reasons.

Instead of pulling away as she would have if she'd known what he'd been thinking, Sarah slumped against him as if the pain was too great for her to bear it alone. Her arms slipped around his waist, her hands gripping fistfuls of the back of his shirt. The front of it was already damp with her tears.

"She was my best friend, and she's dead...because of me."

Her anguish touched him in a place he'd barred anyone access to since Mark's death. A place of guilt and shame. A place where public absolution and the pointing finger of self-blame could never be fully reconciled. But he couldn't let her torture herself with the belief that it was all her fault.

He rubbed slow circles on her back. "Come on, you know that isn't true."

"And *you* know it is." She shook her head against his chest.

"We don't even know for certain that Brooks is a suspect."

Sarah pushed him away and then crossed her arms. "She died the same day she was trying to reach me. Maybe even at the same *time* she was calling me. Isn't that suspicious enough for you?"

He pressed his lips into a thin line. Okay, the guy was at the top of his suspect list, too, but then he'd been given more information than the other police agency might have had. And there were no coincidences in law enforcement.

As Sarah shared more details from the detective, each added another layer to the lump of dread building in Jamie's gut.

"And the police knew to call you because…?"

"They pulled Tonya's phone records."

"They know who you are?"

"Only that I'm Sarah Cline. I made up the address."

He swallowed. False reporting. Just another string added to the tangled web of her lies, and another legal liability. Anyway, if those detectives were worth their salt, they would already be tracking Sarah through pings to cell phone towers, but she didn't need one more thing to worry about.

"If an arrest hasn't been made or if the case hasn't been closed, we don't know anything for sure."

Did he really believe that would somehow keep her from being frightened? He was scared enough for them both.

Sarah paced across the room and turned back to him, leaning against the filing cabinet. "Believe what you want, but I know the truth. If Tonya didn't know me, and hadn't helped me to get away from Michael, she would be…alive…right now."

He nodded, his eyes finally filling on behalf of a woman he would never meet. He could never repay Tonya for her sacrifice, but he intended to honor it by helping to ensure that Sarah stayed alive.

"So, let's say that Tonya really was trying to warn you when she called that day and that the suspect who attacked her was Brooks." He took a breath and then voiced the questions that were swirling in his mind. "Do you think he's figured out where you are? *Who* you are?"

"He's smart. If he hasn't yet, he will soon."

"Then we have to assume he already has."

She let her head fall forward. "If he overheard Tonya calling me, and it went to voicemail, then he already knows—"

"That you're Sarah," he finished for her, a chill climbing his arms.

"And he has Tonya's planner—"

"Where, I'm guessing, there's a listing for *Sarah* in it."

She covered her face with her hands, her fingers splayed so nothing hid the fear in her eyes. Finally, she lowered her hands, but only to grip them together.

"He's coming for Aiden and me. And he's had *six days* to find me. Do you think he's already in Brighton?"

Jamie didn't want to give an opinion on that.

"Well, I can't stay here like some sitting duck, just waiting for him to come after us. I can't let him get to Aiden. I *won't*."

She was already rushing for the office door when Jamie rested his hand on her shoulder. She tried to shake it off, but he held on as gently as he could until she stilled.

"Wait, Sarah. We need to think this through. We need to plan."

Reluctantly, he lowered his hand. Instead of rushing out the door as he'd expected she would, away from him and his offer of support, she turned back to him.

"We?"

She'd dismissed that word so easily that morning. He couldn't allow himself to read too much into the fact that she hadn't pushed him away now. Desperate people did and said all kinds of things.

"Of course, *we*." He guided her to one of the guest chairs and sat in the other one.

"You said Brooks is smart. Do you think he would show up here without a plan?" Jamie shook his head. "I don't think so. Besides, he's on parole. He can't even leave the state without special permission from his parole officer."

"You think that would stop him?"

"Maybe not, but I do think he would work out as many details as he could beforehand, since he can't afford to get caught and have his parole revoked. He probably thinks he has a lot of time, too. He has no reason to expect that you were made aware he'd been paroled. And he had to figure it would take a while before the news of Tonya's death would reach you."

"Do you think he had a plan when he went to… Tonya's?"

"Your guess is as good as mine. The murder could have been premeditated. Maybe not. But then that situation is different, too. There isn't anything obvious that the police could use to connect him to Tonya." He held his hands wide. "On the other hand, he was married to you."

"If the police figure that part out."

"They will eventually."

"Well, Aiden and I just need to disappear again. I have to pack. Exchange coins in my jar for paper money. Throw a dart at the map."

With each item Sarah ticked off on her list, Jamie's panic built.

"Are you ever going to stop running?"

She blinked. "What do you want me to do? Wait for him to kill me and take Aiden? Because it's what he will do when I refuse to go back to him. And I won't go back."

She clasped her locket and twisted it, as if the fragile piece of metal could somehow keep her grounded.

"If you run, I can't help you."

He hated the plea in his voice, but he'd never stated the truth so plainly. Yet she said nothing for so long that he wondered if she'd heard him.

"You could go with us."

She'd whispered the words but might as well have shouted them, as they shook him so forcefully. His sternum felt as if someone was standing on it. He tried to make eye contact with her, but she stared at her necklace, continuing to twist it.

"It's a lovely invitation. A few days ago, I might have

jumped at the chance to just be with you and Aiden. Even if it meant walking away from everything else that mattered to me. Even if it meant that I would always have to run, too."

He lowered his chin to his chest. "But everything is different now."

"How is it different?"

"You know how. Tonya's *dead*. We now know that Brooks has no qualms about killing to get what he wants. He's desperate. He has nothing to lose."

Jamie pushed his shoulders back and set his jaw. "I can't take a chance that you'll be next. Or Aiden, if he gets in the way."

She lowered her forehead into the cradle of her cupped hands. "What do you expect me to do then?"

"Stay."

That one simple word was both an offer and a plea. It was proof that he was all in, though he could admit now that he had been since the first day. That piece of pie. The note that changed everything. Even before.

This time she looked right at him and lifted her chin. "Why would you ask me to do that? You know I can't. It would be like giving up, and I owe Aiden more than that."

"It wouldn't be giving up. It would be fighting back." At her dubious look, he pressed on. "I know it's hard for you, but you said you trust me, and now I need you to really do it. I'll be right there with you, but I need you to turn yourself in. You can tell the whole truth and then ask the court for leniency. There are mitigating circumstances, and you'll be helping the police to solve a murder. Those things have to count for something."

She'd shot him down the first time he'd suggested

it, so it didn't surprise him that she started shaking her head before he could even finish his argument.

"Look, Sarah, if you run now, you'll never be able to stop. Because he'll never give up trying to find you. He'll always be waiting in the shadows around the next corner or watching you from outside the window at night."

"But I can't risk losing my son. What if a judge decides my reasons for doing what I did weren't good enough? What would happen to Aiden if I had to go to jail?"

"It's the only way. Shouldn't Brooks have to pay for his crimes? For what he did to Tonya? And doesn't she deserve justice?"

Again, she shook her head. "Tonya would understand. She went to great lengths to protect us."

"But she couldn't keep Brooks from figuring out how to find you. The truth is I can't protect you, either. At least not on my own."

"Why do you feel like you have to?"

For a few seconds, Jamie could only stare at her. She still didn't know. How could she not after he'd worked tirelessly to win her trust, he'd sheltered her secrets though it had cost him, and he'd loved her with the desperation of a man who'd touched heaven, only to learn that he wasn't allowed in?

"You still don't get it, do you? I'm in love with you." He cleared his throat, his heart beating frantically in his chest. "What happens to you is critically important to me."

Sarah was the one staring this time, as if she couldn't quite believe what he'd said. Why was she surprised? Didn't she know how amazing she was? How precious?

This wasn't the way he would have preferred to tell

her. In a moment of crisis. But at least now she knew, and he wasn't sorry he'd told her.

If she left tonight, he might never get another chance. He tried to tell himself it didn't matter how she responded to his plea and his confession, but the stakes were high. Her choices tonight went beyond whether she would have a future with him. If she chose wrong, she might have no future at all.

"Okay."

His mind swam as he tried to find a context for her simple response. "Okay?"

She nodded. "I'll go to the police tomorrow while Aiden's at school."

"Did you agree because of what I said?"

"Does it matter?"

Hell, yes, it mattered. But did it really? He didn't care why she was doing the right thing if it improved her chance of survival.

"But you promise to go with me, right?"

"I'm off tomorrow. I'll do whatever you want me to do."

"Then could you kiss me now?"

Because he could deny her nothing, especially when his heart cried out for her, he turned his chair so that it faced hers. Fitting her knees between his, he leaned forward and rested his fingertips behind her elbows, drawing her forward.

Their lips met for what felt like the first time…then again. He couldn't help it; he tightened his grip on her arms and crushed his lips to hers in a kiss filled with pain and fear and the scariest emotion of all…hope.

Sarah returned his kiss with a similar desperation that went beyond the physical to something spiritual and undefined. She hadn't said she loved him. She might not even feel that way about him. He had to remember that. But for now, this was enough. It had to be.

He was so caught up in the moment with the woman he loved, that the world faded around them. Until someone cleared his throat.

Ted stood in the doorway, grinning and misunderstanding what he'd just interrupted. Jamie pushed his chair back and leaped up as if that could erase what the man had already seen. Sarah's face was crimson, and she was trying to fix her ponytail, but it appeared to be a lost cause.

"Well, I guess the two of you made up." He paused, chuckling. "And to think that I was worried."

Sarah opened her mouth to explain, but Jamie caught her attention and shook his head. The less others knew before tomorrow, the better. He could only hope her boss didn't have a big mouth.

Again, Ted cleared his throat. "Sarah, I was going to tell you that Marilyn was covering your two tables. She owes you. But the Brighton Post folks are here now, and they're asking for you."

"Okay. Thanks."

"You might want to get out there soon, but I would suggest a stop by the ladies' room first."

Ted gestured first toward his hair and then his lips.

Without another word, she started into the hall and took an immediate right toward the restrooms.

"I'm sorry about that," Jamie said, as soon as the older gentleman turned back to him.

"Oh, that?" His gaze shifted to the spot where Jamie and Sarah had been making out only a few moments before. "Well, don't make a habit of it, okay?"

Jamie cleared his throat. "Oh. We won't."

"Let's not repeat the other thing, either."

"Excuse me?"

"You know. All the calls. The tears."

Oh, right. Her boss had thought he and Sarah had been arguing. Jamie couldn't explain his mistake without giving other details, so he told the part of the truth he could tell. "I won't."

"Sarah's a gem," Ted continued, crossing his arms. "I think of her as a daughter. She and that boy of hers deserve wonderful things. I hope you have good intentions…"

Jamie's cheeks burned as the man stared him down, evaluating, warning. Like the next best thing to the father Sarah had lost.

"The best intentions. I promise." They might not be speaking about the same things, at least for now, but Jamie meant every word.

Ted nodded, appearing satisfied.

"If you're planning to join your friends, you might want to head out the back door and come in through the front again. Like I said before, nobody's business, though you might want to stop by the men's room on the way out, too."

Did he look as disheveled as Sarah had?

"Oh. Okay. Thanks." Jamie slid around him and stepped into the hall.

"And Trooper Donovan?" Ted waited until Jamie glanced back at him once more. "Good for you."

Chapter 22

"You sure you have everything you need?"

Sarah had already asked her houseguest that question but couldn't resist posing it again. From the safe distance of the kitchen. Where she was too far away to touch him. She couldn't keep a clear head if she fell into his arms again, and she needed to think tonight. About sweet Tonya. About monsters who reached out in the night. And about the confession she had to make to the police in a few hours.

"I'm fine. Again." Jamie fluffed his pillow and pulled up the blanket that he'd folding in half like a sleeping bag. "You're the perfect hostess."

"You sure you don't want me to open the bed? It's right inside the couch you're on."

"That's okay," he said in a strained voice. "Thanks for the reminder, though."

"Sorry."

Sarah's face heated. Leave it to her to make a clumsy comment about him sleeping in her bed when they'd been blissfully together in *his* fourteen hours before. Even if that truth had been on her mind since he'd offered to stay at her place for extra protection in case Michael showed up.

"It's fine. You should get some rest. I probably wouldn't have gotten much sleep before, but now I'll be wide-awake and guarding my post all night."

That made two of them, except for the post part. How could she sleep when so much emotional upheaval had been squeezed into one day? After a sunrise of freedom in Jamie's arms had turned to a sunset of possible captivity and separation from her son. And after tonight's glimmer of hope peeked through her afternoon of despair.

Jamie loved her. Why his confession emerged from the tangle of so many significant events and discoveries, she wasn't sure, but it still shamed her. It didn't matter that she loved him, too, and that she'd begun to imagine a future with him and Aiden, where they could all live together without fear. How could she think of her own happiness today of all days?

"You never told me what Aiden said when you let him know I would be staying on your sofa and you would be taking the top bunk in his room."

"You think I told him either of those things? He would still be awake now if I had." She shot a look at the bedroom door and found it still safely closed. "Also, I would have had to explain why."

"You're going to need to tell him *something*, especially about tomorrow." He lifted his arm and used his other hand to flick the light on his watch. "I meant later this morning."

She swallowed. "I'll figure out something. But remember, you have to be out of here in the morning, so I can send him off to school and get to work. Ted will pick me up. Then you can meet me at the diner after the morning rush."

"I know. I still don't see why you're going to work tomorrow morning. They can survive one morning without you."

"The cinnamon rolls. The customers expect them." That it might be her last chance to make them for Casey's clientele could also have had something to do with it, but she didn't share that part.

Jamie nodded, though he clearly didn't understand her insistence on keeping the schedule as normal as possible on a day that would be anything but. She didn't want to analyze it herself.

"One more thing," he said. "I wanted to apologize again for that text at work. I was just worried about you staying alone tonight."

He held his hands wide, his trademark grin appearing on his face. "Bad timing, I know. Anyway, I felt terrible when you dropped that tray."

"No big deal. Only two plates." She lifted her shoulder and lowered it. "I was already jumpy, serving the officers at your table after…you know. I also don't usually receive texts from guests at one of my tables."

"We were just glad the only plates that bit the dust were Vinnie's and Dion's and not ours."

"Glad I could help out. At least Ted didn't fire me. I gave him enough reasons to today."

"Fire you? I think he wants to *adopt* you."

"Oh, no." She squinted and pinched the bridge of her nose. "What did he say to you after I left?"

"He just wanted to make sure I had your best interests at heart. I assured him that I do."

Their gazes caught and held in a way they never had before. Where they'd been using conversation to fill the vacuum in the room, now it seemed unnecessary. Unwanted even.

Just fifteen steps. She blinked as the calculation appeared in her thoughts, but that was exactly how much effort it would take for her to reach him now. Just one good-night kiss. That was all she needed.

Her lips lifted of their own accord. Who was she kidding? If she hadn't been able to stop with one kiss from Jamie so far, she had no chance of pulling away from him tonight. On a night when her heart ached with the loss of her friend and her skin craved the warmth of his touch, if only to prove she was still alive.

"Um, Sarah…"

As his words broke the silence, she blinked, her head shifting. "Yeah?"

"I need you to stop looking at me that way and to go into that bedroom and shut the door." He cleared his throat. "And once you're in there, I'll stick my head in the freezer to cool off."

"Oh. Okay."

"And like I said, get some sleep. Everything's going to be fine. I'll make sure you and Aiden are safe."

It took more strength than she knew she had to slip inside the bedroom instead of going to him, despite his request, but soon a door separated them. She stood with her hand on the knob for a few seconds, both to get her bearings in the room, lit only by moonlight, and to catch her breath. Then she started up the ladder at the end of the bunk bed. The wood creaked when she was halfway up, but Aiden didn't even turn over.

Once she was under the covers, she finally allowed herself to replay Jamie's promise in her thoughts. He would keep them safe. The strange thing was that she believed him. She could trust him with their lives just as she'd entrusted him with the delicate care of her body. She could even rest if she wanted to, knowing that Jamie had the situation under control and would do whatever was necessary to protect them. Including putting himself in danger.

But how could she let him? Didn't she already have enough blood on her hands after her best friend had risked her life…and lost it? Could she live with herself if something happened to Jamie while he was trying to protect them?

No, she couldn't, and she also couldn't let him take that chance.

Now the pieces of the puzzle that had eluded her since she'd first agreed to go to the police with him appeared in the darkness, the peninsulas and gulfs of their shapes clicking easily into place. *Because* she loved him, she couldn't go to the police with him. She couldn't make him Michael's target.

She had to run again. Without Jamie. It couldn't matter that he would never understand. That he would believe she'd run to save herself from a prison sentence, though that was only a small part of it. She couldn't let someone else she loved risk his life for her and Aiden. She couldn't, and she wouldn't.

Her decision made, Sarah nodded into the darkness. If only the image of Michael squeezing the life from her friend hadn't appeared in her thoughts, cutting off her own breath. She shivered as she stared up at the glow-in-the-dark stars and planets on the ceiling. She refused to let panic overwhelm her this time. She needed a second plan, one that didn't involve Jamie, but it surprised her to realize she'd been forming it in her mind all night. Her determination to work in the morning had been just part of it.

Jamie had been right about one thing: Michael would never give up looking for them. He would keep coming after her with his bastardization of love. The kind that destroyed and maimed. But Jamie's other prediction, that she would have to keep running forever—he was wrong about that.

She was tired. Of running. Of being afraid. Of blaming herself for mistakes she'd made a lifetime ago. She couldn't do it anymore. This time if Michael caught up with them, she would stop him from getting to Aiden, even if she had to kill him herself.

The scents of cinnamon and yeast bread that wafted from the oven as Sarah pulled out the first batch made her stomach roll. Maybe it hadn't been the greatest idea to insist on keeping the morning schedule the same, even if she'd needed Jamie to go home to shower so she could pack the two bags that would be the only possessions she and Aiden took with them. At least he'd bought her theory that Michael was too smart to come after her in broad daylight.

She managed to slide the trays into the cooling racks without dropping them, then and rushed into the ladies' room to slap water on her face. She closed her eyes and waited for the nausea to pass.

Feeling a little better, she started back to the kitchen, only to have Ted call out from the office as she passed. "Hey, you okay?"

She turned back and leaned in the doorway. He sat next to the desktop computer where she'd been researching intercity bus schedules, stations and ticket-purchase sites an hour before.

"I'm fine."

"And you're still sure you want to go through with all this?"

She wiped her face with a paper towel and met his gaze steadily. "I am. Are you? Because if you don't want to do it, I can just take a cab to the bus station."

"Clear to downtown Detroit? You don't have the money for that."

Since they'd already planned a stop at one of the few locations where travelers without credit cards could pay cash for bus tickets, she appreciated that he didn't mention using a shared-ride service.

"I can still figure out something."

"No, I'll take you…if that's what you want."

"It's what I want."

"So, you just want me to pick up Aiden at school and then swing by to pick up you and the bags at your apartment?"

They'd already been over the details twice, but she nodded, anyway. If only there was an uncomplicated way for someone without a car to catch a bus out of Brighton, when all the major bus stops were more than forty miles away. She should have realized how trapped they would be when she'd settled in the small Detroit suburb.

"Glad I'll get to see my little buddy before you go.

Maybe the two of you will come back and visit sometime."

She smiled, her throat feeling thick. Saying goodbye
to her friend would be almost as tough as leaving Jamie.
Her chest ached over the quick kiss she and Jamie had
shared as he'd slipped out her apartment door that morning. He'd promised her that he'd see her in a few hours.
She'd known the truth.

"Sure you don't want to go with me to the school?"

"I still need to take care of a few things at home."

It was also best that no one see her and Aiden leaving
the school together, but she didn't add that.

"What are you running from, Sarah? You've been
running the whole time I've known you."

She shook her head. "Don't ask, Ted. The less you
know, the better."

"Then why don't you let Trooper Donovan help you?
I've seen the way that young man looks at you. And after
what I saw in here yesterday, well…"

"It's complicated."

"It must be. Otherwise, why would you leave the guy
who's finally put a sparkle in your eyes? And made you
drop a whole tray for the first time ever."

At that, her eyes filled with something besides sparks,
but she forced a smile anyway. "He told me you were
giving him the third-degree last night."

"I just want what's best for you. I believe that the
trooper wants that, as well. That boy's in love with you,
and I would say the feeling's mutual. You know how
lucky you are to find that?"

She did. That was the problem. But she couldn't think
about that now, couldn't wonder what it would have been

like if she'd met him when she was free to love him the way he deserved.

"Can we not talk about this? Look, I want good things for Jamie, too. All good things. That's why he can't know where I'm going."

"Are you going to tell *me* where?"

"No. I love you too much for that." She pointed down the hall. "Now let me get back to those cinnamon rolls and that pie, so we can get out of here before…well, before customers come clamoring for them."

She hurried away before he could ask more questions. Before she told him something that might put him in danger.

She went through motions of making more yeast dough and giving it time to rise before treating it to the magic of butter, brown sugar and cinnamon. She would miss this and all the people she'd met while living this ordinary, wonderful life, even for a little while. Jamie, Ted, Nadia. Even fellow workers like Marilyn, Léon and Marty.

Later, when all this was over, and she and Aiden had safely vanished again, this time in a big city like Atlanta, she would allow herself a few minutes to mourn all she'd lost.

Chapter 23

This was taking too long. The words repeated in her head in the rhythm of her footsteps as she hurried the last block to Heatherby Elementary School. She was supposed to wait for them at the apartment. That was *her* plan. She knew better than to change it at the last minute.

The bags were ready by the door, two bus tickets from Detroit to Atlanta tucked in the outside pocket of hers, but something just wasn't right. She'd felt it from the moment she'd gone to her bookshelf to pack her precious family photo album and found it missing. When she hadn't been able to find it, other possibilities had slipped into her thoughts. Could Jamie have taken it? Had someone else come into her apartment?

Neither of those ideas made any more sense than her impulse to call Jamie with her worries, when she had no right now that she'd left him. Then Ted had been running a few minutes late, and here she was, showing up like a cavalry officer who'd lost her horse.

There were plenty of reasons they would be running behind, anyway. Maybe something had happened at the diner, forcing Ted to pop back over there. Or maybe school officials had caused the delay by questioning Ted's authority to pick up Aiden, even though his name was on Aiden's emergency card.

Both of those were at least more reasonable than her theories about the missing photo album, but only when she reached the school parking lot could she release the breath she'd been holding. Ted's sedan was parked in one of the guest spots, just as it should have been. If they moved quickly, they would arrive in Detroit with even enough time to grab lunch before their three o'clock departure.

The car was there, but the two of them were nowhere in sight. No one was entering or exiting through the main entrance, and even the playground was deserted, so the students couldn't be just coming in from recess. She started toward the school entrance, anxious to solve the mystery.

But movement in her peripheral vision drew her attention, and her stomach dropped as she caught sight of the two men wrestling a man and a boy into the open sliding door of a white cargo van. Then the child—*her child*—screamed.

"Aiden!" The name felt as if it had been ripped from her soul. "Ted! Let them go!"

Both men, one of them so familiar, looked back at her from outside the van. The distraction gave Ted the chance to shock the other guy with an uppercut, which he paid for when the man returned a knife-hand strike to his throat that dropped him to the ground.

Sarah sprinted toward them on shaky legs, seeming to make no progress, as though she was running through sludge. Her heart felt like it was trying to punch its way out of her chest. But she had to reach them. Her son. Her friend. She had to stop those men before—

Her mind froze as the man from her nightmares stepped out from between two of the other cars and right into her path. She tried to stop, but the momentum was her enemy as she smacked into Michael's chest. She recoiled as the pungent scent of unwashed male invaded her nostrils. She tried to hold back a scream, but a muffled wail escaped her anyway.

"Honey, I'm home."

"But my friend. My son…"

Using both hands, she pushed against his chest so that she could see past him, but he was wider than he'd been when they were married. He only tightened his hold on her back. Always stronger than her. Even stronger now.

"*Your* son, Maria? Or should I call you… *Sarah*?"

Even braced against him and even knowing that he was aware of her alias, she couldn't keep herself from shivering at his use of that name. She'd become *Sarah* after she'd found the strength to escape him, and he had no right to call her that.

But his next words mattered far more than anything he could have called her, and he practically growled them.

"*My* son will be just fine."

Her breath caught as she realized he hadn't said the same thing about Ted or her. In trying to keep Jamie from being involved, she'd included her other friend in the mess of her life. She couldn't imagine what Ted must have been thinking then, but she would protect him and make it up to him. For now, though, she had to play along. Finally, she lowered her arms to her sides.

"What are you doing here, Michael?" She ground out the words. "What do you want?"

"You, of course, *darling*. Always you. And little Andy."

"Please let them…go. Our…son has to be so afraid." She could force herself to say that, but she wouldn't call him "Aiden" around Michael because that might make her son think the man should know him. Michael never deserved to know him.

"As I said, he'll be fine. I can't say the same for his mother."

He'd loosened his hold, so she jerked back to look up at him. The grinning face she'd once found handsome. His jaw was covered with several days' growth, and his dark hair was greasy and badly in need of a cut. But when she tried to shove him away again, fingers encircled her arm and squeezed until she winced. Then he turned around until he was standing next to her where they could both see the van.

"We'll have to take time for a proper hello later. After I deal with my friends here."

The man she thought she recognized had already started toward them with a huge roll of duct tape hanging from his arm. The other guy slid the van door closed, locking Ted and Aiden inside, and followed him down the sidewalk, his steps slower, more reluctant.

"Hey, you made it, Brooks," the first guy said. "Look at what we were bringing to you."

The man gestured first toward his partner and then

the van. Sarah's eyes widened as she came to face-to-face with one of the officers who'd chosen his informant over her life.

"So, who told you to bring in an owner from a crappy little diner?"

The officer sent a nervous look to his partner. "He came with the kid."

"Then I guess you know what you have to do with him."

Sarah shivered, and not just about the threat, which she hoped beyond reason was just that. If Michael knew where she worked, just how long had he been in town? Had he been following her this whole time? Did he know about her and Jamie, too?

She needed to stall, had to hold at least a few of the cards, when Michael had always hogged them all before.

"Hello, Mrs. Brooks."

"Hello, Officer." She couldn't remember his name, and she didn't care to find out.

"It's Larry." He indicated his partner, who was taking his sweet time getting to them. "And that's Clint."

At closer inspection, Sarah recognized the other officer as Larry's partner, apparently in work as well as in crime, though the guy had probably gained thirty pounds since she'd last seen him testifying in court.

"Sorry to interrupt your little social gathering here, but we need to take this party to somewhere a little more private. Especially since someone's probably called the police by now." Michael smiled at the two dirty cops standing just opposite him. "Officers who still settle for their state-employee wages, anyway."

Then he leaned in close to Larry's ear. "I thought I

was supposed to make the contacts once we had a location."

"Oh, we just wanted to help out," Larry said with a nervous chuckle.

"Here, follow us." Michael turned back to Sarah. "Don't try anything stupid, or I can't guarantee what happens to those in the other car."

She nodded. Oh, she'd done enough stupid things to last a lifetime, and now she had to do something right, or she might lose her son and a friend, whose only crime was to care about her. She let Michael push her into the passenger seat of a filthy car. She couldn't run and leave Ted and Aiden behind, but there was something she could do. She pulled her cell phone from her pocket, found the list of recent calls and tapped on the last one. Then she stuffed the phone in her waistband, just as Michael opened the driver's-side door.

At least she hadn't dumped the phone, like she'd planned to after the call from the police yesterday. But no matter how he felt about her after she'd betrayed him, the man who answered the call on the second ring would at least try to help.

"Just listen," she said, in a voice that she hoped wasn't too loud as Michael slid behind the wheel.

Just like she hoped he would, Michael took the bait as he pulled out into traffic. "Oh, no. *You* listen, you lying whore. Who do you think you are, trying to leave me when I was away and didn't have a say?"

"That was wrong of me. I'm sorry."

Her words of appeasement grated on her in a way they never had before, when she'd been too broken to ever defend herself. She couldn't do it now, either, but this time she would protect two people she loved and give the third enough time to reach them.

"You think that's going to be enough? You took my son away from me and…everything I care about. You made me *look* for you. You hid under a fake name."

"I'm so sorry," she said, to fill in another pause.

Michael made several turns in quick succession, as if he was familiar with the area, and soon they were heading into a more rural section of Brighton Township, where the houses were farther apart and the possibility of help more remote.

"Sweetheart, you had to know I would find you. You're my wife. We belong together. With our beautiful little family. Always."

"You're right. We do belong together," she said, falling so easily into that singsong cadence she'd used to avoid injury when he'd been the drunkest. Or angriest. Sometimes it had even worked.

Not this time. The strike came fast, like it had sometimes before. A hard backhand across the mouth that gave her no time to prepare. No time to shield her lips. She bit down and tasted blood, the sour, metallic flavor both familiar and crippling. Would she fall back into old habits instead of just pretending to do that?

"Were you so sure that we belong together when you were lying on your back for your little boyfriend, giving it up to him and everyone else, for all I know, when you'd already promised to give it only to me…until death?"

Her hand went to her mouth, the pressure only causing more pain to her already swollen lip. Her fingertips were immediately wet, so she had no doubt he'd split it. Again.

"You think I don't know about your little *cop*? Guess we've both been in bed with the police, haven't we?"

"I'm sorry." Her words were more a whisper now, both because it was what he would expect from her and because she couldn't speak that lie out loud. She wasn't sorry. Just like she didn't regret trying to protect Aiden from his father, she would never regret loving Jamie for as long as she could. Even if it would never be long enough.

"I did get a little more out of it than you did. You'll see. If you make the right decision. And I know you will."

His words weren't making any sense. She'd guessed that there were some shady business deals. Was that what he was talking about? This time when he paused, she searched for something to fill the silence.

"It didn't mean…anything." She swallowed, realizing she'd gone too far, and she'd failed.

"You can't even lie about it without giving yourself away. You were so hot for him that you practically took him on right there in front of the window. I *saw* you."

"What? Where?" But her memory quickly filled in the blanks. Precious, private moments that lost their shine with the truth that they'd been watched.

"Don't worry. You'll get over him. And then things will be just like they were between us. Better."

"How…how is that?"

This time he reached over and brushed his fingers over her chest until it came to rest on that place where her seat belt covered sternum. She braced herself for the touch to become more invasive, but he only slid his hand away again.

"You'll see. But a few people have to go away first."

Her arms automatically crossed. "Go away?"

"You know. Like your boyfriend."

He lifted one hand off the steering wheel and held it wide, as if his plan was obvious. "You led me right to him, sweetheart. Just like your friend led me to you."

"You killed Tonya." She squeezed her eyes closed, fresh tears threatening again. "I knew it was you."

"Now I didn't say that."

Sarah didn't realize that her hand had slid to her waistband, where she'd tucked the phone, until she caught him watching her. She tried to be nonchalant as she shifted, but in that lightning-fast way he always struck, Michael hit with the back of his hand again, his knuckles striking the plastic.

"You bitch!"

She grabbed at his hand, but he quickly dug the phone out from beneath her shirt and tucked it between his ear and shoulder, all while keeping the car mostly on the road.

"Hello, Officer," he said into the receiver.

Sarah held her breath. Maybe Jamie hadn't been on the line this whole time. Maybe he hadn't heard enough of a confession to get them both killed.

But Jamie's voice came through loud and clear. "Brooks."

"So, I hear you've been getting off on my wife. She's a pretty little piece of ass, isn't she?"

Sarah could only cover her face with her hands. She didn't know how or even if Jamie would answer. His inherent decency wouldn't allow him to abide ill treatment of women, but she'd hurt him, so though she could expect him to do his job, she shouldn't rely on him to defend her honor.

"It's not like that, and she's not your wife."

Cleary, Michael hadn't expected him to answer his shocking statement, either, as he gripped the phone so tightly that he should have crushed it.

"Well, she's mine now. The whore has always been mine."

Jamie's voice came back immediately this time. "If anything happens to Sarah, or that boy of hers or Ted, I can promise you that I'll never stop hunting you down."

Ted? How did Jamie know that he was with them? Had he already gone by the diner and discovered that her boss was missing, too? For the hundredth time that afternoon, she wished she'd kept that appointment with Jamie, if only to say goodbye to him. Now she wouldn't get the chance.

"Her…name…is… Maria."

As soon as the words were of Michael's mouth, he tossed the phone out the window. A moan escaped Sarah as she stared in the side-view mirror at the plastic carnage strewn on the country road behind them. The probability that they would get out of this situation alive dropped with it. If Jamie had been looking for them, and his words to Michael gave her that hope, he had no way to track them now.

For several minutes, neither spoke as Michael made several more turns, the white van carefully following about two car lengths behind. Sarah had nothing to say. She couldn't even honor Tonya's memory now by assuring she hadn't died in vain. She had no reason to believe any of them would get out of this alive, except Aiden maybe, and he would be sentenced to life with his dad, which was hardly better than death. At that, she couldn't control her tears, which came in a rush. Hot. Wet. With a level of hopelessness she'd never experienced before.

Finally, Michael pulled the car off the road and followed an unpaved drive that went along a soybean field. When he reached an open area with a huge bank of trees beyond it, he parked the car and shut off the engine.

"Your friend sounded like that, you know, just before," he said, still looking at the windshield.

For the first time in her life, Sarah pummeled Michael, with fists that he pushed away like he was swatting gnats.

"I wish she was still here, so I could thank her."

"For what?" She didn't want to know, but she couldn't help asking, either.

"Oh, that's simple." He smiled over at her. "For bringing my wife back to me."

Chapter 24

The moment that one of Michael's partners pulled the duct tape off Aiden's mouth, he started calling out for her. Since her legs weren't taped, there was nothing her captors could have done to stop Sarah from going to him, except shoot her. At this point, she would have done it, anyway.

"Everything's okay." She sat on the ground and wrapped her arms around her son, crooning to him with the empty promises that other mothers facing tragedy had shared with their children. "It's going to be okay."

One of Michael's partners yanked the tape off Ted's mouth, leaving a red, raw mark over his lips. Neither bothered to unbind the older man's hands and feet. It would probably be easier for them to shoot him if he couldn't make a run for it. No one had tied Sarah up at all. They wagered correctly that she wouldn't go anywhere as long as they had her son.

The three men stood about twenty feet away in a tight circle, discussing with heated voices. Occasionally, they glanced their way, making it clear they were trying to figure out what to do with them.

When Aiden calmed, Sarah leaned closer to Ted and spoke in a quiet voice. "I'm sorry for involving you in all this. I thought you could just drop us off at the bus station, and I could vanish again. I never intended to put you in danger."

"That's why you blew off Jamie today, too. To protect him."

She shrugged. "He'll never understand that."

"Maybe not."

He was watching her so closely that she shifted, uncrossing and then folding her legs again.

"What?"

"Maria?" He shook his head. "Nah. It doesn't fit you."

"Who's Maria?" Aiden asked, as he looked up at her.

"No one," she told him honestly. Not anymore.

Her son lifted his brow as if he didn't believe her. After today, he would never believe anything she said.

Aiden shifted so his mouth was near her ear, and unlike usual, when his whispers weren't really whispers, he lowered his voice. "Is he my father?"

She considered lying to him as she had all his life But she found she couldn't do it.

"Yes, he is."

"I thought so." He settled next to her again.

That gave her the chance to turn back to Ted. "How do you know about Maria?"

"There were a couple of Chatty Cathies in that van."

"Then do you know why they're all here? It can't all be about Aiden and me, can it?"

"I think it's something about money. Isn't it always?"

"What money? I don't have any money."

"They weren't *that* chatty."

Michael glared at them. "Quiet over there, you two."

Ted shot a glance at their captors and then whispered, "Don't worry. He'll be here."

The knot that had formed in her stomach the moment she'd seen those two men and the van tightened even more. Didn't Ted understand that her phone had gone out the window, and with it, any chance they had of being rescued?

"I'm sure he will," she whispered. She couldn't bear to tell Ted the truth that they were on their own.

"Maria, could you come over here?"

She licked her lips. "Can I bring… Andrew?"

"No. Leave him there."

She couldn't bring herself to look back at Aiden now and see all the confusion she was responsible for putting there. Not only didn't he know his mother's real name, but he also didn't know his own.

Her posture as straight as she could manage, Sarah crossed to the three men, who were all looking at her strangely.

"What is this about, Michael? Because if it's only about us and our son, then we're right here. You've found us." She pointed to the other two men. "Why are they still here?"

Larry held his hands wide and looked back and forth between the other two men. "Does she really know nothing about the money?"

"What money? I don't have any money. You think if I did I would have been living in that dump?"

"You won't have to do that anymore," Larry said with a laugh. "You two will be getting your share of a lovely little nest egg. A little over $750,000 in all."

Michael's gaze narrowed in that way she'd come to recognize—and fear—during their marriage. She'd never come away without cuts, bruises or even a broken bone after he'd had that look. Obviously, his partner didn't realize that this was the kind of news Michael would have wanted to deliver himself. He would hate it that Larry stole his thunder.

"Do you guys have the book?" Michael asked.

"Sure, buddy," Larry said, and started toward the van.

"No." Michael waited for the first man to look back and then pointed to the second. "Him."

Clint looked confused but nodded and walked to the vehicle. He returned a few minutes later with a photo album. *Her* photo album.

"Hey, that's mine. Where did you get it?" Her hands were already sweaty, and he hadn't even admitted yet how they'd been able to get inside her apartment. What else had they touched or taken?

"Your building's super was especially nice to police officers," Clint said. "Isn't that right, Larry?"

"Very nice," Larry agreed.

Sarah shivered over the violation, though she suspected she would learn details that were so much worse that day.

Larry rubbed his hands together. "Well, let's get on with it. You're going to love this, Maria. It was your husband's ingenious idea to make you the key…"

"The key to what?" she asked.

"The money."

"Stop. Now."

Larry jerked his head to look Michael's way, and found a gun pointed right at him.

"What the hell, Michael? You don't point that at people. What's wrong with you?"

"You've got a big mouth. You've always had a big mouth."

Larry lifted both his hands in a defensive move, but he was too late. A single shot to the forehead dropped him to the ground.

Sarah was too shocked to scream. She couldn't even look at the body. She sneaked a peek at Aiden, who was curled up next to Ted, the older man wisely tucking the boy behind him to limit what he witnessed and, she suspected, get his help in loosening the tape on his hands.

"Now, where were we?" Michael said, as he tucked the gun back in the waistband of his pants.

Sarah swallowed, aware that he had been carrying it all along and could have used it on any of them whenever he chose. She was relieved that Jamie wouldn't be able to find them. Her ex had nothing to lose. He would have no qualms about putting a bullet through Jamie's head, as well.

Clint, whose face had paled, chewed his lip. "We were talking about splitting the money two ways."

"Or maybe just one."

The other officer closed his eyes, waiting.

But Michael only chuckled until Clint opened them again.

Sarah cleared her throat. "This money… I don't know

anything about it. Well, not much anyway. And I don't need to know any more about it. You two can just head off in one direction, and I'll go in another. Please. I'll never tell—".

Michael shook his head to interrupt her. "It can't be that way, Maria. The money was for us, so we could make a new start."

"Like someone said, you're the key," Clint chimed.

This time, instead of reaching for his gun again, Michael nodded. He took three steps closer to Sarah and reached for her throat. Her thoughts flashing to Tonya, Sarah steadied herself and hoped it was quick.

Instead, Michael took hold of her locket and yanked it from her neck. He opened it, popped out the black-and-white photo of Sarah's grandmother and flipped it over. On the back were the numbers 3, 46 and 17. No hyphens between them.

Sarah leaned in and took a closer look. "What is that?"

"It's a safe combination," Michael said.

"And I've had it all along?"

He nodded. "I had to put it in something I knew you'd never get rid of. You never took that damn thing off."

"That's why you've had your friends hunting me for six years?"

He shook his head, smiling. "Of course not. That's only part of it. I had to bring my family back together."

"Now the album?" Clint asked.

Michael held out his arms until his partner cautiously set in it in his hands. Immediately, he opened the book to the back, pulled up the glued binding and lifted out a small key. He tucked it and the combination in his pocket.

"It was there all along, too?" she asked.

"You always held the keys to the money and my heart.

Now you can have both." He nodded as if that settled the matter.

"If the combination and the key are here, then where's the safe?"

"That's the best part of all. It's in the last place your parents would look. You always said it would take a backhoe to get all of the stuff out of their overstuffed basement, and an act of Congress to get them out of that house, so I took you at your word." He shrugged. "All that money, and it's right there waiting for us."

Sarah didn't miss the irony that he'd placed not only the keys but the safe itself in locations connected to her family. He'd forced her to forfeit a relationship with her parents to be with him, and with this, Michael had given them one more giant middle finger.

"Well, this is all real romantic and all," Clint began, drawing their attention back to him, and the gun that was suddenly in his hand, "but for me, it's not personal. It's always just been about the money. And two shares really do look better than one."

Michael lifted his left hand. "Now, Clint, you want to think about this. So far, you haven't killed anyone. If you get caught, you'll go to prison, but you won't die there. Are you brave enough to take a life…or four, since we're all witnesses?"

Clint held his gun steady for several seconds and then started to lower it, but just as he did, Michael pulled out his, aimed at the officer's head and fired.

"I didn't think so."

Sarah made an involuntary sound in her throat, her gaze shifting from Aiden to Ted as she tried to determine who would be next. There was no way she would let it be either of them. This was her fight, not theirs.

Michael had been her mistake alone. She'd escaped from him before, but she was done running. She would stop him from hurting the others, today, or she'd die trying.

Jamie had been moving as quickly as he could through the grove of trees, trying to get in position, just as the sniper and two other officers were doing, farther down. But when a gunshot broke the silence a second time, he couldn't keep from racing forward. Brooks was running out of victims before he started on the people Jamie cared about. Even with the heads-up from Ted and the later one from Sarah, they weren't moving fast enough. They were almost out of time.

"Please, Sarah, don't do anything stupid," he whispered as he neared an opening. Anything else, that is, when she'd already done enough today.

He would try to follow his own advice. Already he was acting with more sense than he had from the day Sarah had passed him that note. He'd called for backup, and with all the troopers, off and on duty, helping out, they'd already covered more ground than he ever would have been able to on his own.

One trooper had gathered descriptions of the two men in the cargo van for the Amber Alert on Aiden, someone else had pulled Brooks's mug shot, and another trooper had followed up on the call from a concerned neighbor about two cars that had pulled onto a nearby property, helping them to get a more exact location.

Now all he had to do was keep from rushing in too quickly and getting one of them killed.

As he reached the edge of the clearing, he crouched low, drew his weapon and waited, hoping the other officers were in place. Beyond the trees, he had more backup from patrol cars that had come in silently, but from where he stood, it looked as if he was going in alone.

Aiden was the first one to notice him as Jamie crept to the back the cargo van. He touched his index finger to his lips, and the boy turned back without acknowledging him. With two victims already down, Jamie couldn't afford to make a mistake and end up causing a third.

Sarah saw him, too. He knew it from the way her shoulders lifted just the tiniest bit, and she purposefully didn't look his way as she continued the conversation she'd been having with her ex.

"…and we could go open the safe at my mom's, take the money and go anywhere you want, just the two of us. We can disappear. For good this time."

"That does sound good, doesn't it?" Brooks said.

Something looked odd about Sarah's mouth, and Jamie couldn't help but watch it for several seconds. When he realized her lips were swollen and turning blue from being hit, and that red line was dried blood, it was all he could do not to rush in and kill the guy himself.

Brooks moved the weapon—probably a .40 mm Glock—from hand to hand as if testing the weight of it.

"So, let's go right now. We'll just leave those two behind and start out on our own adventure," Sarah told him. "No kids."

This time he looked from the weapon to her. "Until you don't think it's fun anymore."

She shook her head. "Now why would you think that?"

"Because that's what you always do. When something happens, you blame me instead of admitting that you made me do it."

"I promise I'll be different now."

"And leave Andy? What kind of mother leaves her kid?" Brooks asked.

"One who's tired of all the work and just wants to have some fun."

A mother who was prepared to give her own life to save her son's. Jamie's chest ached over Sarah's bravery, but the risk she was taking made his hands sweat. He would have time later to dissect what else he thought about her and the way she'd betrayed him today, but now he had to make sure that she didn't have to make good on her promise to her child.

He crept farther forward, coming up with a plan to disarm Brooks. But the suspect must have heard something, for he suddenly shifted and started scanning the area beyond the two vehicles.

Before Jamie could move, Aiden scrambled up off the ground and walked right up to Brooks.

"Are you my daddy?"

Brooks barely glanced down. "Of course, I am. But you would know that if your mother hadn't hidden you from me."

He shoved Aiden out of the way as he passed, causing the boy to trip and fall to the ground.

Jamie couldn't help it. He lunged forward and aimed his weapon at the man who'd taken so much from the woman he loved, and who would do the same from that precious child if given the chance.

Brooks bent and yanked Aiden in front of him, holding him beneath the chin, and pointed his gun at Jamie.

"My wife's little police lover has come to play the hero. Where's your uniform, Officer? And what are you going to do now? Can you risk missing me and hitting the kid?"

Jamie refused to lower his weapon. "Are you talking about your *son*? The child you're using as a human shield?"

Sarah rushed toward Brooks from his left, stopping only when he waved his weapon her way.

"No, Michael! Please! I told you I'll go with you. I'll do anything you want. Just let them go."

"Maria, sweetheart, do you notice that your cop boyfriend has a gun pointed at me, too? I don't hear you pleading with him for my life."

Aiden tilted his head back and looked up at his father. "You leave Mr. Jamie alone."

"Shut up, Andy," Brooks warned.

"I'm Aiden."

Brooks shifted the gun to his son's head. "Look how you've brainwashed him. I would drop that gun if you want to see this kid walk away."

"You will…let him walk? Let all of them go?"

"Sure, why not. I'm feeling generous."

Jamie's instinct told him it was a mistake, that the man had no honor, but he had no choice. He lowered his weapon to the ground and kicked it away from him as instructed.

When he stood vulnerable, with his hands up, Brooks smiled at him.

"You're a fool to think you can just swoop in and take my life from me. He's *my* son. And she's *my* wife."

Well, this might be the end for him, but he wouldn't go without a fight. As the other man lifted his weapon and aimed, Jamie lunged for him.

"Aiden, duck!"

What he hadn't counted on was that Sarah would dive in at the same time, putting herself in the line of fire.

Two shots rang out, so quickly that Jamie wondered if he'd imagined the second one. Time seemed to freeze as a surreal haze enclosed them, a momentary gift before the cruel truth set in.

"Mom!"

At Aiden's shout, Jamie's mind cleared. He lifted his head and found Sarah crumpled on the ground not ten feet away. The woman who'd stolen his heart had just risked her life for him. Maybe given it. He'd landed on his stomach, his forearms thumping against the hard earth, but he scrambled to his feet and stumbled over to her.

"Is she alive?" Aiden asked, his voice catching on the last word.

Jamie needed to check, but his limbs felt heavy, as if they needed him to delay the answer that could kill him. He was vaguely aware of Brooks's body another fifteen feet beyond, blood seeping from a hole in his chest, and he would get to him, but Sarah came first.

Finally, he gathered the courage to rest a hand on her shoulder, but just as he reached farther to check for a pulse, she turned her head.

"Ouch! That's…going to leave…a mark."

"Mom, you're okay."

"No, but she will be." Jamie hoped that saying it out loud would make it true.

Both he and Aiden came around her, so they could see her face. Jamie swallowed when he caught a glimpse of just what would be leaving that mark.

A red stain was spreading on her right shoulder. He pulled off his shirt, balled it and pressed it against her wound.

"Sorry," he said when she hissed in pain. "But we need to stop the bleeding. What were you thinking, jumping between him and me like that? You could have been," he paused, glancing at Aiden, "hurt."

"I know it was stupid."

"At least we can agree on one thing, but thank you," he said, smiling.

"You're going to be okay." He didn't know whether he was saying those words to himself or Sarah. Even if he couldn't be with her after this, she had to be all right. "The ambulances are already on their way."

As it to confirm his comment, an ambulance and a fire-and-rescue vehicle started up the long drive toward them. Sirens in the distance suggested there would be more.

"Ambulances, plural?"

Because her real question wasn't the one she'd spoken aloud, he stepped over to Brooks, whose body lay outside her line of vision. He looked as though he'd fallen straight back with no attempt to soften his landing. And now the blood on his shirt had spread to cover it from a telltale sniper wound to the center mass of his upper chest. Jamie checked unnecessarily for a pulse. The threat had been eliminated.

He resisted the temptation to close the man's eyes for his son's sake and drew Aiden away from the body instead.

"The suspect is deceased," he told Sarah, when he reached her.

"Does that mean dead?" Aiden asked in a shaky voice.

"Yes, it does."

"Jamie, I'm so sorry," Sarah called out in a pain-roughened voice.

"Don't try to speak. We can talk later. We need to get you to the hospital first."

"Will we?" She paused, wincing. "Talk, I mean."

"Sure." But he wasn't sure at all. What could he tell her when he didn't believe they had anything left to say?

He was relieved when the EMTs rolled a gurney over, so he could put distance between them. He needed to get some perspective. He had allowed himself to love Sarah and Aiden, and he could have lost them that afternoon.

But because he still had to get through this day and the inevitable questions that would come about what he knew, when he knew it and why he'd never told anyone, he stepped back to Aiden. The boy was watching too closely as the EMTs zipped Brooks into a body bag.

Aiden pointed to the gurney. "He was my dad. He didn't know my name."

"Yes," Jamie said, confirming both statements.

"He and those other men were bad."

"Sometimes people make poor choices."

"Like Mom jumping in front of the gun? And Mr. Ted trying to cover me once he got the tape off his hands?"

"No, those were *risky* choices."

"I started talking to *him*, so he wouldn't see you." He pointed to the man in the body bag.

"That was really risky. But brave, too." At the boy's confused look, Jamie explained, "Sometimes risky things are also brave."

He had to force himself to calmly answer all of Aiden's questions. Like him and Sarah, the boy would have to learn to live with a tragedy from his childhood. Jamie could only hope the great kid never believed that any of it was his fault.

"He hurt my mom," Aiden said, after a long pause.

"Yes, he did. But he won't anymore."

Chapter 25

Jamie stood outside Sarah's hospital room, a bouquet of flowers in his hand, but he couldn't bring himself to go inside. Even forty-eight hours and reams of paperwork later, he still had no idea what he would say to her, especially if she asked him again to forgive her.

He'd already forgiven her for lying to him, if it had all been a lie, or just fear, which he had no doubt was part of it. Either way, there was a difference between forgiving and forgetting. And he couldn't forget.

Figuring he couldn't stay in the hallway forever, Jamie entered the hospital room, a single, though it was small. Sarah was asleep, her shoulder bandaged following surgery to remove bullet fragments, and an IV drip was attached to her arm.

For the longest time, he could only stare at her from across the room. She looked so frail, with her skin paler than normal and her hair curling around her face. But he would never again think of this woman who'd stepped in front of a bullet for him as fragile. Now trust was a different story. She still trusted no one but herself.

He watched her for several more seconds and then started to back from the room. That was when her eyes fluttered open.

"Hi."

He cleared his throat. "Hi. How are you feeling?"

"It's not too bad. Thanks for coming. Are those flowers for me?"

Jamie glanced under his arm, where he'd tucked the bouquet. Though he'd forgotten all about it, he pulled it out now and set it on her dining tray.

"Thanks."

He stepped to the window and scooted the visitor's chair closer, but not too close.

"Has Aiden been by to see you?"

She nodded. "Last night with Nadia. Ted came by this morning. I felt so bad about those cuts on his hands."

"That's what you get when you use a tailpipe to cut through duct tape around your wrists."

"Guess so."

Neither mentioned anything about the injury to her shoulder, which was something people got when they jumped out in front of loaded guns. Or worse.

"I'd kind of hoped you would have stopped by yesterday."

He shrugged. "I was busy. I had a few things to answer for at work."

"I'm going to be dealing with some stuff, too, but my attorney said I might be able to get probation. Mitigating circumstances. Mom said she would help out, too."

He blinked. "Your mom? The same mom who cut you off?"

"Same one. After the police contacted her to search her basement for the safe, she asked them where she could reach me. They told her the hospital, though I'm surprised they didn't just give her my room's phone number, as often as they've been calling. Especially the detective handling Tonya's case, who will be coming here tomorrow to take my statement."

He'd been half listening to the details, but one struck him as more significant. "Wait. You said your mother reached you at the hospital. How?"

"I'm registered under my real name." Then she pointed to the dry-erase board. "I told the nurses I prefer to be called Sarah. If you didn't know, how did you find me?"

"Ted gave me your room number. He's been updating me."

"He just wants to help out. And he adores me."

"That he does."

They could keep dancing around topics, and he could leave without saying the things that needed to be said, but he couldn't help asking a few more questions to delay leaving her a little longer.

"So, what happens now? Will you and Aiden go back to Illinois? Will you stay with your mom? Will he even go by Aiden?"

"Let me unpack that," she said, chuckling. "Aiden wants me to legally change his name to Aiden, and he's not a big fan of his last name, either. And, let me see, I'm just living day-to-day for a while. Mom has offered to set me up in an apartment near her until I get my feet on the ground. We both have regrets and want to make up for lost time."

"Maybe that would be good for you two to go to Illinois."

"It would make it easier on you."

He straightened, his shoulder blades touching the back of the chair. "What's that supposed to mean?"

"Look, Jamie, I have a lot of regrets. And not going with you to turn myself in was one of the biggest. I should never have run. Or *tried* to run."

She held her hands wide, and it must have caused a twinge to her shoulder because she winched and settled back against the pillows.

"It was just another lie, and you were an expert at telling them."

She flinched, though she hadn't moved on the bed. "I meant it when I said I would go with you, but then I got scared, and I fell into old habits."

"Because you could only trust yourself. I even told you I loved you, and you couldn't trust me enough to let me help. I can't be with someone who doesn't trust me."

"You've got it all wrong. I didn't leave because I didn't trust you." She took a deep breath. "It was because I…love you. Tonya was already dead, and I couldn't risk someone else I love *dying* because of me."

"That's all pretty easy to say now that it's past, and you're not looking over your shoulder anymore."

"Easy?"

The word came out so loud that they both shot a look toward the hospital room door. She'd also come up off the bed, so she squeezed her eyes closed for several seconds as she settled back against the pillows. When she spoke again, she had lowered her voice.

"Nothing I did with you was *easy*, and that included

letting you be the first man I'd trusted with my body since…"

Jamie pressed his lips together. He did know that had been significant for her, and some of the most precious moments in his life.

"But then, when things got tough, you ran," he said. "You couldn't even tell me you were going. I had to find out from a voice-mail message from Ted, telling me to track his phone."

"So that's how you found us so fast."

"That and a citizen who called about two cars on a neighbor's land."

"I'm sorry I ran, but I can tell that this isn't all about trust." She shook head several times, pursing her lips. "In fact, I don't think this is about me at all."

"Now this I've got to hear."

"You lost Mark. It was devastating for you. I get that. But you've been protecting yourself ever since. From getting too close. You live in fear of losing someone else you love because you don't think you could survive it."

"There's only one problem with your theory, Dr. Freud."

"And what's that?"

"I did let myself get close to you. And I told you I love you. First. Then you ran."

"Yes, I ran. From a man who tried to kill me and succeeded in murdering three other people. So perhaps my fears were well founded."

"You didn't let me protect you." He didn't know he was going to say it. Had never considered it. But now that the words were out there between them, he knew that it was the most honest thing he'd ever said to her, other than that he loved her. He'd needed her to need him, but like always, she'd relied only on herself.

After all the things they'd said to each other, this was the one that made her cry. At first her eyes only filled with tears, and then they overflowed, and the rain kept coming.

"Look, Sarah, I'm sorry. I should have waited to have this conversation with you. Until maybe we'd both had time to think it over. The timing is terrible. You just lost your— Well, your ex-husband just died."

"I hear what you're saying, but you're wrong. I have been running for years, but I'm not running anymore." Sarah tilted her head to the side and pinned him with her stare. "You might ask yourself who's running now."

Jamie held out his hands. "What do you want from me, Sarah?"

She stared at her hands for few seconds and then looked up at him again. "Nothing. Everything."

Jamie pushed open the door at Casey's, the bells grating on him more than normal. On the other hand, everything had annoyed him lately. The dining room was so deserted that he almost wondered if the place was closed, but a restaurant serving American cuisine wasn't the destination of choice for Cinco de Mayo, either.

"There he is," Ted called out as he emerged from the kitchen. He crossed to Jamie, and they shook hands. "I'm so glad you could make it. It's been a while."

Just over two weeks since the double homicide and officer-involved shooting, but who was counting? Not that he'd thought about it every day since then, and about Sarah fifty times more often by a conservative count. Of course, he hadn't seen her since that day at the hospital. By choice. How was he supposed to get over her if he saw her in person, as if in his mind wasn't enough?

They slipped into one of the booths, with Jamie facing the front door the way he always preferred because of his training. The sound of the swinging doors opening still bought him around. One of the other waitresses nodded as she carried out a tray with two water glasses.

"I told you she wasn't working today."

Jamie nodded. It had been the only reason he'd agreed to come.

"In fact, she won't be coming back to work. She's moving to be near her mom."

He swallowed. "I told her that will be good for them."

"Now don't sound so enthusiastic about it. Why don't you just admit that you're miserable?"

"Is that why you invited me here today? To ruin my Saturday?"

He started to stand, but Ted gestured for him to stay seated. "Word from the other Brighton Post guys is that you're ruining all their Saturdays, but, no, that wasn't why I invited you. This was." He stopped and executed a two-finger whistle.

The office door opened, and Aiden came running down the hall.

"Surprise!"

"Hey, buddy!"

He ran to the table and slid in next to Jamie.

"His mom needed to do some packing, so I offered to keep him around here for a few hours."

Aiden must have taken the lull in the conversation as an opportunity, for he leaned over and snaked his arms around Jamie. "I've missed you, Mr. Jamie. Why haven't you been at the center?"

"I've missed you, too. Sorry. Just been busy."

Busy brooding at his house. Busy feeling sorry for himself. That still counted, right?

"Did you hear we're moving?" He waited for Jamie's nod. "To be with my grandma. I didn't have a grandma, but I do now. She'd be nice. She gives me jelly beans from a bag in her purse."

"Well, I guess she's a keeper then."

"Want to see a picture of her?"

"I guess."

Aiden bounced out of the seat, raced at his usual full speed back to the office and returned with his backpack. From it, he pulled out a small framed photograph.

"Here it is. Mom said I could keep it."

Jamie accepted it and immediately regretted it. Aiden's grandmother was pictured with a teenage Sarah. They were both smiling, so he guessed it was taken before their relationship had soured.

"Isn't she pretty?"

"Yeah," Jamie said, and then cleared his throat.

Aiden stuffed the frame back in his pack and was off on another adventure, this time to help Marilyn fill the saltshakers.

"I bet the boy didn't even know you weren't talking about his grandma," Ted said.

Jamie frowned at him, but turned as Belinda came out of the kitchen, carrying a tray.

"Oh, I forgot. I ordered pie for us," Ted said.

The waitress set plates of apple amaretto in front of them.

"But I thought—"

"No, Sarah hasn't been back to bake. But I froze this one. She made it special the day she thought she had to leave. I figured the intended recipient should at least get some of it, so I saved it."

"She made a goodbye pie for me?" But already he was shoveling the first bite in his mouth, remembering as well as savoring. Even when she'd believed she had no choice but to run, she'd thought of him.

"Tastes better than a Dear John letter, I'm thinking. "Now there's one more thing I need to say to you before—"

"Give it a rest, will you, Ted?"

He nodded. "I will. Absolutely. After I say this last thing."

Jamie set his empty plate on the edge of the table and sat back, crossing his arms. "Go ahead."

"I know a lot about being alone. Since my wife died, I've had a lot of it. Now if I had the chance for one do-over for the mistakes I made with my brother, I would take it." He cleared throat and pinned Jamie with his stare. "I know you were hurt that Sarah bailed on you, but you need to give her one chance for a do-over. And give me one chance for the daughter and grandson I never had."

Jamie shook his head. "Ted, I know that you care about her, but—"

Aiden returned to the table then in a flurry of energy. "Mr. Jamie, can I ask you a question?"

"Sure."

"Is it risky or brave to love someone?"

He glanced sidelong at Ted, but the other man raised his hands in a gesture of innocence.

"Why do you ask?"

"Because I need to find someone to love my mom."

"Buddy, I think love is one of those things that might be both risky and brave."

Jamie might have said more, but the front door opened then, and the woman who'd been the topic of discussion all afternoon stepped inside. Her arm was in a sling, her hair was in a messy ponytail and she didn't wear a stitch of makeup with her jeans and T-shirt, but she'd never looked more beautiful.

She startled when she noticed him and then smiled as she approached.

"I only said she wasn't working. Not that she wouldn't be here."

Jamie didn't even look Ted's way to answer. "Thanks, my friend."

Sarah slid in the booth next to Ted, and the four of them laughed together for another hour.

She was oblivious to the fact that with her presence alone, she'd completed two different conversations. But Jamie knew now that if anyone needed the chance for a do-over, it was him. And Aiden didn't need to find someone to love his mom. Someone already did.

As Sarah answered her apartment door that Sunday afternoon, butterflies were completing aerial dives in her stomach. Great acrobatic moves that would be crowd pleasers but dives nonetheless. Something had changed with Jamie yesterday at the diner, and she didn't know what it meant, but she was tempted to feel a little hope.

"Wow, that was fast," he said, when she opened the door.

"Just two locks these days." She indicated the door with a game show hostess move. "I leave three unlocked most of the time, like I don't have a care in the world."

"Keep that up and you'll have squatters in here in no time."

"Or they could just rent the place."

"Oh. Right."

She couldn't believe she was leaving, either. Maybe he'd only meant packing when he'd offered yesterday to come by and help. She'd probably read the other part into his words. The part where he begged her not to pack, but to unpack and stay with him.

Maybe he was just trying that whole post-relationship-friendship thing, which at that moment seemed over-rated. She couldn't be with him without wanting to really be with him.

"Well, where do you want me to start?" he asked.

Sarah turned away, refusing to acknowledge the burning behind her eyes. She couldn't let herself cry. He'd told her how he felt. He'd been up front with her that it was over between them. It wasn't his fault she'd been convinced that he'd changed his mind.

"I guess you can start in the kitchen. With this sling, I'm having a rough time getting up and down to pack the stuff from the lower cabinets. And the upper cabinets…" She paused, pointing. "Forget about it."

"Then I'm your man."

She swallowed and turned away again. Was he being intentionally cruel, or did he just not get it? She wanted so much for him to be *her man* and a wonderful male role model for Aiden. But life, it appeared, really wasn't fair. And choices, whether whimsically or desperately made, had consequences.

"Oh, I forgot. I bought a box of tools in case we have to take some things apart."

"You brought a box of stuff?" Even feeling a little

sorry for herself, she couldn't help smiling at that. "You do understand that the point is to take boxes out of the apartment, right?"

"Oh, I've got it. Don't you worry."

Still, he passed by her and slipped out the door, reappearing with a medium-sized and heavy-looking box. He took it right into the kitchen and set it on the counter.

"When did you say that Aiden will be back?"

"I didn't. He's spending the afternoon with Nadia. She's so sad to see us go."

Sarah waited, hoping he would say he was sad, too, but when he didn't, she resigned herself to the truth. He really was here only to help her pack. To give herself a few minutes to accept that truth, she moved to the bedroom and started emptying the dresser. But she was on only the second drawer when he appeared in the doorway.

"Sarah, would you mind helping me for a minute in the kitchen?"

She nodded, following him. But outside the bedroom door, when he moved to the side, she found a candlelit dinner on her tiny dinette table, complete with a white tablecloth, a carryout bag of food and extra-thick paper plates. A bottle of wine was chilling in the ice cube bin, and a box of chocolates rested next to it.

The butterflies were at it again, times ten.

"What is all of this?" She hoped she knew, but she didn't know, and if he didn't say something soon, she was going to explode.

"I thought I would give you a proper send-off."

"Oh." The word came out before she could stop it, her disappointment encapsulated in two little letters.

"Or not."

Her gaze had lowered to the floor, but his confusing comment had her looking up again.

Jamie was on one knee next to the table, and in his hand was an open jeweler's box with the most beautiful solitaire diamond nestled inside.

"Oh, Jamie."

He set the box on the table, guided her into one of the kitchen chairs and took both her hands in his. "Sarah, I dreamed of you before I knew you, and then when I met you, my dreams paled next to the real flesh-and-blood woman.

"I am so in love with you. With all of you, the parts I know now and the parts I will meet in the next sixty years. Be my partner in life, my lover, my confidante and my friend. Will you marry me, Sarah?"

She was already crying, but she needed him to know what she was feeling. "Jamie, I love you. I was afraid to be myself when I met you, and you would accept nothing less. You taught me that I not only can love, but that I am worthy of love. You value trust more than anything, and I trust you implicitly."

He grinned at her as he rose to his feet and pulled her into his arms. "So…do you have an answer for me?"

"Yes. Yes. And yes."

He pressed his lips to hers in a kiss filled with passion and so much more. It was a promise of the vulnerability, partnership and joy they would share. When he finally broke off the kiss, both of them were breathless.

"I know we have a lot of things to talk about." He strode away from her and then back. "You're leaving to be with your mother. After you just found her, I can't ask you to leave her again, so I'll try to find another law-enforcement position there."

"Or she could move here." She smiled. "And Ted's looking for another partner at Casey's, so…"

"So, you could bake, just like you dreamed."

"And Aiden's just going to hate this news."

She was laughing as she said it, but Jamie suddenly became serious.

"You know I love your son like he's my own, and if he wants me to adopt him, I will. I would love it."

"He would, too," she said with a smile. "But we don't have to decide everything right now. Not when we have this place to ourselves…all afternoon."

"What can we do? Oh. Right. More packing."

He drew her into his arms and started something wonderful that wasn't at all like packing.

"Oh, one more thing we need to decide," he said, pressing his forehead to hers.

"Today?"

He nodded. "We need to decide what your name will be."

"Maria? Sarah?" She shook her head. "I don't care as long as it ends in Donovan."

"You, my love, will always be Sarah to me."

* * * * *

*Don't miss Dana Nussio's next
Harlequin Romantic Suspense romance from her
True Blue series, fall 2019.*

ROMANTIC suspense

Available March 5, 2019

#2031 COLTON'S CONVENIENT BRIDE
The Coltons of Roaring Springs
by Jennifer Morey

Decker Colton agreed to an arranged marriage but when his new bride, Kendall Hadley, is nearly kidnapped, they'll have to dodge danger and navigate a relationship that's gone from business deal...to pure pleasure!

#2032 COWBOY DEFENDER
Cowboys of Holiday Ranch • by Carla Cassidy

Clay Madison has set his eyes on single mom Miranda Silver, but when she's kidnapped, it becomes a race against time to save her.

#2033 SPECIAL OPS COWBOY
Midnight Pass, Texas • by Addison Fox

After a one-night stand leads to a pregnancy and with the threats against her escalating, Reese Grantham turns to Hoyt Reynolds for protection. Can he stay committed to his plan to remain unattached while keeping Reese and their baby out of the crosshairs?

#2034 TEMPTED BY THE BADGE
To Serve and Seduce • by Deborah Fletcher Mello

History teacher Joanna Barnes has been charged with a crime she didn't commit. Private investigator Mingus Black has no qualms about getting his hands dirty to prove her innocence—but more than his career is at risk now...

HRSCNM0219

Get 4 FREE REWARDS!

We'll send you 2 FREE Books plus 2 FREE Mystery Gifts.

Harlequin® Romantic Suspense books feature heart-racing sensuality and the promise of a sweeping romance set against the backdrop of suspense.

FREE
Value Over
$20

The silence on the car ride to the public hearing at the Chicago
Board of Education building on Madison Street was jaw-dropping.
Mingus maneuvered his car through traffic, his expression smug
as he stole occasional glances in her direction. Joanna stared out
the passenger-side window, still lost in the heat of Mingus's touch.
That kiss had left her shaking, her knees quivering and her heart
racing. She couldn't not think about it if she wanted to.

His kiss had been everything she'd imagined and more. It
was summer rain in a blue sky, fudge cake with scoops of praline
ice cream, balloons floating against a backdrop of clouds, small
puppies, bubbles in a spa bath and fireworks over Lake Michigan.
It had left her completely satiated and famished for more. Closing
her eyes and kissing him back had been as natural as breathing.
And there was no denying that she had kissed him back. She hadn't
been able to speak since, no words coming that would explain the
wealth of emotion flowing like a tidal wave through her spirit.

They paused at a red light. Mingus checked his mirrors and
the flow of traffic as he waited for his turn to proceed through

the intersection. Joanna suddenly reached out her hand for his, entwining his fingers between her own.

"I'm still mad at you," Joanna said.

"I know. I'm still mad at myself. I just felt like I was failing you. You need results and I'm not coming up with anything concrete. I want to fix this and suddenly I didn't know if I could. I felt like I was being outwitted. Like someone's playing this game better than I am, but it's not a game. They're playing with your life, and I don't plan to let them beat either one of us."

"From day one you believed me. Most didn't and, to be honest, I don't know that anyone else does. But not once have you looked at me like I'm lying or I'm crazy. This afternoon, you yelling at me felt like doubt, and I couldn't handle you doubting me. It broke my heart."

Mingus squeezed her fingers, still stalled at the light, a line of cars beginning to pull in behind him. "I don't doubt you, baby. But we need to figure this out and, frankly, we're running out of time."

The honking of a car horn yanked his attention back to the road. He pulled into the intersection and turned left. Minutes later he slid into a parking spot and shut down the car engine. Joanna was still staring out the window.

"Are you okay?" he asked.

Joanna nodded and gave him her sweetest smile. "Yeah. I was just thinking that I really like it when you call me 'baby.'"

Don't miss
Tempted by the Badge *by Deborah Fletcher Mello,*
available March 2019 wherever
Harlequin® Romantic Suspense books
and ebooks are sold.

www.Harlequin.com

Love Harlequin romance?

DISCOVER.

Be the first to find out about promotions,
news and exclusive content!

Facebook.com/HarlequinBooks

Twitter.com/HarlequinBooks

Instagram.com/HarlequinBooks

Pinterest.com/HarlequinBooks

ReaderService.com

EXPLORE.

Sign up for the Harlequin e-newsletter and
download a free book from any series at
TryHarlequin.com.

CONNECT.

Join our Harlequin community to share
your thoughts and connect with other
romance readers!
Facebook.com/groups/HarlequinConnection

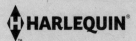

**ROMANCE WHEN
YOU NEED IT**

HSOCIAL2018